THE LA]

"Well-developed characters and plot make this historical fantasy a true pleasure to read and become lost in... A very unique and fascinating story. I definitely can't wait for this series to continue!"
— Cecily Wolfe, author of *Throne of Grace*

"Effie is an amazing character. I loved following her journey and seeing her change and grow."
— I Heart Reading

"The book was a one sit read for me. I loved it and would recommend it to everyone. The characters were well developed and deep with an original story."
— Read Day and Night Blog

OAK SEER

"Comer weaves a riveting tale of intrigue, magic, and romance in a steampunk-flavored Scotland packed with evil creatures, scheming politicians, and vicious bigots. But the real highlight of OAK SEER is its heroine. Effie of Glen Coe is one feisty freedom fighter!"
— Wendy N. Wagner,
Hugo Award Winner & author of *An Oath of Dogs*

"A fantastic sequel, OAK SEER plunges you willingly into the fey underworld of Victorian Scotland."
— Garrett Calcaterra, author of *Dreamwielder*

BARROW WITCH

"In BARROW WITCH, the stakes are steeper, the danger more dreadful, and Effie is more exciting than ever. Comer concludes his trilogy with flourishing aplomb... It's quite the accomplishment for each book in a series to improve, but with BARROW WITCH we reach the ultimate high of fey steampunk fantasy that the series has always delivered."
— Ahimsa Kerp, author of *Empire of the Undead*

"Brings human and magical beings together brilliantly! . . . This intricate tale is woven with much lore, mysticism, clever banter, and incredible characters that readers will instantly love!"
— InD'tale Magazine

Effie of Glen Coe

"This is a fantastic steampunk story that hints at a much larger world of fantasy & magic where all the Queen's men are bent on rooting out the last of the fey—a personal favorite of mine."
— Jonathan Jacobs, Editor in Chief of Nevermet Press

THE ROADS TO BALDAIRN MOTTE

"I was drawn into the world of Baldairn Motte at once by the rich prose and the promise of high adventure, but it was the characters and the fast moving story that held me literary hostage. I hope there's a sequel!"
— James P. Blaylock, author of *Lord Kelvin's Machine*

"Whores become heroes, farmers become freedom fighters and healers strike down the unjust against the backdrop of a land in turmoil. The authors have created a rich world that leaps off the page..."
— Misty Massey, author of *Mad Kestrel*

"The prose is crisp, and the characters fleshed out as real people, not archetypes. The book had an epic feel...."
— Rogue Blades Entertainment

"For a heroic fantasy novel written by not one, not two, but three authors – Garrett Calcaterra, Craig Comer, and Ahimsa Kerp – The Roads to Baldairn Motte is a surprisingly well-structured, remarkably cohesive tale that actually benefits from the different voices, without seeming fragmented."
— Beauty in Ruins Blog

Also by Craig Comer

The Fey Matter Trilogy

THE LAIRD OF DUNCAIRN

OAK SEER

BARROW WITCH

THRALLS OF THE FAIRIE
and Other Tales

THE ROADS TO BALDAIRN MOTTE
(with Ahimsa Kerp and Garrett Calcaterra)

A Dagger Among Friends

CRAIG COMER

COPPER POT
BOOKS

This book is a work of fiction. Names, characters, places, and incidents either are products of the author's imagination or are used fictitiously. Any resemblance to actual events or locales or persons, living or dead, is entirely coincidental and not intended by the author.

A DAGGER AMONG FRIENDS

All Rights preserved. Except as permitted under the U. S. Copyright Act of 1976, no part of this publication may be reproduced, distributed, or transmitted in any form or by any means, or stored in a database or retrieval system, without the prior consent and permission of the author.

Copyright 2023 © by Craig Comer.

Copper Pot Books / First Printed August 2023

Print Edition ISBN: 979-8-9886951-1-0
eBook Edition ISBN: 979-8-9886951-2-7

For Martina

CHAPTER 1

I spied the attack too late. My hand reached out and pulled back. "Am I dead now?" I blurted, lamenting the mistakes I'd made. The blunders and missed opportunities. The false starts and lies I'd swallowed whole.

I grimaced. I'd sounded way more chipper than intended. But at least I was finally getting somewhere.

Above, the large Edison bulbs of my cousin's game shop hummed. Their amber hues battled the streetlight flooding through the shop's front windows. Beckett Cooper, my never-again pity date, wilted. He clearly hadn't expected such glee. An urgent need to study the floor overtook him. Mousy-colored locks fell over his bony face. A twinge of guilt rattled through me at his abused-puppy-dog reaction. My cousin, Case, tittered at my lack of social grace. The three of us occupied a table in Roll For It's front corner, the one normally used for demonstrations and a weekly role-playing club. An uber-nerdy board game sprawled before us. A couple cans of Sprite and a bowl of pretzels hinted the air with citrus and salt.

Some date…Though to be fair, Beckett's plans weren't entirely crazy. Even in my forties, I still loved tabletop games. Each one was its own enigma, with dueling pieces and traps to spring. But I couldn't get into this one. My mind was fixated on the rejection letter I'd received from Miley University. It'd been my one hope for medical school. My only plan for the future. The whole reason I'd added the word "temporary" to every decision I'd made since retreating home last spring.

Without medical school, my midlife crisis was less like a reboot and more like that abrasive clicking noise just before complete system failure.

Case's phone buzzed. He silenced it without looking. I frowned at his lack of curiosity—odd for him—and he laughed harder. Clearly, my embarrassment provided a greater source of entertainment. His cheeks puffed, full of pretzels. My cousin grazed like a goat with a tapeworm. A Samuels through his father, his mother was my dad's sister. We'd grown up together as kids, drifted apart in our thirties, and reconnected over the last year.

Leaning over the board, I let his derision pass. Time to move things along. All I wanted was a hot shower and something with a splash of rum. Or vodka. Or really anything with the word "proof" on the bottle. I wasn't picky. Snatching my game piece, I shook my head. The plastic figure was supposed to be a Valkyrie, but Case's painting skills had left it closer to a lady of the docks. The violet mascara reached her hairline. Her lips blazed like a fire engine. The bosom was shaded perfectly, of course.

It looked nothing like me, except for the blonde hair. Lithe, angular, and with the grace of a drunken gazelle in thirty-inch heels—that was closer to my truth. I'd inherited my mother's hazel eyes and dark brows, and my grandfather's resting smirk face. I'd once reigned as Miss Harvest Falls in our small Pacific Northwest mountain town, but the jury had been rigged. My mother had spearheaded the Women's League at the time, and they'd funded the competition.

"You're unconscious, technically," said Beckett. He tried to wave the figure back into place but fell short of actually touching me. He sniffled to punctuate the end of his ruling like a radio operator calling out the end of transmission.

Only unconscious. Bummer. I replaced my Valkyrie and slumped in my chair.

My first date since the big breakup with Mason, and I so wanted to be dead.

Beckett took no notice. "A hush falls over the wooded vale as you crumple to the leaf-strewn ground," he intoned. He sniffled again, this time with a pause for dramatic effect, before toppling my Valkyrie with a flick of his pinkie. The figure clacked against the game board. Case's barbarian figure, complete with raised hammer and wolf-pelt cloak, stood alone against a dozen thorny green monsters I'd already forgotten the name of—again.

Case's phone buzzed a second time. My eyes darted to the screen, trying to snoop the caller's name. But he clicked it off before I had the chance to read anything. The bastard relished my discomfort way too much. A couple years my junior, he and Beckett had been best friends since birth. But where my cousin kept himself looking sharp and tidy, Beckett lurched about like Inspector Gadget's goth brother. With a black duster and unkempt hair, the few freckles painting his cheeks made him pleasant enough to look at, though his shoulders tended to hunch. For our date, he'd selected a T-shirt that read "Tall, Darth, and Handsome."

Yep, that's right. And here I was without a bat to fend off other suitors.

At least he'd made an effort. He smelled nice. He must've used soap with plenty of eucalyptus in it. Or maybe he'd just scrubbed himself with an air freshener. Either way, the scent flew at me in gusts when he waved his arms. Case's wafts tended toward an upmarket cologne. Whatever his gents' magazine told him to buy.

My own scent probably resembled the chocolate cookie I'd had for lunch. I'd eaten my emotions. Or at least I'd tried. The pickings had been slim since I'd not gone shopping in a couple of weeks. I'd planned to pack up and leave Harvest Falls by now. I hadn't planned to stay past summer, let alone past Halloween.

When I didn't respond, Beckett glanced at my chest. I'd worn a black V-neck, simple and comfortable. A pair of jeans and low-cut gray boots completed the outfit. There hadn't been much thought to it. I'd only said yes to the date with Beckett to get Case off my back. But his schoolboy leering made me question my life choices.

I'd been doing that a lot lately. Like how I'd not bothered with any exercise in a month. Okay, more like two. Or my hair, as another fine example. Over the summer I'd cut it short, and it was only starting to come back to shoulder length. I don't know why I'd mangled it. I didn't like the way it looked.

My mother would've hated it.

I slugged the rest of my Sprite. I definitely needed

something stronger.

"Do you want to drink a healing potion?" asked Case. His gaze twinkled blue. The way he leaned on the table made his arms and shoulders flex. He was thick all around but no longer rotund like he'd once been, more like a Shetland pony with a honey-brown crew cut.

"I thought I was unconscious," I snapped back.

Beckett's head bobbed as he contemplated the breach of rules. In a romantic gesture, he decided to be congenial. "It's okay, I'll say you can manage it. Maybe, like, as you're passing out."

He sniffled.

Well, crap. My sigh could be heard in a galaxy far, far away. Metal screeched as I shifted my chair. I scoured the walls for a clock. Case's grin broadened at my squirming. Beckett studied me, still hopeful. Shame flushed through me. This date had been a horrible idea.

Thankfully, my phone lit up and did its jingle. It saved me from making a decision. I grabbed it with gusto. I rose from the table and stepped into an aisle of shelved games, the artwork on the shrink-wrapped boxes screaming for my attention.

Case hollered, "Charlie, don't leave me! We can win this!"

I held up an index finger, begging him to wait a second. The static coming through the line made me jerk the phone from my ear. Male voices mumbled. The scuff and crunch of boots stomping over dry leaves and gravel.

"Sweet pea?" My dad's tenor popped through the static. He was the only one who'd ever called me a vegetable and meant it as endearment. I'd tried to correct him in my early twenties but had given up over the years. Parents would always be parents. "You there?"

I let him know I was. As chief of police for Harvest Falls, he had a habit of calling me at odd hours. Since I'd taken a summer job in the station's administrative pool, those check-in calls had become less frequent. But I wasn't surprised to hear his voice.

"I have a big favor to ask," he said. "We're a bit short staffed tonight, and uh..." He paused to bark something at Vin D'Amato, his patrol officer. "There's something at The Oak Grove tavern I can't take care of. I need you to check how serious it is. Can you do that for me?"

I balked and stared at the phone as if tiny aliens had crawled out of it, all thorny and skittering about, with impossible-to-remember names. Returning the phone to my ear, I made my voice polite. "Dad, you know I'm not a real cop. What am I supposed to do?"

"I know, I know." His voice strained. "I'm not asking for you to do any police work. Just make sure James has it handled. If he doesn't, if it's serious, call me, and we'll come right over."

Hmm. Curiosity jabbed me politely on the shoulder. "Can you tell me what's going on?" My shoulders rose, as if my confusion would ooze its way through the line. "Where are you? It sounds like a forest road."

Case stood and eased his way next to me. My words and tone of disbelief must've piqued his interest. Anything out of the norm always seized his attention. As a boy, he'd once spent an entire night searching for an owl because its hoot didn't sound right. Beckett remained hunched over the board game, but I could tell he listened as well.

"We're out along the highway," Dad said. "We're going to be here all night."

"And?" I was going to need more than that.

A long beat of silence followed. I thought he'd hung up, but he came back sounding distracted. "Sorry, sweet pea. It's chaotic here. Anyway, a call came in from Helen Tait. She's at the tavern and says a couple out-of-towners are causing a stir. I called James, and he didn't answer. I need eyes. Can you do that for me?"

Ah. At least part of the odd call fell into focus. Helen Tait took issue with a sunny day. I was sure that at some point, she'd filed a complaint about one too. In the months I'd worked at the station, I'd watched her grouse about everything from untrimmed trees to a speck of mold marring a park bench. Dad's crazy ask started to make sense. Such was living in a small town like Harvest Falls. This old dingbat had to be taken seriously because she happened to be good friends with our mayor.

Yet it certainly sounded like my dad had real policing to do tonight.

"Just walk over and make sure there's not a brawl going on?" I asked. "No fires or rampaging geese?" The last time he'd ignored one of Helen Tait's complaints, she'd had her stitching circle post flyers to have him recalled, despite the fact that he was appointed, not elected.

"I tried Case," Dad said. "I can again."

"No worries, he's right here." The admission made my cheeks flush.

"Oh. I thought you had a date tonight."

"Yep, he's here too." My cheeks burst into flame.

Dad gave no response. Through the line, I heard a car pull up. Tires ground gravel. Doors opened and slammed. More voices came, none I recognized.

"Charlie, I have to go," Dad said.

"I'll...I'll call you in a few," I replied, stumbling over the words. He never called me Charlie. It gave me pause, and I wondered just how serious things were. If I were to turn on a TV, would I see an image of our little stretch of highway lit up by floodlights, Dad warning news reporters to stand back in that sweet yet stern manner of his?

The static cut to silence. This time, he had hung up.

CHAPTER 2

"Bar fight?" Case asked as I pulled the phone from my ear. He clapped a fist into his other palm, and I choked back laughter. A fighter my cousin was not. Excitable and easily swayed, absolutely.

"Time for a field trip," I announced. I filled him and Beckett in as I shrugged into my jacket. Beckett didn't mope, to his credit. He seemed to take the change of plans with the same edge of excitement as Case, knocking into the table as he scrambled to fetch his duster. Monsters tumbled. They would have to feast on my Valkyrie ass another day.

Outside, the wash of autumn colors had started to fade away from Harvest Falls. The leaves of Second Street dropped at the slightest kiss of wind, their bronzes and scarlets not as bright as they'd been a month before. Cold had returned to the night and seeped its way into the greater part of the day. A scent of mildew and wetness clung to the air. A tourist waystop nestled in the Coast Range of Oregon, the town had once found glory in its mineral baths and forested lodges. But those days had long since faded. The town survived now on summer tourists who swarmed the streets searching for ice cream, antique trinkets, and an easy jaunt to our breathtaking waterfall.

As we walked, the pounding thrum of the town's namesake called like a siren. I heard it in the distance, comforting yet powerful. Often, I caught myself meandering in the direction of the falls, lost in thought, only to snap alert when my shoes hit the grassy edge of the park nestled at its base.

Case nudged me, shoulder to shoulder. "They give you any grief," he said, making a show of cracking his knuckles, "and I'll be more than happy to…call the chief for you." His hand turned into the pantomime of a phone.

"My hero," I said, breaking myself from the spell of the falls. He hadn't bothered locking the shop this late in the evening. In the autumn months, when the tourists had long since vanished, the streets were empty. Anyone you saw you were likely to know. Besides, we weren't heading far. My gaze focused two doors down. The Oak Grove's barely lit sign hung above an even dimmer brown door. A place for locals, its standoffish exterior belied a cozy and cheery interior made up to mimic an English-style pub.

I listened for disturbances as we ambled closer. But nothing spilled onto the street, no clatter of chairs being thrown or grunts of ever-loving pain. My stride became more confident. Helen Tait might've just rescued me from an awkward night's end.

Beckett shoved his hands into his pockets. His shoulders pressed almost to his ears. "This is your place, too, right?" he asked. He didn't mean anything by it, but I grew defensive all the same.

"Huh?" I glanced away. I am a master wordsmith when put on the spot.

"The three families that own the town," he said. Sniffle. "This is, like, your block, I heard. After your grandmother passed—"

"What? Uh, no. I don't…" For the second time in minutes, my cheeks burned. I didn't want Beckett in my business. Sure, it was public record, but my name wouldn't be on the title for long. That was the plan, at least.

Of course, medical school had also been the plan, and I'd managed to bungle that like a giraffe doing the limbo.

For the second time, my subconscious kindly reminded me. I'd been premed in college. Then Mason Purdy had happened, and I'd fled family expectations only to wind up right back where I'd started twenty years later. Only this time with shorter hair and larger jeans.

Case pulled the door open and held it for us. I rushed in to avoid any follow-up questions from Beckett. Warm, yeasty air melted my flesh. The place was more crowded than I'd expected for a Sunday night. Swaths of flannels and jeans mingled amid an assortment of hoodies and long-sleeved shirts. The colors popped against the dark wood of the tables. The Timbers' green and gold were well represented at the bar. Above them, a pair of TVs played a soccer match.

My heart thumped. I scoured the screens, searching for any breaking news crawling along the bottom or inserted into the closed captioning.

Nothing showed.

"Looks like a false alarm." Case broke my attention. He mumbled through a gnashing of peanuts. "I don't think Helen Tait's even here." He had a toddler's instinct when it came to loose food. Somehow he'd found this trove of nuts and crammed it into his piehole before I'd even started looking for Helen.

A few heads had turned when we entered. I recognized all of them. I smiled and waved at those who still looked my way. They waved back or nodded. A few raised a beer. Despite the crowd, the place was quiet. A gaggle of geese would put the din to shame, rampaging or not. Only the clink of glasses and groan of floorboards rose above the steady murmur of conversations.

"There's James," I said and started for the bar. I could spot James Bryson anywhere. He had an easy manner that soothed and a tall, sturdy physique that incited. With blue eyes, blond hair, and the perfect amount of scruff on his cheeks, he was the first boy I'd ever mooned over at school. Not that he'd had the scruff then. He'd kissed me at our eighth-grade graduation dance, and my toes hadn't touched the ground for a week.

Beckett sniffled beside me. Fate can be a hairy arse like that.

James caught my approach as he finished pulling a stout. Dimples flashed. "What's up, buttercup?" he asked. He'd always had a barman's persona, even in school. He'd taken on managing his uncle's place as soon as he came of legal age and now owned it outright. The bar, at least. Technically, I was his landlord. Snatching a rag, he wiped circles on the bar top in front of me. Its dark grain gleamed like a chocolate mirror glaze.

"Chief said he tried calling you," I replied. I grabbed one of the cardstock coasters from a stack on the bar and tapped it absently.

His head cocked in confusion. He patted the back pocket of his jeans before slouching in defeat.

"Leave your phone in the back room again?" I asked. James had not taken well to modern technology. He had a habit of mislaying his phone anywhere he could.

"Ah, in the basement," he admitted. "Tapped a fresh keg of Seven Devils, though, if you want some." Grabbing a tumbler, he didn't wait for a response. He poured a frothy ounce and slapped it in front of me. A strong, malty scent overwhelmed my nose.

"Try it," he said. "It'll put hair on your chest."

His gaze became a playful challenge. Blue eyes lit up the room. I snorted in a very sexy way and grabbed the bar rail for balance. *Dream about that tonight, Mr. Bryson!* But I wasn't about to let him win. Rallying, I tossed the coaster and reached for the beer.

My fingers stilled as they met cold glass. The reflection of some maddening commercial bounced off the bar's surface and distracted me. The TVs enthralled my attention once more. I had to know what was going on along the highway. But I refused to peek. Instead, I clamped my eyes shut and shook away the heebie-jeebies.

"Helen Tait." I managed to sputter the name. I scolded myself for forgetting about Dad's task so easily. Damn those eyes and their dimple cousins.

"Right," said James. He drew out the word. He understood the unspoken question. Spreading his arms wide, he leaned on the bar. It did wonders for his muscles. A quick flick of his gaze let me know Case and Beckett had found their way behind me.

"She was here earlier, snipping and snapping," he continued. "Asked for ice in her pinot gris, then complained it was too cold. Waddled out of here about a half hour ago."

"See?" Case nudged next to me and wiggled a finger, indicating for James to pour him a Seven Devils. "And you thought there'd be trouble Sir James couldn't handle."

James' brow rose. "Trouble I couldn't handle?" He locked onto Case. "Did you tell me about the Twinkie? Er…wait." His face fell. "No, it doesn't work that direction." He slapped the bar and looked away.

Case bellowed, deep and wide mouthed. Beckett snickered behind me. I caught the lame *Ghostbusters* reference too—the Twinkie line was one of my favorites—but only shook my head in mock pity. Though secretly, I scored him points for trying. At school, Case had started a history club and roped me and James into it. All we did was watch 80s movies, and ever since we'd played an unspoken game, trying to crack each other up with quotes—and mostly misquotes. James was a master.

A roar came from the Timbers fans, and my heart punched my throat. *Great flaming meeples!* I'd turned jumpy as a flea. Goose bumps spiked on my arms. My fist clenched the tumbler. I was lucky it hadn't shattered. I shot the beer, swallowing hard. Its thick head fizzled down my throat.

"Have you heard about anything happening along the highway?" I asked, trying to deflect the curious glances of my compatriots. I pulled my phone from a hip pocket and hit Dad's number. I'd have to let him know everything here was fine. That, and pry more information from him on what he was doing.

James shook his head, and Case filled him in on the earlier call.

As he listened, James ran a hand over his chin. I caught a flash of the white scar near his wrist. It was from Winter Ball, sophomore year of high school. He'd gone stag with some of the other guys on the basketball team. They'd dared him to vault a park bench near the falls, and he'd failed utterly, landing himself in urgent care. The whole school had laughed about it for months afterward, but what I remembered most was how my mother described the incident. She was old school. She cast shade in whispers: the greater the perceived shame, the lower the volume. James's injury had warranted a low hum of disapproval and an exaggerated eye roll.

It placed him forevermore in the camp of undesirables, in her mind.

She'd never explicitly told me not to date James—that was not her way—but after the injury the judgment had been there, as solid as a brick wall. He didn't have enough ambition in her eyes. His dreams weren't suitable for her daughter. They were too contained, too mundane. One moment, one decision completely benign and childlike, and that had been it for his chances with one of Harvest Falls' Most Desirable Daughters. The moniker brought a twinge to my gut. Just like it had every time my mother had uttered it.

I wondered these days whether I'd latched onto Mason as an act of rebellion. Spent years of my life with a man who had no ambition just to prove a point. That I could stand against the tide of expectations. Of course, the joke had landed on me, and my mother hadn't been around to witness my defiance anyway.

The call to Dad went to voice mail. I took a breath to speak, but Case pawed the phone away from me and hung up.

"Let's go out there," he said. He jiggled like a fifth grader eager to raid a stash of Halloween candy.

"What? Why?" I blinked and stared at my empty palm. "I can leave a message. We don't even know where *there* is."

"We can find it," said Case. "Look, your father, the chief, deputized you to investigate and report on this situation. The job isn't done until he holds that information in his head." He tapped his temple. "Besides, don't you want to know what's out there?"

"He did not deputize…" I took in his unfocused grin, the slight sway of his body. "Were you sneaking shots earlier? How many have you had?" I shook my head. "And for the record, no, I don't want to go out there. Whatever it is, we'd only get in the way."

And yet, even as I spoke the words, I knew I lied. I wanted to know what was going on as much as Case did. Probably more. Dad had clearly been distracted by something big. But if we showed up, he'd only send us away. He didn't need another headache, and I didn't want to cause him any grief.

"You think it's something serious?" James asked. His lips twitched as he forced away a smug grin. After a dramatic pause, he leaned over the bar and whispered at Case. "Do you think the faeries have returned?"

Case's excitement soured. He gave James a not-so-kind

gesture. "That was one time, like ten years ago. I said I *thought* I saw a sasquatch. If you'd been there, you'd have sworn the same."

Beckett's face popped into my periphery. He blew his hair out of his eyes. "Whatever's out there, I bet we never hear about it. Stuff happens all the time along the highway that you never hear about."

James folded his arms across his chest and stared down at me. "Well, that sounds like a solid challenge, Charlie Goode. You never know, there may be an elk with a busted taillight." He drew us in a circle with his finger. "Best you three investigate."

My gaze narrowed at being drawn in with the other two, but my irritation didn't stick. It never did with James. Damn his eyes. His easy manner. Those jeans he wore. I liked where my mind was headed, but I told it to wait until later.

"So we going?" asked Case. He pounded the rest of his Seven Devils.

"No!" I hollered.

"Oh. Oh, man. Guys." Beckett's face went blank. He studied a text on his phone, the tiny screen lighting his flesh in a pale wash. We fell silent at his tone. My goose bumps returned with a vengeance.

"It's Joyce," he said. His gaze fell on me and quickly darted away. "Addie Newsome's dead. Joyce found her car and thought it was abandoned. She called the police. They discovered Addie in…" He trailed off, tried to meet my eyes again but couldn't.

An electric jolt passed through me. "What?" I urged.

"Someone killed her," he told the floor. "She's been murdered."

It took a moment to make sense of the words. Addie? Murdered? That couldn't be true. I'd just seen her last week. A second irrational thought followed the first—that I was glad my mother would never learn of Addie's death. It would've devastated her. Addie had been the model child in her eyes. She had shoved us together time and again, until in high school our names had been inseparable.

Charlie and Addie, or more reasonably, Addie and Charlie. Queens of the school, who'd barely spoken a dozen words to each other in the decades since graduation.

"I'd better try Dad again," I said. My hands rattled as I swiped my phone open.

James cursed. He had no easy quip. He was lost in his own thoughts. Case leaned over Beckett's phone, swaying slightly. No one asked where the car had been found.

CHAPTER 3

Still in shock, we left James and returned to the game shop. I needed to be away from a crowd, away from cheering soccer fans and the clink of pint glasses. Case followed at my heels, giving me some space. The call to my dad had been short. He couldn't tell me anything, and I didn't have anything to tell him about The Oak Grove. We agreed to talk again in the morning.

Beckett pounded away on his phone, still texting with Joyce Townsend.

Addie murdered. Found in the trunk of her car. Stuffed away like a pair of hiking boots or a spare blanket. Before we left the bar, Beckett had filled in some morbid details from the texts he'd received from Joyce. I pictured the scene: the police tape surrounding her red Audi coupe. The trunk open. Flashes popping from the crime scene photographer's camera. My dad and the other officers, uniformed and plain clothed, talking in subdued tones. They'd be waiting on the medical examiner, eager to get going with the investigation.

I didn't paint in the blood or the body. I wasn't squeamish, but I didn't want to imagine what Addie had gone through. I tried instead to remember the time we'd met up in Seattle. We'd been in our thirties, Addie already on her second marriage. She'd been full of energy, and I had barely uttered a word. But her smile had been the same as it ever was—a mixture of joy and mischief—and I didn't mind listening to the tales of her life. We'd already drifted apart by then, our closeness a thing we remembered rather than continued to experience. Addie had always been a force of nature who left little room for those not living immediately in her wake.

"They're close," said Case. "Beckett and Joyce. Back from their Science Club days."

I nodded. I'd wondered why she texted Beckett, of all people. She was a year younger than him and Case, and I'd barely known of her existence during our school days. From what I knew now, Joyce could be an odd duck. She took fandom obsessions to the extreme. Once, she'd driven all the way to Santa Fe just to meet George R. R. Martin. And that was *before* the TV show.

"She's coming over," said Beckett, finally looking up. He sniffled, and his eyes went wide. "I hope that's okay. I mean, like, we're supposed to be—"

"It's fine," I said. The date was officially over, anyway. Slumping into a chair at the gaming table, I plucked up my Valkyrie and fiddled with it. Had Addie done something to put herself in jeopardy? I cringed at how easy it was to cast blame. And yet, if the murder wasn't random, it'd be easier to solve. That was good for Addie. Something, at least. I sputtered a laugh and almost choked. *Easier to solve*, as if I knew anything more than Vera Stanhope or Stephanie Plum had taught me. Them, and a dozen other heroines on page and screen.

Case and Beckett watched my outburst, their eyes darting

between them. But neither mustered the courage to say anything. I ignored them and studied my Valkyrie. My hands. My shoes. Anything contained within my own private space. After a while, Case disappeared and emerged from the back of the shop with cups of burnt coffee. We slurped in a heavy silence while waiting for Joyce Townsend to arrive.

"Have you figured it out yet?" she demanded as soon as she burst through the door. Her full figure was hidden under a knee-length brown coat. The style of it reminded me of Dick Tracy, like it was better suited as a costume than for practical wear. Her auburn hair was in a bun, with a pair of pencils jabbed through it. Cute, I thought, though trying a little too hard to be on point. She worked as a librarian, after all. Thin lines streaked from her eyes, born from a life of squinting.

She stared at me, and I caught an undertone of something, not menacing, but a challenge all the same. I blinked. My brain cells tried their best, but most decided a slack-jawed expression the best response.

I'm nothing if not quick-witted.

"That's the thing," said Case. He yawned. The hour had grown late. "It could be anybody. The whole town knows the trailhead where you found her car, and the highway runs from the Coast to the Cascades. It wouldn't take a lot of effort for the murderer to be in another state by now."

"Wait, what?" I snapped at Case. "That's what you were thinking about? Who did it? Like you're some great detective?" But my anger faded fast. Case didn't deserve it. Besides, I had to agree with his assessment. I nodded a half-hearted apology and turned my attention back to Joyce. Something in her expression told me she'd held back a few juicy bits of information in her texts. She'd wanted a stage.

"Walk us through it." Beckett wiped his nose. He must've thought the same. He cleared the table and sat backward on his chair. I could see the calculations spooling in his head. Science Club, indeed.

Joyce forced her attention away from me. She took a deep breath to prepare herself before launching into the tale. "I was coming home and saw the car near the Buckner Falls Trailhead." She used her hands to demonstrate. "At first, I didn't think anything of it. But then I noticed it was Addie's car, and I thought, *She wouldn't park there*. It's only a mile from her house, and she hikes what? Twelve miles a day? It didn't make sense. There was no sign of anyone around, so I pulled over and got out to look."

To snoop. I read between the lines.

"Addie Newsome, the Queen Bee," said Beckett. He spoke the name in an awed whisper and slowly shook his head. "It must've been a deal gone bad. Like, way bad."

"A deal?" My head about spun loose from the whiplash. "What's that supposed to mean? Like she was running with some Columbian kingpin or something?" Addie might've done a few things to deserve her reputation, but that didn't mean her memory should be smeared by reckless gossip.

Beckett shrank. "Well, you know. I've heard." Sniffle. "She had money, you know, and the town connections."

Oh, bother. This again.

"What'd you tell the cops?" Case asked, trying to bring focus back to Joyce.

She hesitated. Her gaze flicked to me before finding the corner of the room. "So I had this creepy feeling. You know, like sometimes when you're out in the woods alone and you think you're being watched? I had to get their attention, and I didn't think they'd come out just to check on Addie's car. I mean, they're not known to…"

Her gaze swiveled my way. "You get it, right?"

"Uh, no. Get what?" I was truly dumbfounded.

"Oh, come on!" She all but pouted at having to spell things out for me. "You must know the police don't interfere when it comes to the Newsomes."

"Add the other families," Beckett chirped.

The challenge this time wasn't so subtle. I cocked my head at the insinuation. *Her too?* Where was this coming from? Did she and Beckett spend their free time dreaming up conspiracy theories? A secret cabal of families running the town? Seriously? Irritation mounted, but I did my best to ignore it.

"What did you tell the police? How did you get their attention?" I asked. I had to admit I was now curious.

"So I, uh, said I saw male boot prints leading from the car," Joyce admitted. She grinned, as if giving herself credit for being clever.

"But no sign of Addie's," Case added. He glanced at me, uncertain. "To make it seem like it'd been stolen or something?"

"So they'd be protecting the Newsomes rather than interfering. Smart," said Beckett.

"What?" I was lost. It was like they were speaking a foreign language they'd cooked up in Beckett's basement.

"Well, it was true," Joyce argued. "There were large boot prints all around the car. I just elaborated a bit and made them seem more sinister. And I left out the other, smaller set. A good thing, too, else Addie might've been out there for days." She wheeled on me, as if I were about to throw the book at her. "I helped your dad out. Of course, he won't see it that way."

I tried desperately not to roll my eyes. "You told him you found boot prints…at a trailhead. I think you're safe. And why wouldn't he see it that way?"

She huffed at my lack of understanding.

"You knew her best, Charlie," said Beckett. "Who do you think did it?"

I shrugged and kept my face a blank mask. This whole conversation was getting to be a bit too much. "Like Case said, it could be anybody." Anyone I'd name would certainly be a shot in the dark. The last time I'd seen Addie, she'd just come out of the salon, and we'd almost knocked each other over. Her face had scrunched, ready to snap at me for having the audacity to get in her way. But then she'd recognized me and lit up in excitement. She had to tell me all about her trip to Paris and the bath salts she'd found in a shop along the Champs-Élysées that had changed her life. She had to run, though, and we'd promised to make plans to catch up.

We both knew those plans would never happen. And they hadn't.

But I didn't want to tell Beckett or Joyce that. It would feel like a betrayal, more fuel for their gossip. Fiddling with my coffee, I spun the cup in my hands and studied the dried smears that ran along the lip. I sipped and grimaced. The liquid had turned bitter and cold.

"Her ex-husbands," said Case. "They have to be in play."

I sighed. "Neither live anywhere close to here, and neither owe her alimony."

Still, Case had a point. I wondered if Dad would tell me whether Addie's exes were suspects. Or had they already been ruled out?

"It has to be someone local," said Joyce. She perched stiffly in her chair, daring anyone to challenge her. "I've worked it out. If it was someone from out of town, they would've ditched the car farther away. Somewhere where they could catch a bus or steal another car. This was someone who acted in a rush. They had to drive her car but not be seen, and they wanted to be home in a hurry, so they had to stay close."

"For an alibi," said Beckett. His head bobbed in agreement.

Joyce beamed. "Exactly."

"Okay, Detective Frogger. That's kind of a leap," said Case. He paused for laughs that didn't come before continuing. "I get the rush-and-panic part, but you're assuming the car was moved. You're assuming Addie hadn't met someone there at the trailhead. Someone with their own car."

"Or someones!" Beckett shouted.

"Wasn't it moved?" Joyce asked, with a coy grin. "We could ask the police." Her tone made my skin crawl. I knew exactly who she meant to do the asking.

"No," I barked. "Definitely not."

Joyce batted her eyes while keeping her grin still. The effect was a bit creepy, but I kept her gaze. Obviously, I had let her down. "Good grief, Charlie. It'll become public information eventually." She broke away and pawed toward Case. "Anyway, it's a safe bet the car was moved. I didn't see into the trunk, of course, but there weren't any signs Addie had been killed inside the car, or anywhere nearby. I would've seen the evidence. That kind of mess is hard to hide."

Her eyes widened. A hand went to her mouth, and her head turned back to me. "Oh, so sorry. I know you two were once BFFs."

Uh-huh. Now I wanted to ask Dad about the car, if only to knock the smugness off Joyce's face. Assuming she was wrong. Which I had to admit, she probably wasn't. A bitch, maybe, but definitely clever.

"It's okay," said Beckett, like a knight in rusting armor. "No offense."

"What happened to a drug deal gone wrong?" I flung my irritation his way. "A minute ago you had Addie buying kilos of smack, and now she's being moved around town like a sack of potatoes?" I folded my arms across my chest. "So what's your theory? That someone in Harvest Falls is that cold, callous, and calculating? That someone we all know hated Addie enough to kill her? Like maybe I'll get coffee and say hi to them tomorrow? Or maybe wait next to them in line at the Saturday Market, chatting away about the size of this year's huckleberries? Or maybe…"

Oh, crap! Stop talking! My throat seized as I thought over what I'd uttered. Could any of it be true? Feeling safe officially tucked its tail and hid behind the sofa. A killer was out there haunting our small town. The shop suddenly felt like a meat locker, and I hugged myself tighter for warmth.

Beckett pondered his response before speaking. "She was mean sometimes," he said, meekly. Sniffle. "You know, to people."

And selfish. I grimaced. I hadn't wanted to voice the reasons Addie and I were no longer close, the reasons I hadn't made more of an effort over the years. Not even in my own head. We'd lived hundreds of miles apart and drifted the way friends do. That was the easier version of the tale, especially with someone as headstrong as Addie.

Joyce charged in to fuel the fire. "Do you remember two years ago when Gabby Kemper tried to do that fundraiser for the schools—the trail run? She wanted to use her bakery to cater the whole thing, but once Addie got involved, it had to be Addie's way or no way. She fought Gabby over the T-shirts and the medals, even Gabby's own muffin recipes! And when Gabby didn't back down, Addie had the mayor reject the fundraiser permits."

"I remember that," said Case. "Addie sponsored her own event via her mom and the Women's League. Gabby had to toss out a week's worth of baking when it didn't sell. Her husband was pissed."

"That's the way this town works," said Beckett. "Families with connections."

"You're not half wrong." Case waved off my glare. He ran a hand over his lips like he did when he was crunching out a board game strategy. "But back to those large boot prints, could they be Gresham's? He's pretty chummy with her. Or a boyfriend? I don't remember Addie seeing anyone lately. Not that I'm keeping track."

Joyce muttered something, and they were off again.

I stewed. Perhaps the need to defend Addie arose from regret. Or perhaps it stemmed from a loyalty to the firsts we'd shared. We'd bonded over so many—bras, braces, and parties. But those things seemed trivial now. Surface things that only mimicked a real friendship. Either way, I had heard enough. I lurched to my feet. The chair scraped and clattered behind me.

"It's none of our business!" I shouted. "The police will handle it. My dad will handle it."

Case craned his neck. "Aw, don't get bent, Charlie. We know the chief's on it. I bet he already has a suspect in mind from all the evidence they've collected. There's no harm trying to guess who that is. It's not like anyone would ever find out." He looked around. "It's not leaving this room, right?"

"That's not the point. Addie deserves…" I trailed off. Joyce and Beckett had locked eyes. An unspoken exchange passed between them. They might've shouted for its subtlety.

"What?" I demanded.

Licking her lips, Joyce prepared her delivery. "Well, I know times have changed, but in the past your dad…you know, with your mother."

"Again. What?" My hands clenched hard at my hips. In my head, I heard the click of a pin being pulled from a grenade. *Times have changed. As in, my mother isn't alive to defend herself, you fudding curdberry?*

"Everyone knows her best friend was Charlotte Newsome," Joyce explained. "So there is some conflict of interest. Addie's mom. Your mom. Your dad."

"The thing is," Beckett jumped in, "there have been times in the past when…" Sniffle. "Well, someone independent might have reached a different conclusion than the Harvest Falls police department."

The words exploded through me like buckshot, and I staggered back. "You're calling my dad corrupt?"

Joyce's eyes widened in feigned shock. "Charlie, the town loves your dad. For the most part. He's been a staple of this town for decades. But even you have to agree we'll never know the truth about Addie's death. Not the whole truth, anyway."

"You just said it'll be public information!"

"Only what they want us to know," said Beckett.

"Wh-what?" The absurdity of the statement floored me. Yet rather than fueling my rage, it released it. I was too tired, too sad, and too pissed to make sense of anything. Tension bubbled up from my gut, shoved through my throat, and erupted from my lips like the barking of a seal. A mad, foaming-at-the-mouth, barking seal.

Beckett pressed his hands out to form a barrier between us. "Look, it's happened before. You know, years ago with Addie's dad. People say he shot himself out of guilt. It was a big cover-up in the day. Too much corruption. In fact, it's generally accepted as the real truth."

"By morons." I enunciated each syllable at full volume. Marc Newsome's suicide was almost forty years ago. Addie and I had been kids, the whole thing coming out of nowhere. I didn't know what Beckett meant by the guilt part, but I wasn't about to ask.

"There's also your mother's accident," said Joyce. "The

official police report is rather thin on details."

"Not to mention four years ago," said Beckett. "He arrested members of that bird-watching group, you know, for protesting against logging contracts. Locked them up without charge. Even the mayor made a stink about that one."

"And just last year," Joyce leaped in, all too eager, "the funds from the summer parking tickets that were meant to go to the library wound up paying for a new squad car. That didn't happen by chance."

I stopped listening to the lunacy. Detaining three people for vandalizing parked cars, including the old squad car, did not corruption make. To bring up my mother's accident took things way too far, and I didn't need to stand for it. I whipped my jacket from the back of the chair so forcefully that the chair toppled and clattered to the floor.

"Hey," said Case, finally finding his tongue. He blinked, startled, as if he hadn't been paying attention. He probably hadn't, if his gears had started to crank. "Stay a bit. We can figure this out."

I wasn't sure if he meant Addie's murder or Joyce and Beckett disrespecting my father. I'd guess the former. Everything was a wondrous game with Case, and no one ever got hurt. That's part of why he was always single. I wiped a hand over my face. I was flushed and heated. My hands trembled, half in fury, half in embarrassment.

"They're not Gresham's," I said. "The boot prints. Try someone else."

"How're you sure?" Beckett begged. His gaze had turned mopey, like that of a puppy who knew he'd done wrong.

"Trust me." I tried to roast him with my eyes. Though, to be honest, I had no reason to believe Gresham Forthwright guilty or innocent. I just wanted to be contrary, to stop them from soiling the reputation of yet another person I knew.

Charging past their stares, I blew through the door. Case called after, but I had no patience to hang around and listen to crackpot theories. Not if it meant flinging muck about with abandon. Still, I couldn't shake the feeling I might know Addie's killer. That they might be a familiar face around town. And if that was the case, did I know something that would help my dad catch them?

CHAPTER 4

Cold nipped my arms as I stormed up the sidewalk. Moist fog kissed my cheeks. It dampened my hair and jacket. At the end of Second Street, a giant maple cast a dark shadow. Moss shrouded its limbs like an old, mottled sweater. I'd parked my Outback under the maple and had to peel its leaves from my windshield before piling in and cranking the heater.

Despite my efforts to shake them off, Joyce's and Beckett's accusations clung to me like thorns. How could anyone think my dad would obscure the truth? The man I knew would never allow anyone pressure him into hiding anything. Not my mother, and not Charlotte Newsome. Sure, there would always be grumbling. No police chief could survive a single term anywhere without someone being upset. It came with the job. But to point at coverups and corruption? Farfetched was an understatement.

Rubbing my hands for warmth, I forced my focus back onto Addie and the niggle at the back of my head. Was it possible I knew something that would help the investigation? It was hard to tell without knowing more about what had happened. A second, selfish thought followed the first: Would me knowing her killer personally make things any better?

Perhaps easier to explain than a random act by a stranger? But no, I chided myself, there was no explanation that would make what happened easier for anyone.

The notion of Gresham Forthwright being led away in cuffs sprang to mind, but it made me frown. Addie's mother's paramour was a well-known land developer in town. Always with a smile on his face, he had a glad handshake for everyone. He had expensive tastes too: a sports car, fancy dinners, and an open door anywhere he wanted. He and Addie had always seemed to get along, as far as I could tell. But maybe I didn't know him as well as I thought. There'd always been an edge to him, something hidden beneath the surface. He'd wanted to buy my grandmother's land since the day I inherited it—the stretch beneath Case's game shop, The Oak Grove, and the struggling quilting place in between. I'd resisted his charms thus far, but he was not a man to give up easily. His advances felt like a ticking clock counting down to the inevitable.

Not that I had complete control over the decision, to begin with. My grandmother's gift had come with a humdinger of a catch. She and my mother had made me promise certain things when I was young. Things expected of me as a scion of the Danner-Goode family. Things I should've accomplished long ago, like finishing medical school. Things I'd long avoided. Now with them both gone, the weight of upholding those promises squashed my shoulders like a stone gargoyle.

My Outback's tires rattled as I hit a few ruts. I forced myself to focus and slowed a bit. The road ahead, illuminated by my headlights, was lined with tall cedars and dotted with pockets of damp pavement. Upon pulling off Second Street, I headed toward the Harvest Heights complex on Hemlock Lane where Case and I shared a two-bedroom apartment. At the start of summer, I'd returned to find my childhood home converted into a convalescent place—the elegant Danner House, another of my mother's wishes—and I'd needed to move my bed and clothes elsewhere. At the time, Case was sleeping in his shop after a bad breakup. His parents had moved to California years earlier, and I had no desire to move in with my dad. We figured sharing rent would be temporary, just for the summer. Why not? Only now Christmas songs played on the radio, and the days marched ever onward.

The complex was quiet. A few security lights illuminated the beige siding and chocolate trim. The palette gave the buildings the feel of a summer camp. I climbed the exterior stairs, enjoying the silence. None of the people sleeping in their units knew about Addie. Not yet. By morning, that would change. The news would spread like proverbial wildfire.

As the lock clicked, I noticed the lights inside my unit were on. My hand froze. My throat clamped tight. *Had I left them on?* It wasn't like Case to do so. He was a man who knew how to keep a budget.

That image of Addie's red coupe flashed in my head. Trunk open. Beckoning for me to peer inside. I tried to laugh away the tension, but reality sank in. A killer was on the loose, and I was a single woman coming home alone. To an apartment with lights on that shouldn't be. I turned my head slowly and snuck a glance over my shoulder.

Only the cold of night stared back.

Taking a deep breath, I wiggled the key loose and pushed

the door open with a jab of my finger. It swung free and thumped into the doorstop. Day-old pizza and a hint of lemon cleaning solvent met my nose. And lilac. Sweet yet pungent, it filled the living room.

"Hello?" I called, my fear dissolving. I recognized the lilac scent.

A rustle came from the kitchen, and Geraldine Henry appeared. Her dark hair held a tinge of steel. It was done up in a perfect bob. Her makeup was flawless. No shocker there. She always looked immaculate, as if ready for a society dinner.

"Oh, good heavens, Charlie. You scared me," she said.

I remained fixed in the doorway. "What are you doing here?" I blurted. My dad's other half had come to the apartment only once before. She'd found it messy and uncomfortable, I learned later. She must've used his key to gain entry this time.

"That's how you greet me?" Her gaze hardened.

"No," I answered a little too quickly. Unconsciously, I ran a hand through my cropped hair. "Sorry. It's just a surprise. It's late. I thought, with the lights on…it made me think about…" I halted my ramble and reset.

"Dad called you about Addie," I said, starting over. He wouldn't dare not call. Though they maintained separate houses, Geraldine Henry had all but become my stepmother. She and my mother had been best friends for years, when I was young. Along with Charlotte Newsome, the three had been inseparable.

Yep, so there was that.

"Oof." Geraldine clutched her gut as if I'd struck her. She

glanced behind me and beckoned with her free hand. "Come inside and shut the door. Do you want the whole town to hear you?"

I obeyed and set the dead bolt for good measure. Offering Geraldine the pleather armchair, I perched on the edge of the couch. The roses in its pattern had seen better days, but they brought a softer feel to the tiny living room. My touch, in a sea of Case's things.

"Absolutely dreadful," she said, once she settled. She crossed her legs and kept one hand dangling over an armrest. Her fingers no doubt yearned for a cigarette. "This unpleasantness, what a mess it makes of everything your mother strived to build. And poor Charlotte will have to scrap years of planning. All that hard work, gone! I knew that daughter of hers would wind up in some sort of trouble." She lowered her voice. "*More* than the divorces, I mean. It was only a matter of time."

Seriously? I'd never been a screamer, but oh, how I wanted to let loose. But that wasn't my way. Peacemaker—that was the term I preferred. It sounded better than "family doormat." Choking down my outrage, I forced my shoulders to unclench and started a silent chant.

Keep it civil for Dad. Keep it civil for Dad. Keep it civil for Dad.

"You always spoke well of Addie," I said after a moment had passed. "I feel sad for her. Devastated." I had to steer Geraldine a different direction. I couldn't stomach discussing my mother and Charlotte Newsome's grand plans to revitalize Harvest Falls. Nor my part within it. Not tonight.

"Well, of course." Geraldine made a curt humming noise.

"Addie and you were close, like sisters. You must not have seen what others saw. Not that I'd speak ill of the dead." She took in my outfit with a disapproving eye, as if seeing me for the first time. "I'm surprised you didn't call me yourself, when you heard."

I started chanting again.

"I'm sorry. I didn't think of it," I said after a breath. Yet I wondered what had really brought Geraldine to my apartment. She seemed uninterested in offering any real sympathy about Addie. "Does Charlotte know?"

"She knows, poor thing. Your father had to wake her before the gossip mill started. You know how it will be with the riffraff in this town." She leaned forward. "I do hope that nosy busybody who found Addie's car doesn't try and soil the Newsome reputation, but I wouldn't put it past her."

My ears perked up. Maybe Dad had shared more with Geraldine than Joyce had shared at the shop. "Does Dad think she saw something that will help catch who did it?"

"Oh, heavens! It doesn't matter what she saw," Geraldine replied. Her hand came toward her lips, until perhaps she remembered she no longer smoked. She flicked her fingers into the air instead. "It matters what she says. There's more than Addie's name on the line."

My jaw fell slack. Joyce's and Beckett's accusations echoed in my head, but I dared not utter them aloud. They'd only spin Geraldine into a tizzy and wind up doing more harm than good. The last thing I needed was for her to storm away. She'd tell my dad. He'd make excuses for her behavior, and I would wind up the bad guy.

Besides, I didn't want him to hear the slander. He had enough on his plate.

Still, her words made me uncomfortable. A throbbing came to my temple, and I rubbed at it involuntarily.

Geraldine misread my concern. "There's no need to worry, Charlie," she said. "Your father knows his business and will have this whole ordeal wrapped up soon. I'm sure of it." She reached over to pat my knee. "You remember what he always says, right?"

I groaned inwardly but repeated the mantra I'd heard since childhood. "Building a case is not about what happened. It's about what can be proved in court."

"There. Now, doesn't that make everything seem simpler?"

No. No, it did not. In fact, out of context, it made it sound like Joyce and Beckett had a right to be skeptical. I closed my eyes and rubbed my temples with both hands, this time with gusto.

"Well, it's late, and I just wanted to check on you." Geraldine's clothes rustled as she stood. Her footfalls crossed the room, but she paused and called back. "Oh, I'd nearly forgotten. Did you receive anything from Miley University yet?"

My eyes flipped open and rolled to the ceiling. I should've guessed her intentions for the visit. There was no time like a tragedy to remind me of my obligations. Even if I owed Geraldine nothing, she held my mother's whip, and she knew well how to wield it.

"Nope," I lied. I rose and ushered her out of the apartment. She scowled, muttering her disapproval of the postal service.

"Well, it will come," she said. "None of this business changes anything. By next year, you'll have forgotten all about it." She grasped my arms. "One day you'll make your mother so proud. I just know it."

I had nothing to say to that, so kept my lips clamped like a good Thumper. We parted with a stiff hug and air kisses on the cheek. As soon as the door closed, I reset the dead bolt. Case had a key to let himself in later, and I was ready to collapse.

Shuffling into my bedroom, I cringed at sight of the letter from Miley University resting on my dresser. The envelope contained a single sheet of paper. I hadn't even made the waitlist. I guess the decades I'd spent working in San Diego, first for a tourist company and then for a charity, hadn't screamed "aspiring doctor" to them. My undergraduate grades were likewise mediocre. The only classes I'd really enjoyed were anthropology and criminal justice, and those had been electives, the latter audited.

The rest of the room was a hot mess. Since returning home, I'd reverted to my teenage tendencies, and my personal space had fallen victim to a series of miniature eruptions. Shirts, hoodies, and wadded pairs of pants scattered over the faux-pine vinyl flooring. A few of the dresser drawers sat ajar. Sticky notes decorated the pictures I'd hung on the walls. The prints displayed open pastorals and lush English gardens, my idea of bliss. The sticky notes were in Case's handwriting. They reminded me to buy food, get the Outback's oil changed, and to fold my own damn laundry.

The notes were a joke between us, but also Case's way of

showing he cared. I'd dated Mason for so long that adulting for just myself had been a rough adjustment, and I'd needed encouragement to get things done. Luckily, I'd found work as well. Besides the police station, I took pro bono shifts at the game shop and had a regular gig dog sitting. The routine need to be somewhere helped, as did copious pints of Tillamook white chocolate raspberry ice cream.

Slumped on my bed, I yanked off my boots and stopped cold. A hint of neon-green cotton peeked out of an open drawer. It was part of a T-shirt from Malcolm's Arcade. One for the staff, with bold white lettering emblazoned across the chest. I'd worked at the place in high school, and again briefly after returning home, while the summer tourists still lurked.

Addie had spotted me in the shirt and laughed. But she'd also held a knowing look in her eye. She'd understood my situation like no one else in town could. The guilt from failing our mothers' master plans, the trajectory they'd plotted since our first breaths. Her divorces and her own return to Harvest Falls might've been more glamorous than mine, but they'd happened all the same. Both of us had experienced pure humiliation, the kind that shrivels you into a soppy heap and leaves your world in tatters.

At least my mother had not lived to see my shame. I was thankful for that, when I could stomach the guilt. She passed during my second year of college. A single-car accident. I had only recently met Mason, and he became my rock, helping me through my grief. By the time I graduated, he'd joined the navy, and we found ourselves in San Diego. There was no rush for medical school then. I had my own life to live outside my family's grasp.

But that life had fizzled and died a slow death over the years.

Now Addie was gone, too, and it was up to me to redeem us both.

No pressure, right?

My eyes had barely closed when my phone rattled. Dad texted. He asked me to meet a state detective in the morning and play hostess. **Buy him a bagel. Get him to the Newsome house.** *Perfect.* It'd be just like my time as Miss Harvest Falls, my junior year of high school. Only then I'd had Addie at my side and a bright future ahead of me. Not twenty wasted years and a rejection slip atop my dresser.

Maybe I'd wear my sash.

CHAPTER 5

Detective Frank Nichols wore an off-the-rack suit. He had the appearance of a football linebacker just past his prime: muscular, but in a slightly sagging way, with a bulge around his waistline. Maybe a few years older than I was, I guessed. He greeted me with a firm handshake and appraising gaze.

"You Charlie?" he asked. He tucked a leather portfolio folder under one arm. Addie's face flashed through my mind as I caught the lined yellow pages of the pad inside. All her life was distilled into a few scratched notes.

I nodded. We stood on Bywater Street, the town's main thoroughfare, which led directly from the highway to the base of the falls. Second Street, Bywater's hundred-year-old upstart sibling, paralleled the same path a block over. But where Second Street held haunts for locals, Bywater was all for the tourists.

In the summer months, it was near impossible to find a seat in the Sweet Little Buttercup Bakery & Café. But I saw through the etched glass windows that the place was barely half full this late in the year. I clapped my hands together and rubbed them. I'd thrown on a fresh pair of jeans and a sweatshirt, but it was early, and the air outside was frosty.

"Said I'd be fine with the sludge at the station," Frank said. "Bad coffee goes with the job, but the chief sent me here."

"He must like you some," I replied with a smile. "I wouldn't eat anything from the station's fridge either."

Frank opened the door for me. His lips parted in a wry grin. "Shall we?"

Gabby Kemper ran a bright and cheery bakery that echoed her bubbly personality. I spotted her raven-black ponytail swinging as she hustled into the kitchen. Her minute frame lent a false sense of healthiness to the piles of chocolate-drizzled croissants, jam-filled scones, and sugar-dusted muffins that filled the display case at the counter. A pound of butter went into each, and those were the lighter options.

"Chief Goode said you knew the victim well," said Frank.

The victim. *Oy.* Addie would've hated being called that. My cringe must've shown because Frank offered a half smile of condolence.

"Addie have any enemies?" he asked, for only me to hear.

The question echoed what Joyce and Beckett had asked only hours earlier. But where their words had felt greasy, like voyeurs peeping in on Addie's privacy, Frank's felt natural. I wondered how many times he'd been through this routine and remembered how Case and I used to line up our action figures in mock crime scenes. We mimicked what our adolescent brains imagined my dad's workdays were like. I always made Wonder Woman the lead detective, of course. She had the Lasso of Truth. Who better to uncover a killer?

"No enemies, that I'm aware," I said. "A few rivals." One in particular. I searched for the raven ponytail bouncing along like a Gummi Bear hocked up on Gummiberry Juice.

"What can I get you two?" Madison Parker's voice carried from the counter before I found Gabby. She slouched near the register setup next to the display case. Like most mornings, she hadn't bothered with any makeup. She didn't need to. She had natural features that made any style look good, an athletic figure, and round eyes set off by caramel-colored hair.

I greeted her, and we ordered. Madison hadn't reached high school by the time Addie and I graduated but had become friends with Addie later in life. I thought about mentioning that to Frank, but before I could, Gabby pounced on us with full gummi force.

"Morning, Charlie!" Her voice had a slight accent that seemed to come and go throughout the day, as if she were living two separate lives. But the pep—the pep never left. "Who's your man?"

She sidled up to Frank and offered her hand as if he'd kiss it. I bit my lip to keep from snorting. The woman had no shame.

He clutched the hand, shook it, and replied, "Detective Frank Nichols."

Her face lit up. "Welcome to my humble little bakery, Detective." She waved at Madison. "Give them a pair of croissants. They were baked fresh this morning. I know Charlie loves them, though heaven knows where she keeps them on that body of hers." She winked at me like it was a shared secret between us.

"We heard about Addie," Gabby continued as Madison dug into the display case. "Poor thing. I don't know what she would've been doing out there along the highway so late at night. It wasn't like her at all. Have you any suspects?" She waited only half a beat, staring up at Frank, before carrying on. "Oh, I'm sure you can't say. But you find that out, and I'm sure you'll find out all sorts of interesting things."

Frank's brow furrowed. "And where were you last night?"

Gabby laughed and traced her fingers across the front of her apron. "Me? I drove my husband to the airport in Portland. Last-minute thing. He travels so often for work, but I'm sure he can tell you all about it when he gets back next week."

Frank eyed Madison as she reached over the counter to offer the croissants. She shrank back, uncertain. "I was at the Coast all weekend. Drove home this morning. You can check."

"I'm sure Chief Goode appreciates your outside perspective," said Gabby, wresting the attention back her way. "He's not used to this kind of thing, not in Harvest Falls. I mean, a murder, that's a big case. I'm sure it can be overwhelming for the whole force. Don't you think, Charlie?"

My eyes pulled tight, but I kept the scowl from my face. At least, I thought I did. I knew Gabby liked to stir the pot, yet her statement felt a bit more personal. Maybe because it came on the heels of Joyce's accusations. Was she hinting at something else?

Frank rescued me. "Chief Goode is a fine police officer."

"Well, of course," said Gabby. "But you let me know if there's anything I can do to help. As a thriving business owner, I know it takes a whole community to keep it safe. And our tiny police department…well, they can only do so much. I've brought that up to the mayor several times, that we should have cameras installed on the town buildings, safety being the issue that it is. Isn't that right, Darlene?"

A woman inhaled sharply behind me. I spun and found Darlene Devereux peering over my shoulder. Looking smart in cashmere and bangled earrings, she wore a pursed expression but nodded politely to me before striding from the bakery. The whole reaction struck me as odd. I hadn't heard her sneak up, yet Darlene was far from a rude woman. She ran a cute little flower shop and doted on all her customers. I walked her Labrador, Branson, whenever I could, and watched him when Darlene had a busy evening. I presumed her measured departure came from her desire to avoid engaging with Gabby.

"Where are *your* cameras?" I asked, rounding on the baker. I couldn't keep my irritation contained any longer.

Frank waggled a finger to encompass the bakery. "I noticed that as well."

I wanted to kiss him. I wouldn't mind it, either, no sir.

Gabby folded her arms across her chest, looking wounded. "I've asked and asked, but my hubby just says he'll get around to installing them. He's very busy with work." She glanced around the bakery. I couldn't tell if she was looking for an escape route or to see who might have overheard. Gossips don't like to be gossiped about, after all.

"Stabbed, I can't even think about it," said Madison, out of the blue. She seemed lost in a daze, slouching against the counter.

Gabby jumped in fright. Her head whipped from Madison to Frank to me. Her mouth opened, wavered, and closed.

My blood ran cold. Goose pimples frenzied on my arms. It

was a detail I knew I'd learn eventually, but it still brought on a sense of horror. My mental image of Addie's trunk became a great deal grislier.

Frank's face became a stone mask. "How did you come to know that?" he asked. Color drained from Madison's cheeks. Her round eyes widened. She turned to Gabby.

"Vin D'Amato told me," said Gabby. "He was in here when I first opened. He stopped by to get a cruller like he always does. I didn't think it wrong to ask questions. I mean, he wouldn't have told me if it was a secret, right? Police don't do that in these kinds of things."

Her assertion stung. She might as well have said *good* police don't share information. Vin's loose lips must've been what she was alluding to earlier, her digs at the town's police. I began to stew, shifting from one foot to the other. The leak of information added fuel to the fire for anyone trying to call out Dad's investigation.

"Questions can get you hurt," I blurted. I meant it as a statement about being nosy and the emotional damage gossiping can do. But with my hackles up, the words came out far more menacing.

Gabby's eyes bulged. "Is that a threat?" She stepped behind Frank, all dramatics.

Frank's attention swiveled from her to me. He pointed his thumb toward the door, an unspoken command to heel. I did as I was told, wiping the proverbial egg from my face as I slunk away.

"I'm sorry, Detective, if I overstepped," Gabby said, loud enough for me to hear. "I'm overly friendly sometimes, but I know all the juicy bits around Harvest Falls. You just come and ask if you need anything. I'll save you a huckleberry fritter."

Little bells chimed as I pushed through the door. If it'd been a boxing match, I'd have lost the round. I could only imagine what the cooing Gabby would do after Frank left. Slurping my coffee, I listened for the falls. But rain began to patter down, stealing even that simple solace.

Frank emerged from the bakery. I waited for a scolding comment, but it didn't come. He wore a smug expression as he studied me, as if he'd enjoyed himself.

"Let's go," he said. He indicated a dark sedan parked on the street.

"Go?" My head tilted in confusion. "I thought I'd just draw you a map or something. Point the way."

He barked a laugh. The force of it made me startle. "I can google an address. The victim's mother, Mrs. Newsome, asked for you specifically to be there when I showed up. She's already been notified, so this is just for some background. Normally we try to avoid having non-family present, but since you're on the police payroll, your father was able to convince me. Didn't he tell you?"

"I guess I misunderstood." I scanned my clothes and cringed. What had I been thinking? I should've shown Addie more respect than rags snatched from a pile on the floor, even if I hadn't expected to go to the Newsome house. And why had Charlotte asked for me? As a measure of comfort, Geraldine would've been a better choice. They were thick as thieves. I didn't have any answers, but the thought reminded me to tell Frank about Gabby and Addie's history.

"Addie once told me that some of Gabby's famous recipes are stolen from her own grandmother," I said, as I climbed into the sedan. "Those two used to be close, despite the age gap. They'd go hiking all the time and became real fitness junkies. Madison, too, though she was more drug along like a reluctant sister."

"But there was a falling-out?" Frank asked. He cranked the engine and pulled out into traffic. "Traffic" being a relative term in Harvest Falls. There were only a couple of cars within sight.

I nodded. "With Addie, it was better to win than have friends." The statement made me cringe, but it was the truth. "She always assumed she could make more friends. She and Gabby sparred over men, over popularity, and trivial things like fundraiser logos. You asked me who Addie's rival was, and I'd say it was Gabby Kemper."

"Hmm." Frank made a noise but remained quiet thereafter. I evaluated him once again as I pointed out where to turn to get to the Newsome house. His chin and shoulders had a reassuring bearing, and if his midriff had softened a bit over the years, it hadn't stolen any ruggedness from him. I could do worse, I decided. Much worse. Beckett Cooper sprang to mind.

"How come you haven't asked?" he asked as we climbed a steep rise.

My ears burned. I felt like a kid caught with her hand in the cookie jar. "Asked what?" I tried to fathom what the question would be.

The stone mask returned. "Whether we know who killed Addie Newsome."

"Oh, that," I said. The answer came to my lips before I had to think about it. "If you'd known, you wouldn't have asked me who Addie's enemies were."

Outside, the rain stopped as suddenly as it had started.

Frank grunted. His head bobbed in approval. But rather than making me feel proud, the confirmation sent my mind racing. If the case wasn't open and shut, it meant the killer roamed free and might not ever be caught. I'd seen enough detective shows to know the chances of solving a crime went down with each passing day. And here I sat playing mental kissy-face.

I kicked myself. If I truly wanted to help my dad, I'd need to do more than play the obedient daughter. I mean, here I was with the state detective, with his folder of notes and knowledge of the crime scene, and I'd managed to learn only how he took his coffee—black, two sugars. My dad's reputation wouldn't survive if Addie's murder went unsolved. It would always hang over him. People like Joyce and Gabby would see to it. Their interest disturbed me, as did their intentions.

I also had a sinking feeling the town's mistrust ran deeper than a couple conspiracy nuts. Darlene and Madison had acted odd, and even Case hadn't balked at Joyce's prattling. If the police didn't find something tangible, and fast, how long would it be before all of Harvest Falls gathered their pitchforks and torches?

After all, scared people did some awfully stupid things.

CHAPTER 6

Frank stared in awe as we pulled up to Charlotte Newsome's sprawling estate. With over a dozen rooms, the house lorded over at least that many wooded acres. It perched higher in the mountains near a few secluded resorts and other rich homes. Locals referred to the entire area as Above the Falls. The level of derision inflected in the moniker depended entirely on who was speaking.

Gresham Forthwright waited for us on the porch. He didn't lend any favors to the area's reputation. Casual for Gresham involved Italian shoes that gleamed, a Rolex watch that sparkled, and enough product in his curly hair to make an 80s rock band proud. He must have quite the moisturizing routine, too, because his skin made him appear closer to my age than Charlotte's.

As I recalled Joyce's story, my gaze drifted innocently to his shoes. But without knowing the comparison size found near Addie's car, I could make neither heads nor tails of his leather showboats.

Frank kept a muted but polite tone as I made introductions. Gresham, on the other hand, put on a show.

"I'm going to make Charlie this rich someday," he said. He

waved a hand at the house like a *Price Is Right* showgirl. His chompers shone like pearls. "She'll be off to medical school soon, making us proud, and I'll have dollars rolling in by the wheelbarrow for her return."

"That so?" said Frank.

I cringed at the mention of medical school. I was used to Gresham's salesman bluster, but I wanted to hide my head in a hole, all the same. Yet I smiled and played along. I owed Charlotte at least that much. She'd had the worst night a parent could ever have. Whatever sting my personal failures carried, they were nothing by comparison.

Gresham led the way. His bearing became more somber and subdued as we entered the house. The great room was immaculate and full of lush furniture. Sunlight beamed through an array of windows running from floor to ceiling along the back wall. With the trees beyond, a stone fireplace and exposed beams painted a rustic feel, despite the size of the place.

Charlotte welcomed me with a warm hug that plucked at my soul. Lavender mixed with the fresh cotton smell of her sweater. The familiar clank of her bangles sounded as she patted my back. She tried to hide it, but I caught the slight tremble of her shoulders.

She pulled back and greeted Frank. "Detective, I have the photos you asked about. Gresham was a dear and printed some from her phone to go with the older set. He's pulled the video too."

We were led to a couch and seated in front of a coffee table laden with prints of Addie. I caught a few I recognized. Some were from days I'd forgotten. Others were more recent, from events I hadn't been a part of. I pulled one out and barely kept my throat from clamping tight enough to pop my head off. There was a beaming Addie, just a couple of years ago, her arms wrapped around Gabby and Madison. All wore hiking kit, jackets shed and tied around their waists.

"Addie had so much planned for her life," said Charlotte. She sat in a grand chair opposite us, with Gresham hovering over her shoulder. "She planned on opening a day spa and health café for the tourist season next year. We'd only just found a place for it."

A café, eh? I smiled inwardly. The café would've put her in direct competition with Gabby, no matter the spin on health-conscious food. That was just like Addie.

"Sounds impressive," said Frank. He pulled out a notepad and scratched a few things on it. I tried to snoop but couldn't make out what it said without leering into his lap.

Charlotte clutched Gresham's hand. "Oh, it would've been. Addie and I had all kinds of plans to revitalize Harvest Falls, along with Geraldine Henry." Her gaze became distant. When it refocused, she started, as if she'd forgotten we were there. "Oh, Charlie's mother, too, years ago, when she was with us. We wanted to bring the town back to its roots as a place of healing and rejuvenation. You know, that's how Harvest Falls started."

"There are golden waters above the falls, and golden troves to be pumped from them," said Gresham, chuckling. "That's an old family joke."

Slapping his hand, Charlotte scowled. "Now is not the time, for heaven's sake!" She returned her attention to Frank.

"But yes, the minerals in the hills above the falls are the key. That's why it's called Harvest Falls, from the golden hue up there. There are springs, too, that were used for soaking and nourishment for the soul."

"And Addie was vocal with these plans?" Frank asked. "Anyone against them?"

"Well." Charlotte spat the word. "You can start with our mayor, Ruth Radford. She's a squealing cog jamming up the works. And I can't see why. She works against her own best interest, standing in our way. Bringing prosperity back to Harvest Falls would put a feather in her cap, one she could wear the rest of her life."

Frank scratched on his pad. "Why is she so opposed?"

"You'd have to ask her," answered Gresham, as Charlotte shrugged. "She's a woman beyond reason sometimes. Beyond a few other faculties, too, if you ask me. She stopped by this morning to offer condolences and pressed for every detail like she was writing a book. I had to kindly show her out."

"That's true," said Charlotte. "You must've just missed her heading down the hill. Sometimes she's as bossy as a spoiled cat, but that's neither here nor there. I'm sure she's no murderer."

"No," I agreed, breaking my silence and nodding to Frank. I knew the reason Ruth stood against Charlotte's plans. Though bringing in high-end shops would benefit certain business owners, their products and services would be unaffordable to half the town. Our mayor was looking out for the little guy.

Tapping his pen against his leg, Frank considered a

moment before turning to Gresham. "Do you stay over very often, Mr. Forthwright?"

"He didn't last night," Charlotte answered. "I called Gresham here this morning. I needed him. He's the only other one, besides Addie, who knows how to work this insufferable device." She waved toward a large television mounted on the wall. "Show the detective, dear."

Gresham picked up a remote control. "We've watched it already. I didn't remember the camera was there, to be honest, until Charlotte asked me to get the feed. The single camera is mounted on the corner of Addie's front porch." Hitting a series of buttons caused the large screen to flash through a menu until an image appeared. Addie's place. Smaller than Charlotte's house, the porch still held the upmarket furnishings that spoke of wealth. A manicured lawn bordered by roses ran out from the porch. Along the left side, a paved driveway stretched toward a distant street. At such a blown-up size, the image was a bit grainy. A timestamp ran along the bottom. Both the image and timestamp were frozen at early the previous evening.

"Addie installed it a couple of years ago," Charlotte said. "I thought it sent the wrong message about the safety of this town, but now…" She glanced across the scattering of pictures on the coffee table and swallowed down a lump in her throat.

I found a tissue box and handed her one.

She crumpled it in her fist. "There's something you have to see, Detective. When Chief Goode and I spoke last night, I told him Addie had gone out for the evening. She'd told me she had plans. But I didn't know when, or with whom. And I hadn't known Gresham had stopped by her place earlier in the evening."

I went rigid. An image of myself eating crow in front of Joyce and Beckett popped into my head. Perhaps they'd been right to go straight to the only notable man in Addie's life. He couldn't be ruled out so quickly. I'd made an assumption of innocence because I knew him.

But, of course, if he was guilty, would he really agree to come work the recorder?

"Well, yes." Gresham cleared his throat. "I dropped off some papers before meeting Charlotte for dinner near my office. You can see it here."

The recording zipped forward. The sun set, and the image flipped to black and white, with a green tinge. Gresham adjusted the playback to normal speed. At just after seven, his sleek sports car pulled into the driveway. He climbed out and came to the door. After straightening his shirt, he ran a hand through his hair as he waited. The porch light flipped on, bathing the scene in color. Addie answered and stepped onto the porch. I peered closer, leaning on my elbows. She wore sweats and slippers. Her hair was pulled into a messy bun. It was an outfit for staying in, not going out.

What did that mean? She'd told her mother the opposite. Was she meeting someone late? My gut roiled at the possibilities.

The pair hugged in a familial way. Gresham said something, and Addie laughed. He handed her some papers, kissed her forehead, and left.

"We were going to surprise Charlotte," said Gresham.

"The documents for Addie's shop were ready, and she wanted to sign them on her own."

"When you left, you went straight to meet Mrs. Newsome for dinner?" Frank asked.

"Yes." Gresham nodded, then added a bit uncomfortably, "Seen by everyone in the restaurant, and we stayed almost until closing."

I breathed a sigh of relief, thankful Gresham was officially in the clear, at least in my book.

"There's more," said Charlotte.

Gresham fumbled with the remote. The recording fast-forwarded. A few minutes after he drove off, another car pulled up. It was an older hatchback that had seen better days. The driver's-side door opened. The figure that emerged wore dark jeans and a hoodie. I squinted but could make out little else until the porch light flicked on once more. Then I jerked back and pointed, like I was trying to win at charades.

"That's Sera Simmons!" Though the navy blue hood was pulled tight around her face, there was no mistaking the pink-and-green hair peeking out, nor the two silver rings punching through her lip. My brain spun, searching for why Sera would've come to see Addie. I'd always been closer with Sera, though we'd only lightly be called friends. Addie dismissed her at best and openly mocked her at worst.

"I always warned Addie to be careful," said Charlotte. Her nose shriveled. "That Sera was the wrong kind of friend. Someone who'd take advantage of her. And now, look."

Addie had returned to the porch. She did not look happy to see Sera. She kept her arms crossed and her hips all attitude.

Sera shoved her hands into the pouch of her hoodie. Her head bobbed as she spoke. I wished I could read her lips. But I didn't need to, to see where the conversation headed.

Addie raised her arms, hollering something, and Sera stepped back. The pairs' gestures became emphatic and wild. Sera kept stepping back, and Addie followed. They reached the driveway before Sera finally threw up her hands and turned away. She marched to her car and drove off. Addie folded her arms and watched her leave.

"Wow." I blinked a few times. "That was pretty heated. I didn't think they knew each other well enough to get that mad."

Gresham paused the recording. "They had a falling-out recently, after some Halloween party. They'd socialized before that—you know, same age, small town."

"I have a picture of the party here," said Charlotte. She leaned forward and searched through the stack of photos. She found one and handed it to Frank.

I craned my head to look. In it, Addie wore a skimpy Red Riding Hood getup, complete with a cape and shoulderless peasant blouse. She smiled and gave a sexy pose. Sera lurked behind her dressed in a baggy gray jumpsuit. Her mask rested atop her head. I recognized it from an old horror movie, one James and Case could probably quote.

"She's a bad seed," Charlotte said. "She always has been, just like her mother."

I frowned. Despite the costume, I had always known Sera to be more on the free-loving hippie side of life than as a wrathful sort. She'd had a hard childhood. My mother always whispered about the Simmons family as if they carried the plague, but I made a point to be friendly whenever our paths crossed.

Frank finished his scribbling. He took the photo and asked if he could keep it. When Charlotte consented, he asked, "Is there anything else on the recording?"

"Yes," said Gresham. "Addie leaves."

I jumped. It felt like they'd buried the lede. No matter how many visitors Addie had received, seeing her leave the house absolved them all. Or if it didn't completely, it at least opened the door to a million other possibilities, and a million other suspects.

"Show me," said Frank. His tone sounded as strained as my wits.

Gresham complied. True to his word, the image remained clear for the next hour. Then Addie's Audi appeared from off camera, just before nine, heading down the driveway toward the street. Without the porch light on, it was too dark to make out any details of the driver, but a flash of moonlight at the end of the driveway lit up the interior for a brief moment. It was enough to see there was only one person in the car. At least, one person upright.

"The driveway wraps around the side of the house to the garage," I said, at the same time Charlotte explained the same.

"The recording is clear the rest of the night," said Gresham.

Frank tapped his pen. "It's very dark, and the driver's facing the street the entire time. Why do you believe it was Addie?"

Gresham chuckled before catching himself and clearing his throat. "Addie loved that car. She didn't let anyone else drive it."

I opened my mouth, about to fully consume my foot by pointing out the obvious flaw in Gresham's logic, when Frank put a gentle hand on my leg to quiet me. I stilled and noted that I owed Frank another sugary treat from the café.

"Oh, my poor Addie." Charlotte dabbed at her face. My heart tugged. I couldn't image the strength it took to be walking us through this. Reaching over, I rubbed her arm. As I did, another photo on the table caught my eye. In this one, Addie stood before her Audi. It must've been shortly after she bought it, a photo taken to commemorate the event.

"Who would she have met?" Frank asked.

"Oh, I can't imagine." Charlotte searched Gresham's face for answers. He shuffled awkwardly but for once remained silent.

Frank made a note. He tried the question a few more times, each with a slight variance, trying to determine who Addie might have seen. Would she have gone to celebrate the signing? Was she seeing anyone special? Did she like to go anywhere alone to relax?

An odd thing struck me, and I scoured the pile of photos. There were none of her life in Portland, where she'd lived in her thirties. None with either of her ex-husbands. Charlotte had either chosen to weed those out, or she hadn't had any. It'd be just like her and Addie to have destroyed all evidence of the failed marriages. I couldn't imagine doing the same to Mason, no matter how things had ended. But not all women treated being scorned the same.

Rising, Frank thanked Charlotte and offered condolences once more. Charlotte's parting embrace was not as steady as it had been earlier. I thought she might be at the end of keeping up appearances for a while, ready to go into her bedroom and collapse. No one would blame her. I'd do the same in her shoes. Or, at least, I thought I would.

But as we left the Newsome house, my curiosity ran rampant, and I kept replaying the security video in my mind. I couldn't help myself.

"That was something, huh?" I said, once we were alone in the driveway. "Gresham, the fight with Sera, Addie's car leaving." I stressed this last fact. Frank offered only silence in return, so I added, "It could've been anyone driving, no matter what Gresham thinks."

Again, I was met with only silence. But Frank glanced my way quizzically. Or close enough to quizzically that it encouraged me to continue.

I mused aloud. "There's a side door to the garage. If the killer knew about the porch camera, they could've entered through there. Or maybe come to the back of the house and knocked on the sliding glass door. Addie would've answered, if she knew them." I started at my own statement and looked to Frank. "Addie knew her killer?" *Had I done a thing? Actually proven Joyce's point?*

He grinned. "You're assuming two things: that Addie was killed at home, and that the killer avoided the camera on purpose."

Oh, crap. So much for being useful. I heaved a groan, felt guilty about being so callous, then stepped in front of Frank. "Was Addie killed at home? Can you tell me that at least? Do you know?"

"She was," he admitted, side-stepping me. "We found the primary scene late last night. We think she was killed in her back garden, though there's evidence inside the garage too. The techies have been at it all morning."

I swallowed, feeling suddenly colder, but carried on. "But you asked Charlotte a bunch of questions about whom Addie would go to meet. And you didn't correct them about who was driving the car. It's not likely she came home later and parked on the street, out of sight of the camera."

"No," he agreed. "And there wouldn't have been enough time for that before she was discovered at the trailhead, anyway. No, Addic was definitely killed at home sometime in the window between Sera Simmons's departure and her car leaving her house. That's the only scenario that works with what we saw on the video, what we know from the evidence at her house, and when her car was found."

"Meaning, it was definitely the killer we just saw on the video. So you were just trying to, what? Learn more about her friends and habits with those questions to Charlotte?"

Frank nodded.

I didn't know if it was clever or cruel to lead Charlotte on that way, but I jumped to another thought before deciding.

"Was the killer already in the house when Gresham arrived? Oh my God, were they waiting somewhere, or did they have a drink with Addie, or was there evidence in the bedroom of a tryst?"

Frank put up a hand but couldn't keep the laughter from his face. "Slow down. A tryst? Is that what you'd call it? No, no tryst. And we've found no evidence the killer entered the house. Back garden to side garage door, and into the garage. That's it."

"The killer never entered the house." I considered that and switched gears. "But if they left evidence in the garden and garage, why move Addie's body at all? They had to know you'd connect the dots pretty quickly. If they were a stranger, they'd just cut tail and run, taking her car if they needed a ride, and leaving everything else. There'd be no reason for an elaborate misdirection." I recalled Joyce's argument about the killer being local, and I had to admit the pieces were falling that way. "Someone local would be afraid of being recognized driving Addie's car. It makes sense they'd move it only a short distance to the trailhead. But did they really think it would fool you? Or were they just trying to delay the inevitable? But then…"

I trailed off, but my eyes must've turned into saucers.

"What?" Frank waved at me to continue.

"The keys. If the killer approached from the back garden and never entered the house, how'd they start the car? It's not likely Addie came out of the house with them in hand. And as Gresham pointed out, she wasn't about to let someone borrow her car."

"Good question." Frank mocked tipping his hat. "You're spot-on, Little Goode."

I snorted, blurting, "I prefer Goode, the Younger. And for the record, you didn't ask Charlotte about the keys, like if there was an extra set or something."

"That's because I already have the answer." His eyes lit up with a mischievous glint, enough to make my cheeks warm. *Was he flirting? Now? Did I like it?* I was flying too high to tell. A rush of excitement had overtaken me, making my fingers and toes tingle. I wanted to feel embarrassed by it, but couldn't. I was doing something, really doing something. Even if it was only loosely helping Dad and Frank. For the first time in months, I felt a sense of pride.

"You have to tell me," I begged.

Frank considered a moment before speaking. "Addie had labeled keys hanging on hooks in her garage. One hook was empty. The key we found in her car was labeled with her mechanic's name. They've confirmed they would pick up Addie's car for service by entering the garage via a keypad code and using the key found on the hook. They've also been ruled out as a suspect, with a solid alibi."

"That's it? But that doesn't help at all," I blurted. If the key was just hanging there, it didn't narrow the suspect list. What happened to being spot-on? A part of me wanted to be angry for being humored like a child, but the larger part of me wanted to know more. What else had the police learned that they were keeping quiet?

"I'm heading back to Addie's house," said Frank, ignoring my frustration. "I need to see the angles to the street. Now that we know the killer came in while avoiding the camera—intentionally or not—we may find something farther up the road than we'd been looking." He opened the door to the sedan. "You can find your way home from here, I trust."

"Wait!" The word flew out, but I stopped short of adding,

Take me with you! I had the same desire to look at the path from the street to Addie's yard, but my arguments all seemed flimsy. Maybe I'd see something they missed? They were trained and I was not. Maybe my local knowledge would provide them insight? They had my dad and Vin D'Amato.

Frank waited for me to continue, yet his bemused smirk was starting to fade.

"I'll have Case pick me up at Addie's." I piled into the sedan, scouring my thoughts for a reason. Propriety came to the rescue. "I can't just linger out here and not go back inside, and I'd really rather not." I squirmed in the seat. That both statements were true did little to conceal my childish ploy. "Please?"

Frank sighed. "You're not setting foot on her property," he said in a forceful tone that left no room for disobedience.

I wanted to squeal. I wanted to lean over and hug him. It took half a block before it dawned on me I'd just begged and lied to see the spot where my childhood friend had been killed. My gut lurched. What was wrong with me? Wasn't a midlife crisis supposed to include a flashy car and dating a twenty-year-old? Why was mine turning me into a premenopausal Miss Marple?

CHAPTER 7

I leaned against the hood of Frank's sedan while I waited for Case. We'd parked on the street, much to my disappointment. Frank pointed out the square foot of asphalt where I was to remain, before striding off to speak with the crime scene technicians. Their van was parked near the driveway, but I couldn't see much more. Addie's house sat by itself, its front facing a grand view of valley and forest, with the street running along its side. The driveway hooked at its end, dumping into the street a good fifty yards from the house itself. A row of arborvitaes ran along the street and blocked most of the house from view, though from time to time I caught glimpses of movement in the miniscule gaps.

It didn't take long before my toes started tapping, impatient to the last piggy. I mean, the *spirit* of what Frank instructed was what mattered, right? There was no harm in moving a few feet down the road, as long as I didn't interfere. I'd been on ride-alongs with Dad all my life. I knew how to not get in the way. And it wasn't like I wanted to see anything more than what was going on: Frank and the techies in action. That was it.

Addie's street slanted downhill, and I let gravity pull me to the driveway's edge. Her house sat back in the distance. It was a smaller version of Charlotte's, a Craftsman painted white, with stonework skirting its base to a child's height. A tiny black dome hung from the corner of the porch's roof. *Still recording, no doubt.* A shiver pulsed through me. What the camera recorded, and what it did not, told a clear tale. To reach the back garden while avoiding its eye, the killer either had to push through the spider-filled arborvitaes at the side of the house, or scramble down a steep cliff at the far back of the property. There was no access from the far side of the property, not without some serious climbing gear.

But did that mean they'd avoided the camera on purpose? And therefore that they'd been to the house before? And therefore that they'd been known to Addie? It seemed most likely, but it was far from proven.

One of the techies emerged from behind the house. She crawled on her hands and knees, running a latex-gloved hand over the grass.

I swallowed and found my throat dry. *Oh, Addie.* She'd devoted her life to our mothers' machinations. Yet unlike me, she'd finally found a path to success. Charlotte had stated as much. Addie had big plans. She was about to start a new business. No mounting rejections for her. No more pie on her face, as her life remained off track. *Yes, but would she be remembered any better for it?* The thought bubbled up, as confusing as it was startling.

Frank coughed loudly from across the lawn. I jumped, ripped from my thoughts. My shoulders hunched up, and suddenly I was a kid who'd left her English assignment on the bus. He gestured for me to return to my designated spot, before trudging around the side of the house. With a dab more pie on my face, I complied. But the sight of his plodding reminded me of Joyce's tale and the large boot prints she'd seen. She'd seen smaller prints as well. We'd all assumed those would be Addie's, but now I knew they weren't. Two sets of footprints around her car. Did that mean Harvest Falls had two killers on the loose? A flannel-wearing Bonnie and Clyde? Were the smaller prints those of Sera Simmons? Had she made sure to show herself leaving after the argument, parked on the street, and circled back, avoiding the camera? Then what, enlisted someone to fetch her at the trailhead?

I didn't want to think so. I'd always considered Sera a friend. Or, at least, I tried not to judge her the way others in my life did. For some reason, Charlotte and my mother had always disliked the Simmons clan. I never understood why. Sera had been the first in my class to wear makeup, and the first to have her ears pierced. It happened in a flash one morning. Sera strode in as confident as could be, dropped her book bag, and beamed at the rest of us. The tiny studs caught the light; the pink eyeliner matched her shirt and lips. I thought it was cool, but later that night over dinner, my mother had whispered about how shameful it was.

"She'll turn out just like her mother," my mother had chirped. "It's distasteful."

Much later, I'd found out the makeup and earrings had been a surprise to make Sera feel better. Her dad had run out on the family. She'd been understandably upset, and her mom had wanted to cheer her up. I'd felt horrible when I found out about all that, and worse for not standing up for her more. It was the first time I realized how deeply perceptions can wound.

They're as sharp, and as brittle, as a knife's edge. *Confucius? Or maybe* Riverdale.

An engine revved behind me. Tires squealed as they hit the curb. I leaped from my skin, spun, and found Vin D'Amato glaring at me from his squad car. It was a white cruiser with navy blue lettering, one of three the town employed. Dark-haired and square-jawed, Vin was the spitting image of the guys from *Jersey Shore*. He had perhaps as many brain cells too.

He clambered out of the cruiser, reached in, and snatched his baton. Making a show of it, he stalked toward me, one thumb looped behind his belt. His thick neck flexed. His nostrils flared.

My blood got up. I didn't have much patience for Vin on a good day, let alone today.

"You're supposed to be slapping that thing in your hand," I said, nodding toward the baton. "It's more menacing that way. Don't you read *Yokel Cop Monthly*?"

"I see what you're trying to do. Making me look bad." He thrust a meaty finger at me. "You ratted me out."

My face scrunched. This was not the accusation I had expected.

"You're going to have to clarify," I replied. Holding my ground, I folded my arms across my chest. Vin didn't scare me. He was a bully, the type of guy who loved women who drooled over his biceps and saw as a threat any who didn't.

"Talking to the detective about what I said, what I didn't say." He stepped closer. "You're not a cop, and you're not on this case. You're nothing but a low-rent call girl. Like, I call for coffee or a file, and you fetch it. Got it?"

Ugh. Gag me with an 80s cliché.

But I read between the lines. He meant what Gabby and Madison told Frank this morning. How Vin had spilled the beans about Addie being stabbed. His loose lips must've come back on him already. Yet arguing I hadn't ratted on him, that I hadn't mentioned his name at all, wouldn't do any good. So instead, I smirked as childishly as I could. "You might want to tell the state detective that. We've been having a great time doing real police work."

Vin snarled. "Think your dad protects you?" His mammoth shoulders pulled up to his ears. His lips pouted. "He doesn't. Maybe he did once, but not anymore. There's a whole world out there just loving your failures. Yours and all the other uptight prom queens who've had everything gifted to them."

"Huh. You should coach Little League." I fired back on autopilot, angry he'd interrupted my train of thought.

"Keep me out of your mouth," he warned.

Seriously? I just couldn't. Laughter spurted out. My gut cramped, and I fell over at the waist. My knees buckled, and I squatted to my heels.

Vin glowered but kept his trap shut.

"Officer D'Amato!" Frank hollered from the driveway. He ran a hand through his hair and dislodged a few clumps. It made him look like a sexier Nick Nolte from *48 Hours*. But his expression cut short my laughter. I remembered where I was, the crime that had been committed, and whom it had been committed against. *Way to represent the family, Charlie!* My cheeks burned in shame.

As Frank directed Vin to bring gloves, tape, and some other equipment to the backyard, he eyed me with a mark of impatience.

I tried explaining myself. "I, uh…Vin thought…he accused me. No, that doesn't matter. What, uh—"

Frank cut me off with a wave of his hand. "I need to speak with Sera Simmons."

My head shot up. "That's perfect. I'm friends with Sera! Er, I was…back in school, we had been. But I just saw her the other day at the grocery store. She was buying muffins." I did everything but wag my tail, feeling like a Labrador waiting to be told I was a good girl.

He snorted. "No, not what I meant. I'm taking Officer D'Amato."

"Vin?" I spat the name. "Whose loose lips already blabbed key information to the entire town? I can keep quiet. I promise. You can deputize me or something."

The corner of his mouth tugged, breaking his stone-faced expression. His voice softened. "Not this time, Little Goode. No badge, no interview. That's the way it works."

My wee bubble burst. But he was right. I was stepping way out of line. I wanted to blame Joyce for putting in my head the need to save Dad's reputation. Or my past friendship with Addie, driving me to find justice. But those weren't really it. Not fully. The truth was I was curious, more so than I had any right to be. I didn't want to hear about things later. I wanted to figure them out now.

Was this how Dad felt all the time?

"Don't take Vin," I said, deflated but still wanting to help. "Sera can't stand him and won't say anything if he's there. She knows how to clam up."

A smirk tugged at Frank's lips. He nodded. "Thanks."

My tail wagged. Just a little bit.

CHAPTER 8

"Whoa!" Case swung us around a curve, driving his Scion loosely with one hand. His jaw dropped low enough that he looked like a Pez dispenser. I'd filled him in on my morning's exploits, everything from the café to the porch camera. He was dressed for work in a Roll For It T-shirt and jeans. The hint of a bacon sandwich and coffee filled the car. The shirt reminded me I was supposed to work at the shop this afternoon. The scents made me want to march back to Gabby's place. Maybe I'd ask Madison what other details Vin had let slip.

But Case didn't take the turn onto Second Street. Instead, he turned toward the lower river area of town. I caught his attention and gestured at the street.

"I've got to pick up something," he explained, a bit sheepishly.

"Where?" I drew the word out. Something smelled fishy beneath the bacon.

"At Sera's."

"Case!"

He squirmed a bit but held his ground. "Okay, I don't have anything to pick up. But we know Sera. Do you really think it's her? Maybe we can clear her, help her out of a jam."

"No, absolutely not. Talking to her can really screw up Dad's investigation." I didn't add that I'd argued to join Frank not ten minutes earlier. What Case didn't know wouldn't hurt him. Besides, me tagging along with an actual detective was way different than Case and me inserting ourselves and revealing information we shouldn't probably know to a suspect.

"So we don't have to go in. We'll just do a drive-by, see what's going down."

I threw my hands up. "Like see if she's out in the backyard burning clothes or washing off a bloody knife with the garden hose? Frank's probably there already. He'll throw us both in cuffs if he see us!"

Case eyed me sideways. "Frank, is it? Our boy James have some competition?"

"Detective Nichols. Fine. And shut up, don't change the subject."

"We're here," he said, making the final turn onto Sera's street. If the Newsome house and Addie's place soared Above the Falls, the Simmons residence definitely crouched below. The weathered rows of houses were built on top of one another, and I wasn't sure you could brush your teeth without everyone in the neighborhood knowing about it. Yet the street definitely had its charm. Worn siding, shingled roofs, and covered porches lent it a cottagey feel. Cute gardens sprouted among those left to rot, with honeysuckle, heather, and roses in their final autumn bloom. Aged pine and cedar trees towered overhead, their needles scattered about. Languid music fell out of a nearby window.

The Simmons house was near the end of the block where the street reached a dead end. Sucking in a breath, I scanned about, only to exhale when I didn't see Frank's sedan. Somehow we'd beaten him here. I slapped Case's shoulder and waved at the empty street. "See? Nothing. Now, let's get out of here."

Case made no protest. He must've heard the warning in my tone. But as he pulled to the curb next to Sera's driveway, ready to turn the car around, the sound of another engine rounded the corner. I didn't need to turn to picture the car—dark sedan, with a now-fuming, possibly enraged detective behind the wheel.

Yelping, I turned my body into pudding and squished myself as low as possible in the seat—a position reached much easier when I was younger. My calves started to cramp immediately. Case played it cooler. After calmly throwing the car into park and killing the engine, he ducked his head into his phone. But I could see his eyes locked on the rearview mirror.

"Nothing to see here," he murmured, as if trying out a Jedi mind trick. "Just a rando visiting the neighbor. Move along."

"Case, let's go," I barked.

"Can't," Case said to his phone. "He'd see us for sure."

The crunch of tires came up behind us, followed by a door slamming. My heart thumped into my throat. *If only Frank had taken me along to begin with...*

"He's taking the bait." Case grinned something wicked. I wanted to pinch his leg, but I knew he'd scream bloody murder.

Peeking over the lip of the passenger window, I watched

Frank ring the bell. Sera answered in a baggy T-shirt and jean shorts. Without the hoodie, I could see her blonde roots sprouting atop the pink-and-green coloring of her hair. She rubbed her eyes and yawned, as if recently woken. Only, she didn't look surprised to find the police at her door. She didn't even look concerned. She leaned against the doorjamb and glared.

"Sera Simmons?" Frank asked. His voice was just loud enough to carry to the curb.

"Yep." Her eyebrow rose.

I blinked, slack-jawed, with an expression of Holmesian shrewdness. Always defiant, Sera had had prior scrapes with the police. But to stand there so brazenly—could she really be involved with Addie's death? I couldn't picture it. Or maybe didn't want to. I wanted more to remember the rambunctious girl who once tried to stage a sit-in against the fried foods served by our school's cafeteria. The girl who wore ripped jeans to prom.

"I need to ask you a few questions," Frank was saying. "Do you mind if I come in?"

A smile came to Sera's lips, and not a kind one. "If I do mind?"

Frank adjusted his stance. "We can talk right here, or you can come down to the police station."

Sera peered over Frank's shoulder. She stared right at me and pointed.

Oh, crap! I ducked low and missed her response. Case whimpered, fumbling his phone into his lap. He reached for his keys hanging in the ignition before stiffening like a petrified chipmunk. He held his hands up in surrender. A rap came at the window.

"You are a dead man," I whispered through clenched teeth.

He whimpered again.

"Step out, Charlie Goode," said Frank, as deadpan as RoboCop reviewing his taxes. "Just you," he added, when Case made a play for his door.

I climbed from the car, and not knowing what else to do, awkwardly bowed my head. With a deep sigh, Frank stepped close enough I could smell a mix of croissant and grass from Addie's yard on him.

"Ms. Simmons seems to think she needs a witness to protect her against police brutality," he said. An amused grin passed over his face and quickly vanished.

"I didn't tell her to say anything, I swear! We just got—"

"And you're not going to say anything. Not about the camera recording, Addie's car, or her manner of death. In fact, you're not to say a word." He drummed the roof of the Scion, doubt flashing across his face. "Don't make me regret this."

My gut twirled a little waltz; I was as much confused as elated. "Wait, does that mean…?"

"Not a single word," Frank repeated. He spun on a heel and returned to Sera's door. I followed along behind him, not sure where to look. I didn't buy Sera's ploy for a second, and surely neither did Frank. But whatever her reasons, she'd gotten me in the door.

She glared at me as I approached. "I was expecting your dad. Lights and sirens to make a big show of it, just like he does. I didn't think it'd be you showing up, creeping on my house. That's a surprise. Thought you were serious about the whole doctor thing. Didn't think this town would ever see you again, after the summer."

Her words cut deep, leaving me oddly cold. I made no response. Worse, I felt a bit stupid for wondering about her lack of surprise. Of course she knew about the camera on Addie's porch. She and Addie were friends, of a sort. She would've known their argument was caught of video and that the police would come knocking eventually.

Frank stepped forward. "Let's go inside," he said. It didn't sound like a request, though I knew he couldn't really force Sera to let us into her house. He'd need a warrant for that. But thankfully, Sera relented and backed away from the door. She retreated through a dated living room with paneled walls and faux-pine flooring into a tiny, cluttered kitchen. After pouring herself a coffee, she took a seat at a small breakfast table.

She didn't offer us any coffee. It smelled amazing, but I wasn't about to intrude any more than I already had. Her earlier comments still smarted, and I needed to remain in Frank's good graces. It was best to shut up and listen.

"I'd like to ask where you were last night," said Frank. He took a seat at the table, and I followed suit. It took me a moment to realize he'd chosen a spot out of Sera's reach. I, of course, was in perfect stabbing distance. I tried to subtly scoot myself back, but the legs of the chair scraped and snagged, and I had to snatch the table to keep from tipping over.

My cheeks caught fire, but neither Frank nor Sera glanced my way. They locked gazes, until Sera finally set her coffee down and pressed her hands around it. She stared at the mug, and a bit of the Sera I knew peeked out—calm and caring.

"You've seen the video, that camera on the porch?" She shrugged. "So I was there last night. I came over. We argued like we always did. I left."

Frank pulled out his pad and started scribbling. "What about?"

Sera flicked at the handle of her mug. It sent a slosh of coffee dangerously close to the rim. "We had a lot of stuff between us. We weren't really that close, you know? We were just people who grew up in the same town and ran into each other a lot. Friends in that loose kind of way."

A fair assessment, as far as I knew. I nodded agreement to Frank, but he wasn't looking my direction.

"You two had a falling-out recently, is that correct?" he asked.

"Sure, whatever. Par for the course, when it comes to Addie. She had a way of rubbing everyone the wrong way after a while." Sera's foot tapped under the table. She seemed to flinch at the sound, and it stopped.

Frank set down his pad. He leaned forward and spoke gently. "Okay, Sera, here's the deal. Addie was murdered last night, and by all accounts you two were close friends, not just loose acquaintances. So I'm going to need some details."

Craning her head back, Sera cackled. "Close friends? Right, got it. That must've come from Charlotte. In her eyes, anyone Addie knew had to be a BFF. How could they not fall in love with Little Miss Perfect? And why would it matter anyway? You saw us fight, but you also saw me drive away, right?"

Her eyes narrowed, her expression becoming something

feral and frightening. "You're not going to pin this on me. I had nothing to do with Addie's murder."

Frank didn't budge an inch.

Sera shoved herself back from the table and crossed her arms. "You know why Addie wanted that porch camera? Bet Charlotte didn't tell you that."

"Why's that?"

"To track Gresham's comings and goings." Sera lurched forward and jabbed her finger into the table at each word. This time, the coffee did slosh over.

My lips moved before I could check them. "Why would Addie care about that?"

Sera's face contorted, as if she'd smelled how dense I was. "Think, Doc. It was so she could record the times he came over without Charlotte. Addie complained about how gross he was all the time."

Frank scribbled. "You're saying he made advances toward Addie?"

Rolling her eyes, Sera groaned. "Ugh, that man has tried to hook up with every woman in town. And I mean everybody."

Well, not everybody. I straightened my shirt but resisted the urge to run a hand through my hair.

"That's ridiculous," I said, feeling a little wounded. True, Gresham had always flirted, but it was just his way. Part of his sales shtick. I'd never taken it seriously, nor had he ever crossed the line.

"You've always had your eyes closed, Doc." Sera's tone swung between pity and scorn. "Always too eager to please Mommy and Daddy, never paying attention to what's right in front of your nose."

My jaw dropped. *What the hell? Where was this coming from?* I'd thought Sera and I were cool, even if it had been years since we really spoke.

I'd started to rise, and Frank's hand found my arm. The touch urged me to not take the bait. Taking a breath, I lowered back into the chair.

"Let's get back to last night," said Frank, with a warning in his tone.

But Sera wasn't listening. She glared at me. "I'll prove how blind you are—you haven't even thought about it, have you? You haven't made the connection? Two Newsomes found dead in their cars. Father and daughter."

Frank started to interrupt but stopped himself. His brow pulled tight. I caught his gaze darting toward me, could feel his unspoken questions.

"The two have nothing to do with each other," I said with confidence. I didn't know how they possibly could. One was a suicide, and the other was clearly not.

"What about the other deaths?" Sera asked. "Those poor pawns of Charlotte Newsome's game. She and your mommy snapped their fingers, and your dad made it all go away. That's how it always is, the haves abusing the have-nots." She smirked. "Nothing to do with one another. Right. Tell that to Marc Newsome. Smells like you're doing a whole lot of shoveling, breathing in way too much bullshit."

Anger didn't come this time. It couldn't. It had no room. A torrent of confusion and doubt pounded through me. I'd been young when Addie's dad died, unable to fully understand death. It wasn't surprising I never knew, or didn't remember, all of the details. Yet Sera's attack sounded too similar to what Joyce and Beckett had said: that my dad had acted to cover up some part of Marc Newsome's tragic suicide.

Rumors of all sorts flew around Harvest Falls. It was a small town with a lot of idle minds. I was certain the two deaths weren't linked, but it was clear finding Addie's killer wouldn't be enough to rescue my dad's reputation. There was too much smoke billowing from the past, obscuring things. I needed to find out more. I needed to know why the investigation into Marc Newsome's death incited so much doubt.

And what other deaths? What pawns of Charlotte Newsome, and what did they have to do with my parents? I agreed with Sera about one thing: something certainly stank. But what was its source?

CHAPTER 9

Frank stood. He stretched out a meaty hand to silence us both. "Where are the clothes you wore last night?" he asked Sera.

She returned a blank stare. Wheels turned behind her eyes as she measured her response. She knew the drill better than I did—what a police officer could ask for, what they couldn't. She'd been through it a couple times, and I had no doubt she considered calling a lawyer. I didn't think Frank would have much luck in getting anything more out of her.

But to my amazement, she said, "They're in my bedroom."

The concession knocked me sideways, and I had to wonder if it proved her innocence. Why else would she act so obstinate and yet hand over what could be critical, if not damning, evidence? I'd have to follow up on old rumors later. This was much more interesting.

Frank took the response in stride. At his gesture, Sera led us to the back of the house. Frank kept me from entering the bedroom, but I peered in from the doorway. The room was better kept than mine but still held a scattering of clothes and shoes. Bottles of lotion, a few tubes and tubs of makeup, a tissue box, and some loose jewelry cluttered the surfaces. The bed was unmade. The walls were mostly bare.

My eyes lit up. I pointed at the edge of the bed. "That's the same sweatshirt from the recording!" My excitement gushed, and I shouted louder than I'd expected. But there could be no mistaking the navy blue hoodie. It was from a local ice cream shop and had the Rosie's Tasty Cones logo stamped across the front of it. The thing didn't look dirty, but it certainly hadn't been laundered recently. I could tell from the stretched cuffs and the T-shirt still stuck inside of it. Sera had most likely pulled the clothes off all in one go and thrown them on the bed before climbing under the sheets.

Frank came to the same conclusion, and I realized he'd asked about the clothes as a simple test. It was very clever. If Sera had refused to show us, or if she'd washed them, or they had something suspicious on them, it would've strengthened her as a suspect. The fact that she'd given over the clothes freely, and that they appeared untainted, meant…what?

My mind spun. She could've taken the hoodie off at some point. She could've been careful and kept it clean. I bit my lip. I had to admit I was out of my element. I needed to step back, take a breath, and leave my emotions out of it. To think like a detective.

Sera hadn't been ruled out, clever test or not. Until she had, she was a suspect.

I studied Frank as he bent over the sweatshirt. He ran his eyes over every inch of material but was careful not to touch it. Staring at the logo sparked a fact I thought helpful.

"That's an employee sweatshirt, right?" I asked. I was careful to keep the question simple and not jump to any conclusions.

Sera nodded. "Yep, everyone has to buy one to work there. It's basically a scam for the owners to make more money. They deduct the cost from your first paycheck. The turnover is so high, some months they must make more selling kit to the employees than ice cream to the customers."

As she explained, I scanned the room again. *Did anything look out of place?*

"Let's go back to last night," said Frank. He straightened and turned to Sera. "What did you and Addie fight about?"

Sera crossed her arms. "Am I going to need a lawyer?"

A few of the tubes of facial cream were high-end, a brand I was pretty sure Sera would never have paid for. But I kept my tongue. Accusing her of having sticky fingers without actual proof would get us nowhere.

She had a folding knife, the size you would keep in your back pocket while camping, set on the nightstand. It didn't look expensive, but the necklace next to it did. Its silver chain held an ornate turtle, the shell a sparking patchwork of emeralds. It looked hand crafted, and as I peered at it, a memory clicked. I'd seen the turtle recently.

"That necklace," I said, interrupting Frank's response to Sera's question. "I saw it earlier in the Halloween photo. The one from Charlotte." I turned to him. "It's Addie's."

Frank pulled out the photo he'd taken from Charlotte and marched over to the nightstand to compare. It didn't take long. The piece was rather unique.

He reached for a tissue from the box near the bed. I thought he'd pick up the necklace and put it into one of those baggies you see on television. But instead, he picked up the knife. Ever so gently, he pried the folding blade out until the lock clicked.

Sera flinched at the sound. Her expression hardened. "I want you to leave now. And you can put that back where you found it," she said. "I know my rights."

♦ ♦ ♦

I bit my tongue until we reached outside, but the dam burst as soon as the doors slammed shut. I rounded on Frank. "Why didn't you arrest her?"

His sly smirk returned. He kept walking. "For what?"

"For...for..." My arguments slipped away. The more I tried to convince myself of Sera's guilt, the more doubts emerged. Her clothes showed no signs of any nefarious acts, and there was no connection between her and the actual event. The only thing we knew for certain was that she and Addie had argued earlier in the night, and that for some reason Sera didn't want to talk about why.

Frank chuckled. "Looks like I'm your ride."

My stammering stopped. I glanced around. The curb stood empty except for Frank's sedan. *That rat bastard.* Case had fled, no doubt as soon as I had disappeared inside.

"Get in," said Frank, saving me from having to beg. I thanked him sheepishly and tried to hide my tomato-red face.

As he cranked the engine, still with his smirk, my fingers tapped my knee. I made it to the end of the block before blurting, "So you don't think she's guilty of Addie's murder?"

"I didn't say that."

"But you don't think there's enough evidence to make a move." I tried to fill in the blanks. *It's not about what happened. It's about what can be proved.* My dad's voice rang in my head. Clearly, Frank agreed.

His smirk widened. "You think I should call in the techies and have them scour every inch of that house?"

"Well, yeah. Maybe. At least the knife and sweatshirt. Wouldn't that determine her guilt or innocence for certain?"

The way his eyes twinkled, I could tell he was enjoying my floundering. "I can tell you we'd probably find traces of Addie in the house. But that wouldn't matter. They were friends. We'd expect to find traces. They saw each other shortly before the crime. No one's denying that. The trick is finding evidence that puts Ms. Simmons on scene at the time of the crime."

"The traces in her house would be easily explained and dismissed," I mused, following along. "But what about the rest?"

"Privileged information. You have a badge on you?" He looked me up and down.

My shoulders slumped, and I remained quiet.

As he turned us onto Bywater Street, he conceded a half shrug. "If we were still looking for where the crime occurred, then maybe. Or if Addie was wearing that necklace during the fight, that'd be something. But I didn't see anything that would warrant the cost. Those kinds of searches aren't done out of the goodness of the techs' hearts. Someone has to pay for them. And finding a strand of Addie's hair on Ms. Simmons' hoodie would only prove what she's already admitted and we've already seen on camera."

That gave me a start. I didn't remember Gil Grissom or Horatio Caine ever worrying over how much something cost.

"You still don't have the murder weapon," I pointed out.

Frank nodded. "Ms. Simmons is coming to make an official statement this afternoon. We'll see what else she'll have to say about the necklace. That was a good find. It might open her up a bit, make her talk about why they were arguing."

I forced a smile but felt exhausted. The stress of consoling Charlotte and confronting Sera had turned my shoulders into knotted ropes. I would need a hot shower to work out the pinches. *Would it be easier if I didn't know either of them?* Maybe, maybe not. And what about Gresham? Did he play a role in any of this? My thoughts strayed back to those large boot prints and how Addie had been found in the trunk of her car. That took strength. Did that mean a man had to be involved? If so, did it help rule out Sera Simmons?

"What do you think about Gresham?" I asked. "Maybe Sera's accusation against him is sour grapes because he made a pass at her, and she feels scorned?" I considered that, and my thoughts derailed once again. "But I'm not sure how that has anything to do with Addie. Not directly, anyway."

Frank pulled the sedan into the small lot attached to the police station. Painted a soothing canary yellow, the brick building sat in a line of city offices that stretched from the new town hall to the aging library.

"You did well, Little Goode, but this is the end of the line for you." Frank's eyes held slightly more than friendliness. A wolfishness had come out, one I imagined had served him well over the years. Strong, yet calm. Hard enough to hold firm, yet soft enough to be tender.

I could do worse, I thought once more. I *had* done worse—a professor at college who'd forgotten my name halfway through the evening. And with Frank, there'd be no attachments. He'd leave as soon as the case wrapped up. Another boon. My flesh started to tingle. He was rugged enough where it counted, I had to admit.

"How long do you think the investigation will take?" I asked.

His gaze drifted lower before lifting to meet mine. "Who knows? With this job, sometimes it just comes down to luck. A tip could come in, and I'd be free for dinner." His expression became playful.

Oh, come on! I groaned but kept a cheerful expression. Still, the cheesy advance was enough to snap me out of the mood. I threw open the car door and clambered out in time to hear a woman bellowing. It was faint. It came from within the station.

My heart lurched. I rushed to the side door, flung it open, and found Ruth Radford ranting like a lunatic. Our mayor flourished a large hunting knife above her head. The thing would make Crocodile Dundee proud. Frank bounded past me. He reached for his service pistol, but I stayed his arm.

"I've found the murder weapon!" Ruth hollered triumphantly. She slammed the knife onto the desk I used while working at the station. My rubber Gumby figurine wobbled and tipped over.

CHAPTER 10

Mayor Ruth Radford maintained a relationship with a few happy pounds. But her rounded figure matched an imposing personality. Clamping her hands on her hips, she stared expectantly at my father. Betsy D'Amato, Vin's mother, tittered nervously from her desk. Normally oozing sweetness, she oversaw the station's administrative pool—basically me. The rest of the station was quiet. A few metal desks sat behind a large wooden counter. Filing cabinets and the chief's windowed office ran along the walls, and a hallway led to a holding cell, an interview room, and a closet where we kept the coffee pot. It was a cozy space with not much room for suspects or criminals.

"I went out to the trailhead myself," said Ruth. "As mayor, I have every right to follow up on how the investigation is being handled. And look what I found just lying there in the bushes." She pointed at the knife.

Dad kept his arm loose at his sides. He was a master at presenting a passive yet reassuring presence. Gray hairs flecked his beard, but it only served to set off blue eyes that studied the world from a giant's height. He wore his chief's uniform starched and spotless.

"Now, Ruth, I'm sure we can get to the bottom of this," he said. He acknowledged Frank and me with a short nod but kept his attention locked on our mayor.

"I want you to make an arrest," Ruth replied. "He's always lurking about near the tourists, causing problems for everyone. It makes an eyesore of the town. My friend Helen heard he had a warrant out on him. For who knows what, one can only imagine. That's something you can look up in that computer system I paid for, isn't it?"

She waggled a hand at the computer monitor sitting on my desk.

Oy, facepalm. What had brought this on? Was she drunk? I felt Frank's disbelief wafting from him.

"We'll look into it," Dad affirmed.

Ruth tapped the knife with a pudgy finger. "If you ask me, Addie went to him to buy drugs. You know how she was, thinking she could get away with anything. It'd be just like her to soil the town without a thought for the rest of us."

I sucked a breath through my teeth. How could Ruth be so callous? She had always greeted Addie with generous gobs of praise, and despite her differences with Charlotte, the two women had always been cordial with one another.

Ruth turned at the sound I made. Her eyes narrowed to tiny slits. Her cheeks held a rosy flush, and her shoulders listed, as if she were taking on water. *Er, probably not water.*

"Why don't we speak in my office?" Dad held out an arm to direct her toward the windowed room along the rear wall. Ruth wavered a moment before conceding and letting him lead her away. She muttered in a terse whisper as they went, but I couldn't make out the words. Dad nodded a couple of times.

"That happen often around here?" Frank asked.

"Not that I'm aware," I said, though perhaps I needed to pay more attention.

Betsy shrugged, noncommittally. She smiled sweetly, looking like a fairy godmother with her silver bun and round glasses. But she would never slander a friend, and I knew she played poker with Ruth on Fridays—part of an old biddy gang that had started as a quilting group.

Frank rested his hands on his hips and swiveled his attention between us both. "Who did she mean the chief to arrest?"

"Sorry, hon," said Betsy. "You heard all I did. Before you came in, Ruth had only asked for the chief and mentioned that knife she found."

"Yeah, mentioned loud enough to wake the…" I cringed at my poor choice of words, but I was as curious as Frank. Who had Ruth meant? Not Gresham. He certainly didn't lurk or cause a bother with the tourists. But as to whom else Ruth considered an eyesore, I couldn't fathom.

I shook my head. "I have no idea either."

Frank grunted. He found an evidence bag and used a glove to pick up the hunting knife and deposit it inside. As he did, I came for a closer look. The blade had a slight curve to its tip and a serrated back. Rust and dirt covered most of it. At least, I hoped it was rust.

"Do you think that could be the murder weapon?" I asked.

His eyebrow rose. "I told you it's the end of the line, Little Goode. You can play Nancy Drew some other time." I huffed in protest at the comparison. He smirked playfully at my discontent and strode away, disappearing into the back hallway. I huffed louder, letting out a tidal wave of anxious energy. It sent jitters down my arms and legs, enough to make me grab the edge of my desk for support.

My computer screen shook awake. I saw the time and cursed. My shift at Roll For It had already started. Yet Case had abandoned me earlier. That eased the guilt a bit, and besides, he'd been the one to egg me on, driving us to Sera's. He wanted to dig into Addie's murder just as much as I did. I just had a better reason for it. Ruth's crazy antics couldn't be ignored. Mayors who believed in their chief didn't go around scouring crime scenes. The act was as glaring as Joyce's and Sera's accusations. I was only glad Vin wasn't around, or the whole town would've known about it by nightfall. His mother was much better at keeping secrets.

But where did I turn now? The other deaths Sera had mentioned? The town's criminal cases were logged in the computer system, even the ancient ones from the 1980s. Only Marc Newsome's case hadn't been a criminal investigation, and even if it had been, I certainly couldn't access it. The same went for any other deaths around the same time. I'd have to look those up another way. My lips made popping sounds as I considered. The library sounded right. Wasn't that where amateur detectives went for information? I supposed they had old newspapers there. Of course, I'd have to time it when Joyce wasn't working. I couldn't let her catch wind of what I was up to. It would only lend weight to her crazy theories.

The front door of the station cracked open, and a frail

hobbit of a woman slipped inside. Addie used to say Helen Tait would live past a hundred out of pure spitfire. I had to agree. The elderly woman crackled with an energy that belied her aging frame. Her thin hair had an almost purple hue. From the permanent pinch of her nose, you'd think garlic a key ingredient of her perfume.

I glanced around. Frank hadn't returned. Dad's office door remained closed, and Betsy D'Amato had expertly timed a jaunt to the copier. *Crud buckets.* I was going to have to deal with this.

Putting on a cheery smile, I walked to the back side of the counter and asked, "How can I help you, Mrs. Tait?" I wasn't impersonating an officer. I'd explained my position at the station a thousand times. But Helen often got confused. Or perhaps she didn't care, seeing me as a Goode first, no matter my title.

She slapped both hands on the counter and grimaced. "That store is stealing from folks."

"Oh, how so?" I picked up a pen and stood ready.

"You know the market off Elm? The one that used to be George's feed store?"

She waited for me to nod. When I complied, she sucked her gums and rolled her eyes before continuing. "You see, they had this big advertisement in their local flyer. Large eggs on discount, it said. Made me want to bake a cake. You know that famous lemon-and-blueberry one I do? Won awards and all?"

She waited again.

"I know the cake," I replied. But really, nope.

"Well, I go down and buy these eggs. But they're not very

large at all, no bigger than a medium, I'd say."

Scratching a note that was more of a doodle, I kept my voice neutral. "Okay, I'll be sure to pass this along to Deputy D'Amato."

Her face brightened. I thought she might be grinning, but I didn't want to imagine why.

"Oh, Vin's such a nice boy," she said. "I'm sure he'll have this straightened out in no time." She leaned forward, and I braced myself in case I had to try and catch her. "Not like our lazy police chief," she added, with another eye roll, "who takes our tax money and does nothing about the traffic in this town. I almost got run over the other day. Not to mention the litter. All of Second Street looks like a garbage pit."

Her breath held a mix of peppermint and onion. I stepped back to get away from it while biting my tongue. Snapping back at Helen would only send her into a finger-pointing tizzy, I knew from experience. Trying to argue in Dad's defense would be worse.

So I went with the third option. "Actually, it's your friend Ruth who manages where the town's tax money goes," I said. "I'm sure she'd love to hear your suggestions for improvement, and I know she's always looking for volunteers to help pick up the trash."

Helen's face pinched tighter. But I didn't back down. I dropped the cheeriness from my face and tried to put on the deadpan expression Frank had used.

To my surprise, Helen relaxed. She nodded. "I'll take it up with her," she said, as Dad's office door clanged open. Her face brightened. "Speak of the dickens."

Ruth stormed toward the front of the station, scowling. When she saw Helen, she stopped to gather herself. The pair greeted each other with gusto, but I could tell Ruth was heaving mad. She eyed me like a prowling tiger and ushered Helen Tait out the front door.

I barely let it swing closed before rushing into Dad's office. He greeted me with a weak smile and leaned back, running both hands through his salted hair.

"What was that about?" I asked. I settled into one of the guest chairs. Because of his lengthy stature, he kept his desk height higher than standard. It lent him an imposing bearing, especially for those sitting on the far side of its lacquered surface. His judgments came, literally, from on high.

"It's nothing," he replied, a bit quickly. "Just a bit of overreacting. Our mayor doesn't know as much as she thinks sometimes. But that never stops her from being passionate about her opinions, and she has every right to them."

I snorted. Dad could find something to praise about a pile of dung. Part of the job, I'd always guessed.

"The 'nothing' is starting to border on obstruction," said Frank. He entered the office with a mug of coffee and leaned against the wall. The roast smelled terrible. I often confused the sludge with axle grease.

Dad waved away the comment. "Mrs. Radford is harmless."

"She took her dogs with her." Frank sipped his coffee. "She and the mutts trampled the whole scene. I just heard it on the radio."

"It's a trailhead off a main highway," Dad replied. "How

many others have left prints and trash there over the past few days? Besides, we already got what we needed, and I don't have the manpower to keep it closed."

Following along, I made myself as small as possible so they wouldn't remember I was there. I gathered Ruth had snooped around where Joyce had found Addie's car. But if that's where the knife had come from, how had Dad and Frank missed it? Unless Ruth had found it somewhere else, and was trying to— what?—frame someone?

"We need to rule him out now," said Frank. "Can't leave it dangling."

"Yep." Dad nodded.

I stiffened in excitement. "Rule who out? I thought you didn't know who Ruth meant?"

Frank leveled a humored gaze at me. "Well, that was ten minutes ago, Little Goode." He took a slow sip before nodding at my dad and slipping out of the office. "Chief," he said, on his way out.

"Dad," I pleaded, whipping my attention to him. "Rule who out?"

Dad's lips drew into a thin line. "You know I can't say, sweet pea. It's part of an active investigation."

"Charlie," I corrected. When he pretended to ignore me, I scoured his face for any crack in the wall he'd erected. But he'd had years of experience playing this game.

I needed to cheat.

"Ruth wants you arrest someone," I said. "But she doesn't know that the murder took place at Addie's own house. So her theory won't hold up."

He didn't flinch, so I kept going. "She suspects a man, and that's most likely because of the large boot prints left near Addie's car at the trailhead."

After pausing, I came back to what had bugged me earlier. "So where'd she find the knife? I mean, theoretically it could be Gresham's. But I doubt it. He seems more like a strangling type of guy than something messy like a hunting knife."

The wall finally broke. Dad threw his hands up to stop me. "Whoa, sweet pea. That's not something you need to be thinking about, or accusing of others. We have it handled. This is dangerous business, and I'm sorry I brought you anywhere near it this morning. I shouldn't have. That's on me."

Sweet pea. There it was again, him treating me like a child. I shifted in the chair. Pressing my weight on my hands, I tried to find a comfortable position. I wanted to tell Dad I could handle anything. I wanted to tell him all I'd already done while helping Frank. But none of that was as important as the need to tell him why I had to help—that his integrity had been called into question. Inhaling, I readied to lay it all on the table. But I already saw the response that would come. He would deflect and dismiss, change the subject, and ultimately ignore my concerns. That was his way. When asked by those in town when he'd retire, he'd reminisce about the old chief before him, his mentor. When asked about my mother's car accident, he'd bring up the need for sturdy all-weather tires.

When I'd asked about Addie's father, back when I was young, he'd only tousled my hair and told me that if I ever felt sad or scared, to remember that he was there to protect me. And somehow, I'd always left it at that, never questioning further. My hands gripped the chair until my knuckles turned white.

"Dad, what happened to Marc Newsome?" I asked.

His expression changed. It became more guarded. "That's a strange question."

I cocked my head. "Is it? Doesn't it seem odd that both he and Addie were found in their own cars? What led up to his death? I was so young I don't remember."

Dad sat straighter. "I can't say I knew what was going through Marc's mind when he did what he did, but I can tell you it has nothing to do with Addie."

"How do you know?"

He didn't bat an eye. "Charlie, some things are best left alone. There's no need to dredge up memories of things you can't change. What's this about, anyway?"

The odd response made tiny icicles dance along my arms. I didn't know how to take it, nor his demeanor. Beyond not making sense, it sounded like a warning. But how could that be? What wasn't he saying? I studied my hands. They'd gone numb, and I worked the blood back into them.

"You should remember the good times," Dad offered, watching me. "Marc and Addie will always stay with you, you know. Just like your mother."

Hmm. A Hallmark card. The sentiment made me a bit miffed.

"Do you remember the time he took you girls to see—what was it? The one with the girl who wound up with a cocaine problem." He waited, but I didn't remember the movie's name. I only remembered the yelling that happened that night between my parents. A harsh quiet had fallen on our house afterward, one that lasted for weeks.

Dad chuckled. "Your mother was so mad. She gave Marc the icy treatment for months. I had to skip two fishing trips to avoid seeing him, just so she wouldn't turn on me."

"I was so young," I mumbled, dejected. Worse than being dismissed, I was being excluded. Whatever the truth from years ago, Dad clearly did not trust me with it.

Mistaking the sadness in my expression, he leaned forward and reached for me to clasp his hands. "I'm sorry about Addie," he said. "You must be a wreck, and I've been caught up in the investigation. I've ignored what you must be going through."

"I'm all right," I said, quickly. "I didn't have to deal with…what you did. Finding her. Having to see her." I entwined my fingers through his. He didn't need to know he'd wounded me. Nor did he need to know how determined he'd made me to find out what happened—to Addie, to Marc, all of it. He could push all he wanted, but I wasn't going to drop it now.

"Hear anything from Miley?"

"Nope." I gave him a caring look. We could both play at secrets. "Are you okay? You knew Addie as long as I did."

"Oh, you know me. I always compartmentalize."

I raised an eyebrow with a bit of skepticism. "That doesn't mean you're doing well, only that you're good at ignoring your feelings."

He grinned. "It's a family trait."

CHAPTER 11

As soon as Sera shut her car door, I pounced. I'd lurked outside the police station for the better part of an hour, hoping the murky clouds gathering above wouldn't soak me to the bone before she showed. I'd thought about heading to the library, but I wanted to hear what I could from the horse's mouth first.

Sera glared and made to storm right past me. Her hood was up, pulled tight about her ears. She hadn't bothered locking her car. Duct tape glinted on the hatchback's windows and bumper. It'd rattled into the lot in wheezing gasps.

I blocked her path. "Sera, I know we haven't hung out since I've been back. Haven't really stayed in touch over the years. But I was hoping you'd answer a couple questions before you went inside."

Her lips pulled back as if she'd sucked on a soiled gym sock. "Why? We aren't friends. For all I know, you're working to pin this crap on me. Daddy's little princess who can do no wrong. Do you know he's arrested me four times? And I'm supposed to trust you?"

"I'm not! I'm not a cop. I'm not working for—"

"Then I don't have to talk to you." She shouldered past

me, roughly.

"Wait," I called after. "Why did you ask me to join Frank—er, Detective Nichols—at your house, if you don't trust me?"

"To screw with him, obvi," she shot over her shoulder, then added smugly, "The chance of getting you into trouble was an added bonus."

I swallowed down a snippy retort and managed to ask instead, "What about Marc Newsome? What other deaths did you mean before? At least tell me that much."

She paused and half turned. Her gaze seemed slightly intrigued. "Always more of a prom queen than you wanted to be, weren't you? You and Addie, queens of the high school—one with her nose in the air, the other with it buried in the dirt."

Ouch. "Please. I need to understand."

She heaved a sigh and glanced toward the falls. It pounded in the distance, whittling away at the hillside as it had done for millennia. Always knowing just what it wanted to do. I envied its sense of purpose.

Sera's aggression fell away, and I realized it'd only been a defensive front. An armor to keep from being wounded. Or perhaps one to keep fear at bay.

"Buckner's Folly," she said, at last.

"That stone chimney thing?" I asked, bewildered. It wasn't the answer I'd expected. The folly stood a few miles outside of town in a dense part of forest. The hearty could hike to it, but it made for a dangerous scramble. How the thing was ever built remained a mystery. As for why, town lore held it was from greed—a grab for more tourist dollars. Old Man Buckner's attempt to create a romantic mythology around Harvest Falls, like the Victorians had done in England. At least I considered him an old man. I really had no idea who Buckner was. As for the romance part, tourists could already buy "I Fell for Harvest Falls" keychains in all the shops. What more was needed?

Sera nodded. "The Newsomes wanted the land it's on. But it's owned by the state. So Charlotte Newsome forced these poor surveyors up the cliff to reevaluate the boundary of the neighboring property. You know, to bully her way in, as if she could magically change the longitude of the Earth."

"What happened?" I hadn't heard any of this before.

"Two men died when the land slipped after a heavy rain. Of course, your dad wrote the whole thing up as an accident."

"Wasn't it? I mean, if it was rain—"

Sera rolled her eyes, letting me know how despicable the whole thing was. "Charlotte had no right to that land. Those men shouldn't have been there. It was dangerous and reckless. They lost their lives for what? So the Newsomes could invoke a greater legacy? How much land does one family need?"

I didn't have a good answer for that. It'd feel hypocritical to try and side with Sera's disgust, but nor would I try and defend my obvious privilege. All the same, biting my tongue brought on a bitter taste.

"I know you didn't kill Addie," I said. "Let me help you get out of this."

She snorted. "And how do you propose to do that, Doc? Last I checked, you were no Veronica Mars."

It was a fair point. I sucked my lip and took a long stare

down the street. My inconspicuous game was crazy good, as long as I stood near a bunch of other sore thumbs. A pride of sore thumbs? A parliament? *Focus, Charlie.*

"Tell me why you had her necklace," I said.

Her gaze hardened. "It was mine. We each had one. Identical, from a trip to Seattle."

The bitter taste returned. "I don't think the detective will buy that," I said before I could help myself.

Her eyes flared daggers once more. "Goodbye, Charlie."

"Wait!" *Crap!* I was blowing this. *What would Frank ask?*

She paused, and I blurted the first thing that came to mind. "What were you and Addie fighting about?" I cringed. I'd hoped to work up to the question better. Slip it in more casually. Less manically.

"Yep, thanks for the help," she said, with just a tiny teaspoon of derision. "I'll be sure to give the detective your regards. Glad you're on my side, Doc."

"At least tell me where you went last night. You know, after Addie's house." I strode after her.

She chuckled as she opened the station door. "Now that is ironic." Ducking her head toward mine, she lowered her voice. "Because I was at your mother's house."

I jerked back, blinking furiously. The sequence didn't rewind my life, so I blinked some more until I was dizzy.

Nope. Not happening.

Lunging forward, I snatched the closing door and followed Sera inside the station. She couldn't just dangle that information in front of me and walk away. It gave her a clear alibi. Why hadn't she said something earlier?

Frank stood up from a desk as I hustled inside. His expression narrowed. I didn't give him a chance to stop me.

"Why didn't you tell us that before?" I demanded.

Sera halted and folded her arms across her chest. She rounded on me and glared. "Why would I need to? I didn't have it out for Addie, not like Gabby Kemper. I'd triple-check her alibi. Not that anyone will, because you've all made up your minds already."

"Miss Goode," said Frank. The tone was low and hard.

I made a wild gesture toward Sera, like I was revealing a woman sawn in half. "She was at Danner House last night. She just told me."

"Miss Goode," Frank warned again, louder.

"It's our old house above the falls where I grew up," I tried to explain. "My mother wanted it turned it into a private nursing home as part of her will. Dad, Chief Goode, set it up that way years ago."

"Stop!" Dad emerged from his office. "Leave it to Detective Nichols."

I threw up my hands. "It gives her an alibi!"

Frank ignored me. He ushered Sera toward the back hallway, steam billowing from his head. I trembled but took a deep breath to steel myself. I didn't need to feel guilty about speaking up. I wasn't a child to cow to my parents anymore.

"Sweet pea, you can't do that. It's interfering." Dad ambled over and leaned against my desk. His tone returned to honey smoothness. Betsy D'Amato found she had work to do elsewhere and followed Frank and Sera into the rear of the station.

"Don't call me that anymore," I snapped.

"What?" He seemed genuinely confused. I'd caught him off guard, and the small victory stoked my fire. He'd never considered the power of those two little words.

"Sweet pea," I repeated. "Don't call me that. I'm not ten. Every time you say it, it sounds like you're putting me down." The irritation had built up for years, and I was tired of shoving my feelings aside. Dad liked the nickname, I'd always reasoned. No need to rock the boat over something so trivial. Always be the dutiful daughter, else the family will fall apart. Well, not anymore, sister! …or father.

He studied me with his deep-blue eyes. I thought he'd find a way to gently scold me. He'd tell me I'd been acting like a child. But he surprised me and nodded. "All right," he said. He drew the word out.

I stared at the things on my desk—the Gumby figurine, the picture of Coronado Bridge I'd snapped during a sunset in San Diego, a small magnetic hedgehog that acted as a paperclip holder. It should've felt good, this act of defiance. But it didn't. It felt like I was giving something up that I'd clung onto for far too long. Something that made home feel like home, even if it'd kept me from moving on.

"I was trying to help," I said.

"I know. But when Frank asked Sera to come down here, he wanted to get her on his terms. Speak to her on his ground. Put her in a certain state of mind."

"So, not combative?" Crap, I really had screwed things up.

Dad didn't laugh. He rested a hand on my shoulder. "You need to play by the rules, just like everyone else in town. No exceptions for being my daughter."

I jerked away faster than I could catch myself. I wanted to scream. *I have been playing by your rules all my life, and where has it gotten me!* But Dad wasn't finished.

"I didn't consider how much Addie's death would affect you, and that's on me. But I think you should take some time off from the station. Let all of this go. Cool down a bit and find what you really want to do with your life."

My jaw dropped. "You're firing me?"

"Focus on getting yourself back on track. Leave this stuff to me and Frank. That will make me happy. It would've made your mother happy too."

Yes, but will it make me happy? Such a simple and obvious question. So why had I never asked it before?

CHAPTER 12

A whirlwind of gusted leaves whipped from my path as I stormed from the station. The ancient cherry trees lining Bywater Street shied away. Squirrels fled in terror. At least in my mind. In reality, I stepped around an elderly gentleman who barely registered my presence and stopped to scratch behind the ears of Darlene Devereux's black Labrador, Branson, who waited for his mistress outside the Sweet Little Buttercup café.

Coffee sounded amazing, but I didn't want to face anyone. I wasn't up for small talk and pleasantries. I needed to be alone.

My feet knew just where to go.

Bywater Street blurred past until I reached the park at its end. The falls thundered good and proper from the park's edge. Spray carried above and through the foliage of maples and cedars. A misty mountaintop rose beyond. I couldn't make out the falls yet, not with the way the rocks jutted and created shadows. They kept their secret for only the adventurous.

Or those needing escape.

I rambled through the trees. Cobbled paths of red brick crisscrossed beneath the canopy, an expense that kept the heavy tramp of tourists from eroding the soil beneath. Wild grass and blackberry brambles filled the open areas between the trees. In summertime, when the berries ripened, the sweetness in the air was cloying. But now in autumn, the sweetness was gone, replaced by something damp and earthen.

The day had become blustery. Maple leaves shook from the trees, falling like snowflakes. I crunched through a light blanket of them as I marched across the cobbles. The rush of pounding water became white noise that filled my ears. But it didn't stop my thoughts nearly as well as I'd hoped. Why was Dad so adamant I stay away from the investigation? Did he have something to hide, after all?

A stupid notion. Catching Addie's killer wasn't my job. I'd been the one crossing the line and getting in the way. But I fixated on the question. It was easier than digging deeper and acknowledging my anger and frustration for what they really were—envy. Envy that it *was* his job—his and Frank's and Vin's—and not mine. A bubble of laughter sputtered out. I stopped and glanced around, realizing I'd been muttering to myself, shaking my head, and jerking my hands about frantically. But only a few sparrows and squirrels were around to witness my lunacy.

My march resumed. My feet found the path to the switchbacks that climbed beside the falls to an overlook. I took it and started the ascent. The cobbles stopped at the base of the switchbacks, and the path turned into rutted dirt and exposed stone. Slick patches dotted the way, dampened by proximity to the falls.

As my breathing labored, the wind shifted. Frigid mist sprayed over me. The damp and cold felt good, set against the burning in my legs and lungs. I needed it all. It'd been a while since I'd forced myself into discomfort.

Addie used to tease me when we were little girls. "You'll wear a badge, just like your dad." She couldn't imagine a worse fate. But I always beamed at the taunt. I wanted to help the town. I'd always wanted to fix things, to make sure everyone was happy. So why not join the police? My dad made a real difference to people's lives. I fantasized I'd do the same.

But those childhood dreams had not survived adolescence.

By sixth grade, Addie had gone the other direction. She'd pocket things from shops all over town. She'd do it with an air of arrogance, too, as if living Above the Falls meant she could get away with anything.

It didn't, and she couldn't.

It only took getting caught once to stop her behavior. But the funny thing was, it was my mother who was livid. She refused to talk about it with anyone. *Anyone.* Not me. Not Dad. Certainly not Charlotte or Addie. She tried to make it seem like it never happened. Addie was the perfect child, to her. And nothing—nothing—was going to shatter that perfect image.

Charlotte hired a lawyer and made it all go away. The ice cream shop that had caught Addie, Rosie's Tasty Cones, received enough cash to repaint the shop and hang a new sign, as long as they never said where the money came from. And, of course, the police never filed any charges.

So maybe Addie had had it right all along.

The cold silence in the aftermath had been the worst part. For weeks, it'd filled the Goode house like a terrifying specter hanging above us. I'd done nothing to create it, yet I couldn't fathom how to appease it. The last thing I wanted was to risk turning my mother's disapproval in my direction.

I rested my hands on my hips, shivering and panting. I'd climbed high enough to peer out over Harvest Falls. Bywater and Second Streets shot like rays from me, toward the highway and all that lay beyond. A golden hue bathed their thick lines of asphalt despite the clouded sky. With the late-autumn leaves and misty horizon, the town looked magical.

The view melted me. Sinking back against the cliff rising higher behind me, I let some of the tension I carried go. Addie might've teased. She might've held better insight about me than I did, but my decisions were my own. They always had been, the drifting away from childhood dreams. It'd made my mother so happy, the night in high school when I told her I wanted to be a doctor. It was the future she'd hoped for me. And for some reason I'd convinced myself it was my responsibility, my duty as the youngling Goode. A way to honor my family. And doctors helped people, right? Wasn't that all I wanted: to help the town? What difference did it make if I wore a stethoscope or a shiny badge?

The sputtering laughter returned. I let it all out, shaking my head and wiping my lips. Had I really been that stupid? Lacing my fingers through my hair, I wanted to squeeze and see if any brains came out. Why had I promised so much—my entire future? It was easy to see now, but I'd only set myself up for failure. My mother praised me when I aced a biology exam and scowled when I refused CPR training because it conflicted with a camping trip. And that became my life until I left for college.

Rosie's Tasty Cones. Clamping my eyes shut, I summoned an

image of the sign. For so long intertwined with Addie and my mother, it now brought me back to Sera, and the hoodie she'd worn. The logo held a pair of waffle cones tilted away from each other, like fingers giving the peace sign. One was topped with a scoop of green ice cream, the other red. Green and red, the best flavors.

This time, my cackling doubled me over at the waist. I staggered a few steps. Dust and pebbles sprayed over the lip of the trail. The drop beyond was maybe a hundred feet. Ahead, the falls still hid from view behind an outcropping of stone. I'd managed to break a sweat without ever seeing the falls. So very typical of me.

The falls overlook was less than a quarter mile up the path. It had a couple of benches and one of those pay-to-view metal binoculars. Switchbacks continued onto a higher ridge above the overlook. Deep shadows had settled over the jagged peaks. I took a step to carry on but stopped myself again. I didn't need to see the falls today. I'd seen them a thousand times before. What I needed was honesty. To admit to myself what I truly wanted. To no longer live in the dark with self-created blinders. And that started with answers. What had Addie and Sera fought about, and who else had Addie angered? Did Gresham Forthwright know? Had he been involved? Who did Ruth Radford want arrested? And had any of it to do with Marc Newsome and a bungled land deal from almost two decades ago?

On the final question, at least, I had an inkling where to start. My feet slapped the path as I made my way down to the park. I felt lighter and broke into a shuffling jog. For the first time in a long while, I had a purpose. I didn't need Dad's approval to protect his reputation, nor his consent to uncover Addie's killer. I didn't need anyone's but my own.

CHAPTER 13

I burst into Roll For It, out of breath and sweaty. Case raised his head. His maw chomped carrots. His stout frame strained his "Meeples Are My Favorite People" T-shirt. He'd been on the computer behind the counter. "Doing inventory," he'd tell me if I asked. But I'd caught him more than once lost in an online conquest of some fantasy kingdom.

"You ditched me, you bastard," I exclaimed, panting.

He leaned against the counter, not fazed by my distress. "I wanted to give you time with yer fella. You get lucky?"

"He's not…we didn't…" *Grr!* Why can family get under your skin so easily? I grabbed a chair at one of the playing tables, threw myself into it, and reveled in the throbbing of my legs and lungs. I hadn't felt so alive in months.

"Drink me," I said.

Case glanced at the clock hanging above the door, noting the lateness of the afternoon, and ensuring I did too. "Three hours late to work and wanting a shot of the sauce." A smirk came to his lips. "What a model employee."

"I work for free."

"I don't think I'd phrase it that way."

"Hardy-har-har." I gave him my best playground snark

before getting serious. "What do you know about the ghosts that are supposed to haunt Buckner's Folly? You know, that story Beckett tells about specters roving the hills?" I'd heard him recount it several times but never gave it my full attention.

Case's eyes went wide. I'd surprised him. "You've become a believer?" He lit up and slapped his hands on the counter. Leaning forward, he begged. "Did Sera show you evidence? Did you see something? Tell me you saw something. Tell me you recorded it!"

"No, no, no, and no."

He deflated. Snatching a pair of red plastic cups, he filled them with a healthy splash of American Honey whiskey. Technically, we weren't supposed to be drinking in the shop during business hours. But technically, we were also supposed to have customers. This late in the season there'd only be a trickle throughout the day, and those mostly to get out of the rain. So it karmically balanced out. He hustled over with the cups, some carrots, and a card game we liked to play that revolved around goods manufacturing.

"Beckett's looking for you, by the way. He was in here just a bit ago," my cousin said while shuffling the cards.

Oh, bother.

"You might've crushed him." Case withheld judgment in his tone, which I appreciated.

"Extenuating circumstances," I replied, something we both knew was a lie. Beckett and I wouldn't have gone anywhere, no matter which way the night had turned. "I'll make it up to him. I promise." Possibly another lie. "Now deal. What's up with these ghosts? Do they have anything to do with the Newsomes and a pair of land surveyors?"

To say Case found the question amusing was to call Mount Hood an anthill. "Why Charlie Goode, have you come to the Dark Side? Just this morning you said solving crimes was none of our business. Wasn't interfering going to mess up the chief's case?" He chucked down the cards, and I helped arrange them into the starting piles. Lumps of coal for us both, and an eager worker.

I sipped the whiskey and enjoyed the sweet burn tracing the back of my throat. Realizing I was hungry, and that afternoon drinking on an empty stomach wouldn't in fact be the adult thing to do, I grabbed some carrots as well.

"I need answers," I said, chomping away. I wasn't sure how else to phrase it. I didn't think I could put anything else into words. Somehow, it wouldn't come out right.

He tried to contain his elation and failed. "In that case, you should know we aren't the only game in town. Joyce has gone full Nancy Drew, and Beckett isn't far behind. I even overheard Gabby yapping about uncovering the real truth. Not that it means much. She'll yap about anything."

Oh, freaking bother. Was there something in the town's drinking water? "You can add Ruth Radford to the list too." I shook my head, but I'd have to worry about the snoops and their gossip later. After scanning my cards, I collected some straw and clay and bought a cattle ranch. I always liked buying cows.

"The ghosts?" I prompted.

Case lofted his cup. "Milling flour. Drink." It was our own house rule. He licked his lips while I followed suit and took a healthy swig. Tapping his fingers on the table, he said, "The ghost tales have become more elaborate over the years, that's for sure. The tellers all want to put their personal stamp on things. And the hauntings now stretch back to the town's founding, if not before. But that doesn't make any logical sense, of course."

"Not make sense? In a ghost tale? Color me surprised."

"What I mean to say is, Buckner's Folly isn't that old. It hasn't been there more than a hundred years. As far as the Newsome land deal, I'm not sure. I suppose it could be connected. Why are you asking? What did Sera tell you, and how does Ruth Radford come into play?"

"Just tracking down the source of some gossip." I rambled on about what Sera had said in the station lot, stopped, and started from when I'd entered her house earlier.

"I'm in," Case said, once I'd finished. He refilled our cups, snatched some chips, and dumped himself back into his chair. "Solving Addie's case, uncovering what happened with the land deal years ago, all of it." When I stammered an objection, he waved me off. "Charlie, you look happier than I've seen you this entire summer. For years, if I'm honest. I'm not missing out."

"Case…" I wanted to tell him he was wrong. How could I look happy when I'd been furious and depressed only twenty minutes ago? But the words fell away. I flopped down my cards and reshuffled the deck.

"No more blinders," I mumbled to myself, then reached for the chips.

He sucked in an excited breath. "We need a murder

board."

"No murder boards. That's not an actual thing."

"You need a hobby." He beamed. "That's an actual thing. All sleuths have hobbies—baking, quilting, cat herding. It helps with the process."

I thought for a moment before perking up. "I play board games," I said. "But I'm not sure how that helps." I lofted my whiskey, stared at my cattle ranch and the cooperage I'd built beside it. "Seems like a distraction."

His foot tapped, fingers drummed. "What Sera told you about Buckner's Folly, that lines up with what I've heard. There were always rumors of dirty deeds done dirt cheap, especially since all of it was swept so neatly under a rug. That's why you asked, right? Checking up on her story?"

I nodded. "It was you or the library, and I didn't want to run into Joyce."

He laughed. Pointing at my worker card, he asked, "Are you working efficiently or inefficiently?"

My shoulders slumped. I had to be honest. "Inefficiently." I flipped my card around and watched my profits dwindle.

Case turned flour into bread. He cackled as he tallied a bunch of points. "So where do we go now?"

"Sera's alibi," I said, then reconsidered. "No. She might be lying about a few things, but that doesn't explain how large boot prints were near Addie's car. Let's focus on Ruth's accusation and the details Joyce told us about."

"The mystery man."

"Yep, I've been thinking about that. There were two sets of prints at the car: one large, one small. At first I thought it meant Addie and a male culprit, but that's been ruled out. According to Frank, Addie did not leave her house alive. So that leaves us with a man and woman as a pair of culprits, with one in a separate car or unnoticeable in the camera footage, or a single culprit with someone else of the opposite sex happening by sometime later. Or maybe not a man at all, but a woman with large feet. Or, I guess, two men, one with small feet."

"Glad you've narrowed it down." Case flipped a card. "Mill. Drink."

I sipped, getting into a flow. "In the security recording, there was only one person visible driving Addie's car, so let's go with the single-culprit theory for now. If the driver wasn't Addie, I'd bet it was a woman from the size. Our mystery man is therefore someone who came by the car, walked around looking at it, and then left without calling the police. Who do we know that would happen by the trailhead in the dark of night?"

"I mean, that could be anyone," said Case. His gaze drifted away. I studied his face, watching it twitch as he thought, until I couldn't keep quiet any longer.

"What are you thinking?"

He put down a card. "I'm going to buy a tannery."

"Case!"

He stretched out his palms in a quelling gesture. "I know, I know. Here's the deal: we have no way to know who stopped by Addie's car. It could've been anyone randomly driving the highway. So maybe it's a better question to ask who our lovely mayor sees as an eyesore. I can think of a few people on her list of undesirables, but what are we going to do, interrogate all of them?"

I moaned. "So we're back to square one?"

Shrugging, Case said, "We could talk to Joyce or Beckett, see what they've worked out."

"No." I snapped the word. "The whole point is to help my dad bring in the killer, not throw egg in his face. Involving Joyce and Beckett would only inflame the rumor mill."

"Heh. Mill. Drink." He drained his cup.

I glared back.

"Okay, got it. Lips sealed." Case shrank back, only to pop up like a prairie dog. "Let's go out to the trailhead and snoop around."

"The crime scene's processed and gone," I said.

"Aye, Captain. But maybe not." He tapped his temple.

I shook my head, not catching on.

"What I mean is," he explained, "Ruth went out there and not only came back with a name but a hunting knife. Where'd that come from? Our mayor might be one to hold grudges, but I don't think she'd plant evidence. It'd get her into some real trouble. She must've found the knife out there. Maybe she uncovered something, and we can too."

I blew out a deep sigh. I had to admit I liked Case's logic. Glancing out the window, I took in the late-afternoon sky. The sun had nearly slunk away. Long shadows stretched over the street and neighboring buildings, washing out the town's deep amber hue. Turning everything colorless and uncertain.

As children, the pair of us had devoured a set of books called *The Mysteries of Little Nibbling*. They featured a badger detective who'd waddle about an English village accusing its denizens of various misdeeds. Inspector Barnaby would often blunder into crucial evidence, but the fun was solving the crime before he did. Case and I used to map out suspects and clues, then race to see who could deduce the culprit the fastest.

A broad grin pulled at my cheeks. I couldn't contain it. Case had been right. As terrible as it sounded—despite Addie's death and all the finger-pointing and slander toward my dad—I felt lighter than I had since returning to Harvest Falls. And if I was honest, lighter than I had in years.

"We'd better hurry," I said. Standing, I grabbed stacks of lumber and added them to my cooperage. Coal and iron went to the smelter. I surveyed. My cows were happy, and the apprentice I'd hired was busy.

Case scanned the cards and pulled at his ears. Lumbering to his feet, he shouted, "Yee! How do you always win?"

I gave him my best "it's a mystery" shrug. The truth was he always played the same strategy. Once I figured that out, countering him was easy. I was always good that way, figuring out an opponent's weaknesses. Maybe there was something to the board game hobby after all. Something to help me catch the killer and save Dad from embarrassment. After slugging the rest of my whiskey, I headed for the door with a bounce in my step.

CHAPTER 14

Gravel kicked up under my Outback's tires as I pulled off the single-lane highway. The sound echoed what I'd heard through the phone the previous night, but I tried not to dwell on that. The lot could hold maybe six cars, though I'd never seen it filled with more than a couple. It was empty now. A brown sign with white lettering marked a wide cut in the foliage. It read "Buckner Falls Trailhead." The path beyond disappeared quickly from view.

Case said something. I ignored him, lost in thought. Buckner Falls was not near as grand as Harvest Falls, but its isolation made it a popular local hike. A place to avoid the hustle and bustle of tourists. It was also on the old Buckner land, in the direction of the folly.

"The night is dark and full of terrors," Case repeated from the passenger seat, this time louder and with a thick accent straight from *Game of Thrones*. He leaned over the dash and peered through the trees.

"I heard you the first time," I said. "Doesn't count. Not from the eighties. Not even the books." I struggled to shake the image of Addie's car and what it must've looked like with crime scene tape wrapped around it, floodlights reflecting off its polished red surface. The trunk open. Police—Dad and Frank—milling about taking notes.

Shivering, I unbuckled and jumped out of the car. It was better to keep moving and get this over with.

"Is cold a smell?" Case asked. He came around the Outback and handed me one of the flashlights he'd fetched from the back of Roll For It.

"It's not that cold," I shot back. But I knew what he meant. The air had a crispness to it that filled the nostrils. I held up the flashlight. "Let's start looking before we need these things." It was dim enough already.

He nodded, and we took off in opposite directions. I wandered over to the trail sign, scanned it and the ground around it. Weeds sprouted along the edge of the gravel. A granola bar wrapper was stuck in one of the tufts of grass. From the faded logo, it looked like it had been there a few months. Pockmarks and ruts scored the gravel lot itself.

The gravel lot. It clicked in my head. Gravel wouldn't leave boot prints. It didn't matter their size. I spun in a circle, not sure what I was looking for until I spied the muddy patch at the far end of the lot. A bubble of excitement sprang forth in a high-pitched yelp. *I'd done a thing!*

"What?" Case begged. He stood at the highway, staring up the road. I waved him over and scoured the patch. But nothing looked like a boot print to me, small or large. The patch was a mire of hard-packed ruts crisscrossed by damp splotches. And I was no backwoods tracker. I doubted I could play one on TV.

By the time Case joined me, I'd near given up. Whatever

had been obvious the night before must've been smeared away by rain. Twilight had settled into dusk, and the tall pines and cedars around us became a wall of dark lines under a murky bluish tinge. I clicked on the flashlight.

Case had his on as well. "I see a trail," he said. He put the flashlight under his chin so it illuminated his face like in an old-time horror movie. "A trail of deception."

"Loser," I said, then flinched in surprise. "No, wait. There is a trail. Look!" A thin break in the foliage had caught in my flashlight's beam. I judged the path's direction. No parking lot shortcut, this one. It ran straight back from the highway into denser forest. The main trail followed the road until it met Little Bear Creek, before heading to Buckner Falls. That was the opposite direction. The two wouldn't cross.

Case and I eyed each other. Our faces lit up like jazz-handing clowns. He gave me the "ladies first" gesture. I shook my head in mock disdain but marched ahead. My flashlight's beam bounced over narrow stretches of exposed dirt and matted grass. Rogue branches snagged against my shoulders and hair, forcing me to slow down and work my way carefully along.

This is stupid. The thought came a little late, as I realized the hulking figure of my childhood nightmares—the man with a hook for a hand, the one wearing a necklace of severed pinkie toes—could be lurking just around the next tree.

My heart pattered to get my attention. It made small pleas, letting me know it needed to pee, warning me that this had been great and all, but it'd be better if we just turned around now and went for a milkshake. I strode forward anyway. The one thing I knew with absolute certainty was that if it came down to it, if my life was on the line: I was faster than Case.

A loud huff came from behind me, as if he could hear my thoughts. It made me giggle. But not for long. In a few strides, the trees closed in, and the forest darkened. My light no longer pushed beyond the few paces before my feet. Cold wrapped me like a blanket. The temperature must've dropped ten degrees.

"What is that?" Case gestured over my shoulder at something caught against the base of a tall cedar. His tone turned hollow. "Is that underwear?"

"Yep," I replied. Calm, like it was a perfectly natural thing to find. Squinting, I stretched my arm in a feeble attempt to get the flashlight closer without moving my feet. I could barely make out the worn cloth, yet the size seemed way too large, way to dingy, and not nearly cute enough. "Definitely not Addie's."

"No, I wouldn't imagine so."

The way Case intoned the words weirded me out a little. I shuffled forward, and my foot thudded against an exposed root. Sucking in a sharp breath, I staggered to catch my balance. As I steadied, I noticed something else half-buried by twigs and nettles: a pink plastic comb.

Case saw it too. His eyes bloomed as round as keg barrels. "This ain't right," he said. "I've got a bad feeling about—"

"Shhh!" I shushed him. My light danced over the comb's pink tines. An odd sense of familiarity had come to me. I'd seen the thing before but couldn't place where. *Was it a young girl's comb?*

A bit of bramble rustled in the near distance. Leaves crumpled. Case yelped. "Run!" he cried, spinning and bolting back the way we'd come.

I did the smarter thing. I froze in terror with lead feet encased in cement, chained to the ground. *Yes, a much smarter thing, as long as that meant stupid.* But my reaction gave me a second to calm down, fetch my heart from where it'd stuck to the side of my face, and shove it back down my throat. I was beginning to feel like I'd need to buy it a leash.

The sound had come from some small critter I'd panicked with my light. Maybe a bird or a squirrel. Nothing bigger.

I took in my surroundings again and realized a small clearing broke just beyond the comb and underwear. Within the clearing nestled more random odds and ends—mostly discarded food wrappers and heaps of plastic bags. A picture came into focus, and I remembered where I'd seen the comb before.

"Case, come back," I hollered. "It's someone's camp."

The crash of his lumbering retreat slowed. I called out again, and this time he called back. By the time he returned, I'd uncovered a ripped coat, a crude cooking stove, and a stash of black garbage bags loaded with discarded tin cans and wadded event circulars—the kind you'd find in free stacks at a café.

Case gulped for air, hands planted on his hips. He tried to scowl while I laughed openly at him, but it only made him wheeze, and he wound up chuckling anyway. "If it'd been a bear, you'd be the dead one, and I'd be the one laughing," he managed to pant.

The statement sent me into a second fit of giggles. Once I

finally quieted, I pointed out what I'd found. "I think this all belongs to that guy who drinks by the secondhand shop, the one off of Church Street. Older, heavyset, a bit of scruff, green denim jacket. I've seen him with that comb before. He flourished it at Vin D'Amato like a fencing sword. Made me almost pee myself laughing."

"Marvin," Case supplied, nodding. "Shepard, I think?"

Of course Case knew him. He'd strike up a conversation with anyone holding a bottle. Once, he gabbed with a German tourist for an hour just to get a sampling of homemade Black Forest schnapps.

I connected some dots. "That fits," I declared. "He's got to be the one Ruth wants arrested, the one she says lurks near the tourists. I've seen him around when the buses arrive. I've heard him shouting a few times too. You know, arguing with the wind."

Case flinched like he'd sucked on something sour. "He's harmless."

"This is our mayor we're talking about," I replied. "His camp is near enough to the trailhead. Ruth had her dogs with her. I bet they found this place, and that's how she got his knife. She went through this pile of stuff."

"Assuming it's his knife."

I bit my lip. "We're assuming everything, but what else do we have to go on?"

Case shrugged. "Okay, I'll buy it. But what does it mean for Addie? Even if the knife is his, it doesn't mean he was near her car."

"No," I agreed. "But think about it. Everything lines up, if it was him." I could picture it in my head, as if the pieces were scattered across a giant game board. "Marvin either heard something or came across Addie's car by chance, after it'd been dumped. He checked it out, left his boot prints, and took off. He's a witness, not a suspect."

Case bobbed his head. "So the large prints are ruled out, and we're going with the single-culprit theory based solely on the set of small prints. Get it? Sole…" He trailed off at my look of exasperation. "We should talk to Marvin," he added, after a moment of thought. "You know, to confirm everything. It'll be easy enough for him to admit, and if true, it'll narrow down the suspects for certain."

We should tell Frank. That was the right thing to do. I knew it but dismissed the thought. He already had Marvin's name thanks to our mayor. He'd all but gloated about it, speaking cryptically to my dad, in front of me. Besides, he'd only tell me to stay out of the way, and we had other leads to follow.

"I should check on Sera's alibi before it gets any later," I said. "Why don't I do that while you find Marvin and chat with him?"

Case seemed eager at the prospect. "Divide and conquer. Smart."

"Yep." I ignored Dad's admonishments and Frank's warnings tolling in my head. The plan was smart, all right—just like throwing turpentine on a dumpster fire.

CHAPTER 15

I leaned against a cold brick wall, one foot propped up like a flamingo. A neon light buzzed above me. An unknown stain made a Rorschach blot on the sidewalk before me. My guess was urine from the smell. It was probably not a dog's.

"So you can't tell me when she arrived?" I asked into the phone. Air wheezed out of my balloon. "Ah, huh. Okay, thank you." I hung up and cursed.

"That bad?" Case asked. He startled me, coming out of Hank's, the other locals' watering hole in Harvest Falls. After polishing off a handful of peanuts, he wiped his hand on his jeans. Hank's glass door rumbled shut behind him. The bar's neon sign flickered. If The Oak Grove aspired to a romantic notion of druids and forest harmony, Hank's swayed more toward grease stains and unpaid alimony.

Pushing myself away from the wall, I crossed my arms to ward off the night's chill. "The woman at Danner House says she remembers Sera being there last night but not at what time. There's a sign-in log, but it's filled in by the visitor."

"The woman doesn't remember anything about Sera's visit?"

"I guess there was a medical issue with one of the other

patients. Sera left late and was the last to sign in. So she could've been there for hours or five minutes."

Case dipped his head back and groaned. "And since she signed herself in, she could've put any time she wanted, as long as it was after the previous visitor."

"Right." I glanced up the street, watched a jacked-up Tacoma zoom past. "She wasn't lying about where she went. But she's certainly not cleared. All she had to do was make sure she was seen. It's a weak alibi at best, and since she's already lied a few times…"

As Case nodded, his brow furrowed. "The nursing home your folks set up in your old house, it's not cheap, right? So how does Sera's mom afford it? They're not exactly a family passing 'GO' with any frequency."

"Life insurance payout from Sera's grandmother," I replied. I'd heard about it from Gabby once. "Apparently, it was all going to Sera until her mom decided she wanted her senior years to have a little more comfort. Can't blame her."

"Ouch, still got to sting though."

My lips puffed as I blew out a sigh. I nudged my head toward Hank's door. "Give me some good news."

Case grinned like a toddler. He hooked a thumb at the bar. "Marvin's in there drinking some piss water from California. He confirmed our theory. Says he didn't hear anything, just found the car abandoned. He tried to see if there was someone sleeping in it. Apparently that happens a few times a month, and he sometimes gets a few bucks by threatening to call a tow truck. He spooked when Joyce's car showed up, and he ran off."

"Nice one, Case! Now, we actually know something!" I sounded like a dunce, but I couldn't help feeling proud. "We're looking for a female who knows Addie's house well enough to avoid the porch camera."

"Well, maybe," said Case. "I've been thinking. If it was a woman alone, how did they get Addie into the trunk? Also, women don't usually commit these types of violent murders. Google says so."

I threw my hands up. "Why do men always assume women can't lift anything heavy? Addie didn't weigh that much, and the killer had all the time they needed at her house."

"Could you lift her?"

My hands curled into fists. "That's beside the point."

"Okay, okay." Case stepped back. "But can you at least allow we're looking for someone small but fit?"

I let my arms drop loose. "Fine," I said. "Now let me call Charlotte and ask about the necklace."

I walked as I dialed. I needed to get away from the stench of Hank's outdoor latrine. Case followed, his gaze tracking the darkened windows and storefronts. Just a pair of do-gooders with nothing else better to do on a Monday night, we were.

My gut clenched as the call connected. My bravado waned. I wasn't sure I wanted to speak with Charlotte again, not after the day she must've had. I imagined her on the couch under a blanket, ravaged by grief. A box of tissues next to a pile of spent ones.

"Hello, Charlie?" Her voice sounded rather cheery.

"Ah…Char…hello?" I stammered, caught off guard.

"Yes, is that you, Charlie?" Charlotte asked. "Your ears

must be burning. Geraldine is here. We were just talking about you!"

I jerked to a halt. *Crap.* Had Geraldine spoken with Dad already? I needed to cross my fingers that she hadn't, else she'd know about my humiliating dismissal.

Case leaned into me. "What is it?"

I waved at him to shush and shoved him away. "You were? She is?" I said, trying not to come off too manic. "My ears on fire. Ha!" I gave a clipped laugh that failed at any semblance of a natural sound.

"Geraldine's offered such wonderful support," said Charlotte. "I don't know how I'd manage without her. Gresham tries, you know, but he just doesn't have it in him to stick around and really be there in a time of crisis. He's more about the appearance than the substance. He's my arm candy, as Geraldine puts it." Charlotte trilled a laugh. It sounded way more practiced than mine had. "But you called me. What can I do for you, dear?"

A clock started ticking in my head. I needed to get answers and get off the phone. There wasn't any time for warming up to the question, so I rolled the dice. "Sorry to bother you so late, but I'm following up on a small detail. Addie had a necklace, an ornate turtle with emeralds. Do you remember where she got it?"

"Yes, funny you should ask. I told your detective fellow all about it just an hour ago."

Oh, crap! I clenched my phone hard enough I feared it might snap. "Right. I'm, ah, just checking again that Addie didn't buy two of them. There's no possible way someone else could have the same necklace?" *Ugh, way to think on your feet, Charlie!*

"No, as I explained to the detective, it's a custom piece, dear, from Beverly Hills. Addie and I went on a shopping trip there last year. It wasn't Paris, but you know, nothing is."

"Nothing is certainly not." I cringed but snatched Case by the arm. Sera had lied once again. Though expected, the news still sent an electrical bolt down my spine. Why was she hiding what really happened? It could get her into a lot of trouble.

"Thank you so much," I said. "I'll be sure to pass on the confirmation to Detective Nichols. Sorry to have bothered you with this."

"Oh, hold on, dear. Geraldine would like to have a word with you."

I yipped. Seriously. Yipped. A ruffling sound came through the connection. My finger hovered over the disconnect button. I willed myself to be strong, but I didn't know whether that meant to cut the call or not.

A second later, Geraldine's voice blared. "Charlie, Charlotte has wonderful news for us. She has a friend at Miley University who's passing through Harvest Falls this week. We'll do lunch. You'll be your impressive self and woo her into granting you a place at their medical school. It's all planned."

I shook my head furiously. "Huh-uh."

"Did you hear me?" Geraldine's tone turned a little sour before resuming its hollow rosiness. "I've asked Gresham to draw up the paperwork for the sale of your grandmother's land. It's all moving forward."

My face pinched. I tried to bubble up some fake

excitement, to play along with the absurdity, but I couldn't muster a drop. "Geraldine, did you go over to Charlotte's house to chat about this today? Really? *Today?*"

"What." It wasn't a question but a flurry of razor blades whirled my direction.

"Sorry," I responded automatically. "I just meant Charlotte must be wanting to think about other things. But I guess this could be a distraction, right? So it's a good thing? And Miley—*yay!*—it will be nice to meet someone, and nice that Charlotte—Mrs. Newsome—can do me such a huge favor. Super pumped for it."

Case flicked my arm, trying to hit my reset button. I ducked away. Silence filled the line for an eternity before Geraldine's harsh whisper sounded. "Your father should never have offered you work at the police station. Look what it's done to you."

My jaw dropped. But before I could inhale, she'd hung up the phone.

"Gwarrr!" I bellowed into the night.

Case shook with delight. "So what did Geraldine have to say?" he asked, singing the question innocently.

Willing him to tumble over with a good, solid leg cramp, I stormed off and forced him to jog to catch up. "She wants me to meet with someone from the Miley University Medical School," I barked. "After all that's happened with Addie, with Dad, I can't believe that's all she cares about. She even has Gresham and Charlotte working on it."

"So why don't you tell her you're not interested?" Case wisely stepped clear of my reach as he posed the question.

I squeezed my eyes shut while not breaking stride, but the sense of continued motion made me dizzy. Popping my lids open made it worse. I grabbed a lamppost for balance, and the world slid to the side. It fled from me, or maybe I fled from it. It was hard to tell the difference.

"Sera lied," I said. "The necklace was Addie's. She stole it."

Case planted his legs wide and leaned back at the waist, stretching. With a grunt, he scanned the street. The streetlights hid the stars above. "I need a beer," he said.

I barely heard him. "I want the truth," I muttered. *From someone, anyone. Even myself.* The thought rattled around my head as if I'd shouted into a giant crevasse. "And I'm going to keep asking until I get it, no matter how long it takes."

CHAPTER 16

"That was fun while it lasted," said Case. "But this is better." He clinked his pint glass against mine. We'd retreated to a table within The Oak Grove. Case had convinced me it was time to regroup. My body had reminded me it preferred not to be so active. I'd conceded on both points, but only until I could come up with a better plan.

The table's polished surface gleamed. James had wiped it down for us, leaving only a hint of stickiness and a waft of yeasty rag water. With a sly wink, he'd hurried back to the bar to pull a few more beers.

One of those was for Frank. The detective perched on a stool at the bar by himself. When he'd seen me enter, he'd raised a glass in greeting. I'd stiffened and angled toward the farthest corner of the room. I stared now at his back and wondered why I'd had such a childish reaction. Had it come from embarrassment? I was tempted to apologize.

But before I could, Darlene Devereux appeared. She hovered over our table, tapping her wineglass with a long, polished fingernail. She kept peering over her shoulder, as if waiting for someone. Bedecked in bangle earrings and cashmere, she wore middle age with a flawless grace.

Something for me to aspire to.

"I heard you and the detective shared some time together," she said. Not an accusation, but I knew her well enough to recognize the unasked question in her tone.

"From Gabby?" I guessed.

"Huh. No surprise there, I guess." She checked her phone. "You know she has it out for you, right?"

"Me? No. Why?" That was a shock. *What did I do?*

But Darlene's head was buried in her phone. Her lips moved as she read a text. When she looked up, her gaze barely met mine. "What? Sorry…I have to…" She spun and started for the door. "We'll catch up later. Come visit anytime. You'll watch Branson this weekend?"

"Of…of course!" I hollered after her. I always jumped at the chance for Branson time. The lovable fur ball owned me, and we both knew it. But I wouldn't wait until the weekend to catch up with Darlene. From her behavior in the morning, and now, she clearly had a secret. Whether it was related to Addie's death was another question.

Case studied her retreat. "*That* was odd," he said before sliding her wineglass closer.

"Should I go after her?"

"Nah, come on. Drink." Case clinked my glass again and took a healthy glug of his own. "Gabby's just winding folks up. It'll be someone else tomorrow."

I sipped sparingly. Gabby's gossip mill wasn't what concerned me, but I decided to let Darlene's behavior go for now. I had higher priorities. Or, to be more honest, other distractions. My gaze wandered back to the bar. Watching

Frank and James trade quips was odd, like seeing characters from my favorite television shows intermingle, each unaware they should be limited to their own timeslot. James wore his normal gentle cheeriness, dimples and all. I couldn't see Frank's face but knew he took in everything around him like a stone Buddha.

Case leaned back and followed my gaze. "You may have missed your chance, you know."

"Huh?" I didn't follow.

"With Boy Wonder. Word on the street says he's getting fitted for a tux. You know, for the Long Walk, the Sweet Kiss of Oblivion, the Final Chapter." Case paused, trying to come up with another lame moniker, before waving his glass toward the bar. "I heard it this morning at the café. Gabby was teasing Madison about it. I guess they're a pretty hot item."

"Wait, what?" I lurched. The few brain cells I had firing decided to give up and ram into each other. Snorts of awkward laughter followed. When I could contain myself, I asked, "You're telling me now? Case! Since when did this happen?"

"We were busy." He shrugged. "I'm just saying what I heard."

I whipped my head back to the bar. "James and Madison? I don't see it. Madison looks like a model and all, but James is…" I trailed off. I didn't want to finish the thought, let alone utter it out loud, not even to Case.

But he knew, the rat bastard. He studied me over the rim of his glass. One eyebrow rose in a not-so-subtle manner.

"I know what you're thinking, but it wouldn't be fair." I sorted through my canned reasons, the ones I'd come up with over the summer. They seemed so clear until I spat them out. "Once I leave for medical school, what then? He'd be stuck here in a long-distance relationship. It could last for years. I mean, who's to say I'd ever come back?"

"Uh-huh." Case drained the rest of his beer.

My eyes narrowed. "Shut up," I muttered. It was easier to be pissed at Case than face the myriad of emotions spawning deep in my chest. There were enough of them to form a union. Whomever said "don't kill the messenger" didn't appreciate an easy way out.

Case set his glass down. He took time lacing his fingers over the barrel he called a stomach. "Do you remember when someone stole the Bywater street sign? You had me pace off the whole block so you could create a diagram of how the thief must've done it. It had every detail drawn out in colored marker. It even had a timeline of the thief's movements. And you were what, nine? And I was six?"

I recognized his obvious gambit—lacing his fingers was one of his tells—but allowed the memory to brighten me up anyway. I couldn't blame him for passing along what he'd heard. He'd probably fretted over protecting my feelings all day. Fretted, and then blurted with abandon—that was Case.

"I'd completely forgotten about that thing. I thought Dad would be proud." I'd hung the diagram on my bedroom wall for a while. It'd lasted until my mother replaced it with this Junior Chemist award, the kind all kids received if their parents shelled out the cash for a hands-on science summer camp.

"I only helped because you couldn't rope Addie into it," Case said. "You were fully invested, though. I'd never seen you like that, a possessed demon child in pigtails."

"I remember. Didn't some girl you liked tease you the whole way?"

Case nodded. "Emily Chambers. I had to pace the block three times before the teasing stopped messing up my count." He smirked. "She made up for it in high school, though."

I refused to engage as he popped his eyebrows suggestively. No doubt she'd merely waved to him in the hall. Allusions toward grand adventures was also in Case's nature. "What made you think of the stolen sign?" I asked and immediately regretted the question.

His head fell to the side. He stared as if I'd asked if vegans ate veal.

"Shut up," I snapped again. But there was more mirth in it this time.

James barked with glee. "Hey, farm boy, you done polishing my horse's saddle?"

Leaping from my skin, I knocked into the table and banged my knee. James had snuck up on us with a second round of beers. *Sneaky, light-footed hobgoblin.* Cursing, I stood and rubbed at the bone. I'd have a good bruise by morning.

"As you wish!" Case replied to the *Princess Bride* line with the classic response. He tittered as he took the offered pints. "Hey, we were just talking about you."

"Case." I shot him my mad-dog glare.

"Oh, yeah? What about?" James looked concerned for my well-being, but the dimples didn't leave his cheeks. "My half-daft craft draft skills?" His grin melted butter in the next state. "Try saying that once."

My face burned. My brain petrified. *If only it were simple…if only neither of us would get hurt*…But I had to shut Case up. I didn't want James picturing anything I wasn't willing to imagine myself. Feeling eyes on me, I caught Frank staring our way. He grinned when our gazes crossed. After finishing his beer, he slid off his barstool and fished a few bucks out of his pocket.

Yes, an escape! An impulse smacked me into action. Not a good impulse, and certainly not a well-formed one.

"Ha! Nice." Case pumped his fist at James's lame but adorable wit.

"I'm going to ask Frank whether he's arresting Sera," I blurted. "I'm sure he got more out of her during the interview at the station. Maybe even the truth this time." I gulped down some beer and wiped my lips. "I'll get him to spill."

James blinked, thoroughly lost.

Giggling, Case winked. "I bet you can, you saucy minx."

Frank reached the door. My throbbing knee wobbled as I staggered off, and I stumbled into James. Strong hands gripped my arms and returned my balance. I reared, knocking him aside. But an impression of the touch remained and made me dizzy—those hands brushing things.

"Sorry!" I yelped. "I-I'm fine. Thanks." I reached out to put a gentle hand on his shoulder, caught myself, and wound up patting his cheek. *Great, Charlie, just like a grandma would do!* He exhaled, confused and silent. Stubble and warm breath tickled across my flesh. As I fled, the growling noise rattling from my lungs put an end to any speculation over my sanity. But Case could sort James out. I needed to pounce on Frank before I considered what I was doing. It was time to reshuffle the deck.

Flying out of the bar, I found the detective already halfway up the block. I hurried after, catching up as he reached his sedan.

"Hello, Little Goode," he said. He opened the driver's door and paused. His expression looked both exhausted and jovial, like a mall Santa at the end of a shift.

I launched in with both feet. "Marvin didn't do it. I think it was his knife, but Ruth had it all wrong. He found Addie's car, and…" I watched his lips tug wider. "You already know this, don't you?"

He tapped an imaginary badge on his chest. "Detective."

Crap. His shield was up. I needed to be cool, real subtle like. Gently coax the information out of him. My mouth opened and threw that plan out the window.

"Are you arresting Sera?" I demanded.

"Good night, Charlie." He climbed into the car.

I plunged into the passenger's side and rambled. "Sera's alibi is weak. I think that gives her opportunity. She's certainly capable, so it really comes down to motive. What was her fight about with Addie, and was it worth killing for?"

"You're making a habit out of jumping in this car." Frank gave me the deadpan stare. His head and gaze flicked to the door, indicating I should climb my ass back out. I doubled down instead, snatching the seat belt and clicking it into place.

"Suit yourself," he said. He started the engine and pulled onto the empty street.

I twisted to watch his expression as he drove. "You

followed up with Charlotte Newsome about the necklace. She told me that. It was Addie's, so why did Sera say she had it? Was it another lie? She told me they both had one, but that's not true."

Frank didn't react to my rambling. "I'm leaving in the morning after a few things. Have to go check in with the homestead."

"What!" My jaw dropped. "You're leaving now? It's the middle of an investigation."

"Don't worry, I'm not going far. These kinds of things take teamwork." He slowed as a signal changed. Another car came up behind us. Its headlights bathed Frank's face in white. His finger tapped the steering wheel. "Your dad's a good man. He'll keep me up to date, and I'll be back soon, if anything pops up or when the forensics come in. Until then, I've got a pile of paperwork sitting on my desk."

My head swiveled and bobbed as I tried to makes sense of his explanation. "So it's not Sera?"

"If I'd gotten anything out of Ms. Simmons, I'd have been home an hour ago." He hit the gas, checked the rearview mirror. His gaze slid my way. "She's not in the clear, though. We just need something more to press the issue, go at her again, and see what shakes out."

"Build a case."

"That's not what I said, nor what I meant, so don't go getting any ideas."

"Got it."

"I'm serious. I already had to threaten those ladies at the café this evening, not to mention deal with your lovely mayor."

He shook his head. "The people in this town have way too much free time on their hands."

"It's the slow season," I said, lost in thought.

The tires *ka-thunked* against the curb as we pulled into the small lot outside the Twin Pines motel. I stared at the gold-plated room numbers screwed against each of the dozen doors. I really hadn't thought things through. We were near the highway at the far end of town. The motel was old and weathered, but with a bright coat of paint slopped over years of wear from rain and wind. My car was back at the game shop where I'd parked after returning from the trailhead.

Frank pulled up in front of one the rooms. He shut off the engine. The wolfish cast from earlier in the day returned to his face. A truck crawled along the road behind us. After it passed, the night became still.

"I've got a bottle of Gentleman Jack in my room. I can rustle up a soda from the vending machine if you want to come in for a drink." His seat belt clicked and slithered off. "We're both adults, right?"

My hand froze over my own release. James's face popped into my head. The memory of his touch returned. But I shook it away, confused and full of self-pity. He'd had his chance. Apparently, he'd chosen Madison. *But had he? And was Frank the next best option?* In the state I was in, I'd be lying if I didn't admit the prospect of being held, of being wrapped in bedsheets and peppered by savage lips, didn't have its attraction. It'd been a long time since Mason and I had shared intimacies. To go from over a decade of closeness to nothing had been a tough adjustment.

I sank back into the seat. Frank would carry on him a hint of beer and sour whiskey, and a hard musk that reeked of confidence. *And he'll be gone tomorrow*, a cruel voice whispered in my head. Wasn't that my summer playbook? No strings. No attachments. No consequences. Wasn't that the very logic that had kept me from James?

Frank leaned over. His hand snapped off my seat belt. "What do you say?"

Little Goode. I filled in the patronizing nickname as I caught a whiff of maple glaze and mint medicinal cream. Donuts and old. Like it had this morning, my delusion shattered. Frank changed back into the salty detective he was, going through motions he'd done a thousand times in a thousand other towns. I shrank back. *This man was meant to be solving Addie's murder!* And he was leaving—if not giving up, he certainly wasn't rolling up his sleeves and digging in for the long haul. What would that mean for the case? Did he care at all?

I couldn't let him touch me. Apathy clung to him like a mold. Apathy and something else. Something more foul. More devious. It nagged at me, all of a sudden, taking hold and not letting go.

"Wait," I said. I recalled his earlier words. "You said homestead. You said you needed to check in with the homestead. You didn't say your lieutenant or the station." My gaze flickered to his bare hand. No tan lines, but that didn't prove anything for certain. Most people lacked a tan in Harvest Falls.

"Are you married?" I asked. I raised my gaze to glare at him.

His grin deepened. A false face, I saw it now. "With three boys," he admitted, without an ounce of shame. "I coach their baseball teams on the weekend, when I can. Doesn't happen that often, though. The youngest has a shot to play in high school; the other two put in a good effort."

My hands balled so tightly I feared I would crack a bone. The rest of his earlier words replayed in my head. He'd said my dad was a good man. That he had every trust in him. They were all on top of the investigation. He'd meant to soothe and appease me. But how much was a snake's opinion worth?

I threw the door open, sprang from the sedan, stomped a few paces, spun, and came back. Grabbing the door, I leaned inside.

"Why did you allow me into Sera's this morning?" I demanded. "Or even Charlotte's, for that matter? You didn't need to, not for the questions you asked. I didn't know what I was doing. Hell, I don't know what I'm doing most of the time, and that's on a normal day."

Frank didn't bother looking sheepish. He returned to a blank mask. But I could tell he only wanted that whiskey and to climb under the sheets. I would've been a lucky bonus, but not something to warrant putting any effort into.

My wheels derailed on their own before he could answer. "You were setting them up, right? Using me as a prop, hoping I'd manipulate their moods?" I mimicked his voice. "Little Goode will have them relax. She'll have them open up and spill their secrets. That it? Well, the joke was on us both, wasn't it? Relaxing people is not what I do!"

"Charlie—" Frank started to say something. I didn't let

him finish. I slammed the door on him. It didn't matter what he wanted. It didn't matter what he thought.

"I'll walk," I hollered over my shoulder. My inner fire raged, and not even the blustery autumn night could cool me down. I only hoped I could focus the flames before they ripped my whole life apart.

CHAPTER 17

As I trudged back into the heart of Harvest Falls, a part of me wanted to throw sanity to the wind and howl like a madwoman. But I kept my rage in check. There'd be time to summon my inner Carrie later. Right now, I needed to figure out what to do next.

What now? Such a simple thought. Yet for the better part of a mile, no easy answers came to mind. I dismissed calling Case for a ride. He'd probably be in no shape to drive, at this point. But I also wanted to put together a game plan on my own. It'd been too long since I'd thought more than a few hours ahead. Well, minutes, to be completely honest. Somehow life had become easier that way.

I slowed my stride. The crisp air felt good on my cheeks. Trees loomed in the darkness all around. The clouds above melded into a thick blanket. I kicked a pebble and barely made it out as it bounced back and forth over the white glow of reflective paint marking the edge of the road. Streetlights were spaced well apart this far out of town. The road had no sidewalk, only a ditch filled with grass and moss, and the occasional tangle of litter.

Talking to Frank had been like talking to a steel door. I

wondered if he'd always wanted to be a detective, or whether he'd fallen into the profession. Could that even happen? It dawned on me that I'd never questioned my dad's passion for police work. Where had it come from, and had it always been the case?

Tires ground the road, coming up behind me. From the motel, I judged. Frank checking on me. When they slowed, I turned and readied a fierce sneer of disdain. But the vehicle wasn't a sedan. The headlights sat too high. A truck, maybe. I blinked against the blinding halogens. My throat constricted. The road was otherwise silent.

Perfect. Way to be an easy target, Charlie!

Thankfully, my lizard brain donned its cape. I didn't wait for the truck to stop. I turned and bolted. A rutted field lay beyond the roadside ditch, and beyond that a thin line of trees. A tempting sanctuary. The truck wouldn't be able to follow me. But I still didn't like my chances. On foot, my pursuer might be faster than me. In the darkness, I might fall and break an ankle.

And then: game over.

I needed the safety of town.

The truck's engine roared. Its headlights flooded the world around me. I fumbled for my phone, but its pleather case slipped through my fingers. The phone banged against my knee and clattered to the road.

Mother fah—! My arms pumped harder. I gulped air into burning lungs. My feet, numbed from the cold, slapped the pavement.

The truck barreled past. Up the road, it swerved to the side of the road. Its tires screeched, brakes squealing, as it blocked my path.

Lizard brain, go! My pace didn't waver. Nor did I angle for the ditch. Anger flared, desperate and seething. A fight response. I didn't want some unknown shadow chasing and catching me from behind. I wanted to face whomever it was, and go down swinging. So I charged.

Sweat streamed down my face, a mix of cold panic and exertion. I blinked it away and strained to focus, but the truck's red taillights blurred in my vision. My legs churned. Dark shadows receded as I neared the royal blue tailgate. One of those stupid Share the Road specialty plates hung beneath the bumper. A sticker in the back window read, "The Illuminati are Everywhere."

Hold on. Lizard brain, recognize?

Beckett. Beckett's truck. It clicked as I tore past the tailgate, racing along the driver's side.

The door swung open. I hurtled toward it, stumbling as I fought to slow. My arms flailed. I shrieked. Beckett jumped from the driver's seat. His eyes went wide. Whirling to avoid me, he smacked into the side of the truck. I managed to catch the open door and swing to a stop.

"What the hell?" I doubled at the waist, gasping.

He clutched his nose, rubbing at it and wincing. "Uh…hi, Charlie. I've been looking for you." It must've been too painful to sniffle.

"You could've texted! Not creep up on me in the dark!"

"Oh, I, uh, saw you coming out of the bar. I thought the detective was maybe, like, driving you home. So I followed. But that's not where you went." He wiggled his nose and snorted a few times. "I really need to talk to you."

Crap. The look on his face was like a wounded otter. Dealing with a broken heart was not what I needed right now. I held up my hand to buy a second of peace, catch my breath, and still my thumping heart. Fetching my phone, I was happy to see it hadn't cracked. That was a silver lining, at least.

"Look, Beckett," I started explaining, "I'm sorry I gave you the wrong impression. I shouldn't have ever…" I trailed off as he flinched. His gaze dropped to his feet. *Oh, boy…*

Backpedaling, I forced myself to remain firm. "I had a fun time until…you know…" *Ugh! Wrong turn!* I tried again, this time with a blunt, "We just don't work."

He blinked. Sad, lost eyes stared at me. "Oh. Yeah. I wasn't thinking. I mean, not about that. I had to find you because I know who killed Addie. I have proof. And I thought you'd want to know first."

"Wait, what?" It was my turn to flinch, not to mention wipe the dozen eggs off my face. A hubris soufflé. "Why didn't you go to the police?" I thought of Frank sipping his whiskey just up the road and wondered how receptive he'd be if I came pounding on his door. Especially after the way I left.

Beckett's head bobbled. "I know, I know. But they won't take me seriously. At least, your dad never has before. Besides, they've already questioned her, and I still don't have the evidence. She does."

"Whoa. Back up. Questioned whom? Sera Simmons?"

"No, not Sera." He wiped his hands on his jacket before tucking them under his pits. "Okay, here's the thing. I bought this live-steel dagger at a Renaissance faire last year. You know, the kind without blunted edges?"

"Like an adult knife?" I prompted.

He drew back as if I'd understated the importance of gravity. "It's really sharp and heavy, and it has scrollwork along the hilt."

"So you think it's the murder weapon?" My balloon of anticipation deflated. Memories of Ruth Radford waving Marvin Shepard's hunting knife flashed through my head. "Wielded by..." I sorted through the short list of *shes* I knew the police had questioned. "...by Joyce?"

That surprised me. Joyce Townsend was certainly capable, but I couldn't fathom a reason she'd want to kill Addie. Nor why Beckett would accuse her. According to Case, the pair were bosom buddies.

"Why?" I asked.

Beckett nodded adamantly. "The dagger is way cool. When I saw it, I knew it had to be modeled on something historical. Maybe from the Knights Hospitallers, maybe even older. Joyce said she'd help me research it, but a few weeks later she told me she'd lost it. Like, it'd just disappeared from the library one day."

He threw up his hands in dismay. I summoned the strength to play along. "So what does that have to do with Addie?"

"Exactly my question. But it's all connected. It has to be. Joyce called this morning and, out of the blue, says she found the dagger. Like months later, here it is popping back into existence."

"And the connection to Addie?" I nudged.

"Don't you get it?" He stepped closer and lowered his voice. "Joyce doesn't have an alibi for last night. The route from the library to her place doesn't pass the Buckner Falls Trailhead. So what was she doing up there? And why has my dagger suddenly reappeared? She's obviously hiding things!"

Oh, good grief. I pinched the bridge of my nose. "If the dagger was thought to be lost months ago, why would Joyce volunteer its discovery the morning after using it on Addie? Wouldn't it make more sense to keep the thing hidden?"

Beckett shrugged. "Things like this happen. People act stupid all the time out of, you know, subconscious guilt and stuff."

I stared into his completely dead-serious eyes and wished I had a rubber chicken. One of those gag ones clowns used to smack each other. Or maybe not a chicken but a much larger bird. Like an ostrich. Something I would need both hands to wield. Something that would make a satisfying slapping sound.

"Have you asked Joyce how she found the dagger?" I inquired, as politely and nonjudgmentally as I could. "I mean, aren't you good friends?"

His head shook. "I didn't want to tip her off. We can't let her know we're on to her. That would be dangerous."

"Right." I was done being cold and tired. I marched for the passenger door. "Get in. Drive me to my car. And have Joyce meet us at Roll For It tomorrow. Tell her to bring the dagger, and we'll sort this all out."

Beckett scrambled for his keys. "Home turf. Greater numbers." He sniffled. "That's clever."

Yep, that's me, sly as a stuffed and mottled fox. I sunk into the passenger seat. At this rate, protecting Dad's reputation was going to take far more than uncovering Addie's killer. I was going to have to convince a town full of emperors they wore no clothes.

CHAPTER 18

I slept longer than planned yet woke feeling unrested. My legs ached. My ankles were tender. A hot shower worked out some of the soreness, and I followed it with coffee and a marionberry muffin. Sugar and caffeine got me out the door. Case had already opened Roll For It by the time I reached the shop.

"You left The Oak Grove way too early," he said in greeting. "Big news. Big." He popped his hands, mimicking tiny explosions, before slurping from a thermos-size coffee mug. The hazelnut scent made me salivate.

My shoulders sank. "Not you too. Beckett told you about Joyce Townsend?"

His face scrunched. "Joyce? I'm talking about the ginormous dustup Gabby had with Addie last week. Full-on cage match, apparently. What're you talking about?"

Ginormous dustup? That was a surprise. Addie's plans for a health spa sprang instantly to mind. If their feud had escalated, it was definitely something worth looking into. I wondered if Frank had left Harvest Falls yet but decided I didn't care. He was the professional. He made his own choices and could follow his own leads. I'd only bug him again if I had something concrete. Until then, Case and I were on our own.

"Come on," I said, "I'll fill you in on Joyce while we do the shelving." My body groaned as I willed it to move once more. I launched into the tale of Beckett's dagger while going along the aisles and tidying the rows of game boxes.

"And you invited her here?" Case begged in almost a whimper. Leave it to him to take Beckett's insane theory seriously.

I chucked a foam burrito at him. They made game components for everything these days. I scanned the shop for a rubber ostrich but didn't spy one. *Bummer.*

"Tell me more about this thing with Gabby," I said, as I started noting what games we'd need to fetch from the little storage room in the back. There weren't many. We'd barely had a handful of customers the last few days.

"Darlene returned and spilled to me and James about it." Case reorganized the endcap the shop had for new releases. He made room for a game where each player managed a brewery. The artwork was surprisingly realistic rather than cartoony. That most likely meant the game would require a lot of math. I made a mental note to try it out, though the number-crunchy ones weren't normally my favorite. I liked the ones where the theme was immersive.

"You know Darlene and Gabby only pretend to be friendly since their shops are so close," I said. I hadn't forgotten Darlene's warning, but I still found it difficult to imagine Gabby had it out for me. More likely, it was an attempt by Darlene to set me against her frenemy, though that seemed out of character for her. She wasn't petty like that.

"She was acting awfully odd last night," I added.

"I know, but the fight had like a dozen witnesses." Case flipped a box around and sent others tumbling to the floor.

"Careful, Mongo."

"Yes, Mother." He squatted to clean up the mess. "So apparently Addie comes into the café and starts trading barbs with Gabby. Just catty stuff at first. Insults veiled as compliments kind of thing. But Addie doesn't let go. She starts talking about some deep conversation she had with Gabby's husband. She makes it seem like something's going on between them, and Gabby loses it. She starts threatening Addie with all kinds of things"—Case made sure he had my full attention—"including stabbing her with a kitchen knife."

A tingle ran up my arms. "Wow, that's serious. But she was taking her husband to the airport, right? She can't be the killer." Unless her alibi didn't hold water. I wondered if Frank had bothered looking into that. Gabby practically made a living massaging the truth. Even Sera had said something to that effect.

"Yeah." Case sounded almost disappointed. "It's hard to picture Gabby as a killer too. Do you see it?"

"No," I admitted, "but I can't picture Sera Simmons or anyone else that way either. And Addie was setting up a rival business to Gabby. If not her, then who? We can't dismiss everyone just because we don't think them capable. Everyone in town has to be a suspect."

Case nodded. "Here's another thing. According to Darlene, if Addie had done anything with Gabby's husband, his cheating would balance the karmic scales. You know what I mean?"

"Gabby cheated?" My jaw dropped. "With whom?"

As he shrugged, Case's face turned white. Dice tumbled from his hand, and he stared past me. I whirled and found Joyce standing in the doorway of the shop. Wayward strands of hair sprouted from the bun atop her head. The lines at her eyes pulled tight. She clutched a long, thick-bladed dagger. She looked hella furious.

Stalking toward us, she kept the blade at her waist. "I hear you've been digging around, Charlie Goode. Going on wild goose chases in the middle of the night, palling around with that detective. Trying to cast blame. But you're just like your old man: quick to get it all wrong. The cops are way off target, and so are you."

"Whoa, Joyce, I'm sure we can work something out." Case backpedaled into a shelf, knocking askew the games I'd straightened earlier. He held his hands up. A Shetland pony in full panic mode, feebly bucking in the stall.

Laughter spurted out of me. I couldn't help it. Joyce glared. Case's face contorted, pleading with me to stop. He jerked his head toward Joyce, his eyes bugged out, as if I didn't see an obvious threat.

"Oh, come on," I said to him. I grabbed a shelf for balance. "So Joyce has this grand plan to off Addie with a stolen Renaissance faire dagger, she involves herself in the investigation by pretending to find the body, plays the shocked bystander with us, and then produces the murder weapon for no good reason? For what, theatrics? She's not that good of an actress."

Joyce startled. A wounded expression crossed her face. *Oh, crap!* I'd forgotten she performed with Harvest Falls' local theater group.

"She's way too smart for such a stupid plan, too!" I blurted. *Nice! Saved it.*

"You said everyone in town is a suspect." Case dropped his hands. "You literally just said it!"

I scoured a shelf for the next best thing to throw but stopped short. He did have a point.

Joyce slumped, her wrath wilted. "I can't believe Beckett thinks I'm a murderer." She glanced around the shop. "Where is he, anyway? He was supposed to meet me here."

Something in her expression made me curious. I strode forward until we stood on opposite sides of the gaming table at the front of the shop. "I'm pretty sure he was too embarrassed to confront you. It's a pretty wild tale he spun." I sat and gestured for her to do the same. "So you have a thing for Beckett, huh?"

She sat and placed the dagger gently on the table. "Not really, no. He's just…nice. Not the easiest to get along with, but at least he's honest to your face. Not like some of the other men in town. Be thankful you left years ago. You have no idea what it's like here."

Nodding sagely, I wondered whom she meant. It was true I hadn't dated much within Harvest Falls. After James, I'd mostly hung out with whatever boys trailed after Addie. High school had been one group date after another. Nothing serious, and then I'd been gone.

"Did you clean the dagger?" Case asked.

Startled, I eyed it closer. A thin layer of oil gave the blade a sheen. The oil looked damp, as if applied recently.

Joyce nodded. "It had rust on it. Seriously, a blade like this you need to take care of. That's how it went missing. Or not really missing. I just kept it for a while. I didn't think Beckett deserved it. He thinks it's some replica from the Crusades. But it's clearly a hand-forged take on Sting. I thought it was a one-of-kind masterpiece."

I balked. "The musician?"

"Bilbo's sword!" Joyce and Case shouted in unison, and not a little exasperated.

The Hobbit. Of course. "So…it's a replica of a not-real weapon?"

Joyce sniffed. "If Beckett doesn't recognize it, and he doesn't want to take care of it, he shouldn't have it."

"Ah…um." I tried to remain sympathetic. "It's still his, though."

"I know." Joyce snapped. Her head lowered. Her arms sprawled across the table, and she spoke to its surface. "That's why I decided to give it back. I couldn't keep it. The guilt was too much. Besides, I found the forge online, and they made like a hundred of them. So it turns out it's not even that unique."

"Market's saturated with knockoffs," Case agreed. He fiddled with a few boxes of cards, a party guessing game.

Of a fantasy sword that never existed! I wanted to bellow at them while driving their heads together Three Stooges–style. But I managed to stay myself. Instead, I asked something that had bugged me since Joyce came through the door. "Why did you say the cops are way off target? Do you know something they don't?"

Her head rose. Her eyes darted to the side, as if she were checking for spies eavesdropping. "I wasn't going to share anything until I had proof. The truth has a habit of getting twisted around here." But her lips tugged eagerly, and I knew she wanted nothing more than to spill the beans. I leaned on my elbows.

"If you know something, you have to share it with the police," I informed her, keeping my expression as serious as I could muster. "You'll be charged with obstruction if you don't." That wasn't entirely true, but it sounded plausible enough for us both.

A deep sigh puffed from Joyce. All part of the act, I recognized. She propped herself up and pretended to contemplate her position. Then her face lit up with giddiness. "Whatever they think, the cops have it all wrong. Addie's death stemmed from one old family taking out the bloodline of another."

"Whoa, like an ancient feud?" Case whistled.

"Exactly," said Joyce. She checked behind her. "But there's more. I watched this program on genealogy, and it got me thinking about the old families that founded Harvest Falls. So I did some research at the library. Did you know there was an Alice Parker killed during the Salem witch trials?"

Oh, dear Lord Sauron. I saw where this was headed. A moan escaped me before I could trap it. It sounded like I'd single-handedly devoured a rafter of turkeys.

"You know the town in Oregon is not the same one, right?" I asked.

Joyce turned to Case, ignoring me. "Apparently, the Parker family has survived to this day. One of them is even a famous actress. That made me dig deeper, and do you know what I found?"

That an expired tin of Spam has a better chance of solving Addie's murder? I studied the beams that ran along the ceiling of the shop.

"What?" Case begged.

"Have you heard of the Eidyn Elders? They're a cult of mystics that use minerals and ointments in their dark rites. Think: evil druids. And minerals, like in the caves above the falls. Can you imagine? What better place than Harvest Falls for such a cult to hide in the shadows?"

Case came forward, excited. "Beckett's mentioned them before. He's found some odd things in those caves. Very odd things."

Putting up my hand, I interrupted the insanity. "Hobbit daggers. Pagan rites. Hidden caves. Even by your own logic, none of it matters unless Madison Parker is a descendant of Alice Parker." I plastered on a pleasant smile. "Is she? Or is there some fiendish cousin living within our midst?"

Joyce scowled. "I'm not sure yet. But it has to be her. It all fits that way. Who else could be the descendant?"

My smile became painful. "So besides being born evil, what's her motive?"

"If I'm right, it has something to do with settling the score between the Newsomes and the Parkers. Something to do with this new generation." Joyce pushed herself from the table. "I'll have to keep digging to get more answers, but do you think I should tell your dad now? Do you think he'd listen to reason?"

Somehow, I managed to keep my face still. I wanted to protect Dad from the town's mistrust. But between Ruth, Joyce, and Beckett, it felt like that was a door that would never close. If their theories got any more absurd, flying saucers would fill the skies, and vampires would glitter under the sun. Still, who was I to say what small detail pointed to the truth? In a town this small, it had to exist somewhere.

"Oh, I definitely think you should take your theory to the chief," I replied. "In fact, we should have them come collect the dagger too."

"Really? The dagger?" Joyce asked. Her gaze dropped to the blade. She reached for it before checking herself.

"Everyone's a suspect," breathed Case.

I bit my lip to stave off giggling. Dad didn't have it easy. Even armed with the truth, his reputation was going suffer from all the rampant speculation gone unchecked. If I wanted to help him at all, I needed to connect some dots. Some actual dots, not those born in a fantasy world. Thankfully, Case's gossip, and my grumbling belly, pointed me in the right direction.

CHAPTER 19

The little bell chimed as I entered Sweet Little Buttercup. I'd left Case and Joyce at the game shop to wait for Vin D'Amato. I didn't have the energy to deal with Vin's ego. At least, not until I had more coffee in me. But more than that, I needed to speak with a certain baker's assistant and get answers to a few questions.

Only a handful of customers filled the café. They sat quietly at tables. Baked sugar and berries assailed my nose. Madison slouched near the register, half-heartedly wiping the top of the display case next to the counter. Strands of caramel-colored hair had pulled free from her ponytail. It tumbled perfectly, as if placed by a professional artist. James would be a lucky man, if what Case told me was true.

Not that I was jealous.

I squinted and pictured her with a pointy hat and broom. Maybe a wart and a tabby cat entwining her legs for good measure. Madison Parker, scion of the Salem Parkers. It kind of fit. Her late mother, Madeline, had certainly held a witchy reputation in her day, and the pair of them were mirror images. Still, I made an unpleasant noise, not quite blowing out a full raspberry, as I realized the inevitable—she could totally pull off the witch look. It was clearly me who was green with envy.

Her brow furrowed. I'd broken her out of some reverie. "What?"

A sign on the counter caught my eye. "What's this about?" I asked, pretending it'd been my focus all along. Written in orange and pink puffy paint, the sign announced that an evening vigil would be held at the café in Addie's honor. Pastries and coffee would be available at a reduced price, of course.

Madison's gaze didn't leave mine. "Gabby, who else?"

"A vigil? Here?" It seemed a bit crass. But all I got from Madison was the slight raise of an eyebrow. She knew who signed her paychecks. I glanced over the display case and picked out a cheese danish. I'd done a lot of running yesterday and had earned it, I rationalized. I refused to think about the muffin I'd devoured for breakfast.

As Madison tonged it into a brown paper sleeve, I leaned closer. "I heard about a fight Gabby had with Addie. It sounded like a real scene."

Madison's eyes rolled. She shoved the last bit of pastry into the sleeve and handed it to me. "You too? Everyone around here's caught the bug, prying and gossiping about Addie. Must be something in our coffee."

Hints of butter and cheese bloomed in the air between us. I wanted desperately to sink my teeth into the danish, but I'd come for answers. Gabby's bouncing ponytail hadn't made an appearance yet, so I gestured for a coffee and hardened my tone.

"So what about it?" I asked, as Madison filled a paper cup.

"Did you see the fight?"

"Nope, don't remember a thing," Madison replied. "Might've been my day off. That, or it wasn't that big a deal. Not enough to remember."

"Did you know Addie had plans to open a health spa in town? She was going to serve food and carve customers away from Sweet Little Buttercup. Gabby knew about it too."

I fibbed on the last bit, or at least I had no proof. But it sounded plausible enough. I watched Madison's reaction, hoping I'd shocked her. She snapped a lid onto my coffee and slid on a cardboard sleeve. Setting the cup on the counter, she lost herself in thought.

I lowered my voice. "What is it?"

When her gaze met mine, her attitude dissolved. "Do you really think Gabby could…?" Shrinking back, she shook her head. "No, it's stupid. She and Addie lived to throw shade at each other. It was painful to witness but nothing more than words. At least on Gabby's end. She only talks tough. It's not her way to be physically aggressive. She wilts at the slightest hint of actual danger."

That surprised me. The Gabby I knew ate mountains for breakfast. I'd never seen her back down from a challenge. "The fight was over Gabby's husband, though, right?" I asked, tapping my credit card against the payment terminal. "Maybe that pushed her to go farther than normal?"

Madison shrugged. "Gabby's really sensitive about him. She probably thinks she doesn't deserve him, or something lame like that." She picked up a rag and stepped a few feet away to wipe the far end of the display case. Clearly, she was done with me.

I shuffled after. "One more thing. I spoke with Sera yesterday. She said the cops drilled her about a necklace of Addie's. Something they thought she shouldn't have. Did you hear anything about that?"

It was a long shot but worth rolling the dice, and I was rewarded. Madison's head fell askance. Her gaze narrowed. "Yep, your detective friend was here late in the afternoon while we were trying to close. Gabby got worked up because I didn't have much to offer. But as I told them both, I was so wasted at that party, I barely remember being there. The whole night's a total blur."

Party? I scoured my brain and did a little hop when something clicked: the photo I'd seen at Charlotte's. "The Halloween party? You were there with Addie and Sera?"

"Not with, but I was at the party."

I pressed against the display case, yearning to tap her forehead until more words spilled out. I must not have kept my poker face in check because she gave the rag a last swirl. Giving up, she tossed it into a sink behind her.

"Ugh, okay! Look, I don't know anything about the necklace. I'm not even sure which one you're talking about, and I certainly didn't witness Addie gifting it to Sera. But if Sera has it, she stole it. I'm sure of that. She's always taking things and playing it off like we'd let her borrow it. She's done that since we were, like, twelve."

I didn't remember Sera ever borrowing more than a pencil from me, let alone stealing something. But I wasn't as close with her as I thought I'd been. Addie, on the other hand, was the kind of person who coveted material things to no end but never grew attached to them. She'd never miss a dress or a pair of shoes, let alone some makeup or cheap jewelry. Yet from what Charlotte said, this particular necklace was special. Maybe Sera's sticky fingers finally *borrowed* the wrong thing. That would certainly explain the big rift they had, and the argument in front of Addie's house.

Addie and Sera, Addie and Gabby. I was beginning to wonder who Addie hadn't fought with recently. It seemed the Queen Bee didn't spare the stinger.

"Hey there!" Gabby's voice trilled. She bounced past lugging a bag of flour that must've weighed more than five of her put together. Seeing her made me wonder again about the vigil. Was it from a guilty conscience? Crassness aside, I needed to come back in the evening, if only to see who showed up, and how they acted.

"See you tonight," I hollered after her. She squeaked in delight and disappeared into the kitchen.

Gathering my coffee and pastry, I paused. "You're not related to Sarah Jessica Parker, are you?" I asked Madison.

Her face scrunched as if I'd broken wind. "Are you off your meds?"

Fair enough point. Truthfully, I'd been off-kilter since the moment I returned to Harvest Falls. Beyond the years of connections and memories I'd missed, I felt like an outsider, adrift as others connected behind my back. But I wouldn't tell that to Madison. She wouldn't care. Staring awkwardly at her made James slip into my head again, and his quirky laugh came to mind. It was directed at me, but not in a cruel way. Rather, it was because he'd thought of some pun to melt away the tension. He'd always understood my insanity. I wondered if he had the same connection with her.

My phone buzzed. I juggled the pastry bag and cup into one hand and fished it out. A text from Geraldine. **Gresham's office. Twenty minutes.** No explanation or greeting. No emoji. The woman despised them.

I reread the cold message and shivered. *Addie.* Something big must've come up. Maybe Dad and Frank had found a vital clue, or even made an arrest.

"What is it?" asked Gabby, startling me. Her head popped through the kitchen door, making it clear she'd been listening. Madison pretended not to care, but I caught her watching from the corner of her eye.

I waved my phone at them both. "Case needs me," I lied. The little bell chimed, and I was out the door. I hadn't learned much from Madison, but perhaps I'd only been fooling myself to begin with. What could I ever hope to uncover that the police couldn't? Guilt niggled at me. I should've had more faith in my dad.

CHAPTER 20

Soft rain trickled from a lifeless steel sky. I let it pepper my face while I hoovered my danish and marched down the street. My boots slapped wet cement. The storefront awnings started to bead and drip. *What had the police discovered?* Images of a press conference and mug shots on the evening news flitted through my head. *And why Gresham's office?* Perhaps Charlotte had chosen the place. Perhaps Dad would be waiting for me with her and Geraldine. The office was quiet, more calming than the police station. That had to be it.

As I worked my way to Second Street, I passed a few empty storefronts that used to hold thriving businesses. Their "For Lease" signs had become all too familiar in town. They spread like fleas, Ruth Radford often lamented. Geraldine and Charlotte saw the signs as opportunity, a way to reclaim the town for their own designs. And they'd roped Addie into their fervor. Her plan for a new health spa had to have enraged a few people. But had it led to her death?

The rain intensified, and I hustled. By the time I reached the gray stone facade of the office building, my face was coated in a wet sheen. The fortress-like stone and darkened windows, glass etched with gold lettering, stood out along the street, as if the building had taken a wrong turn somewhere in Seattle and wound up getting lost.

Gresham's office on the second floor had a thin-lined modern feel, like something out of a pretentious design magazine. Nothing looked comfortable, and nothing was out of place. The assistant's desk sat empty, but the door to his private office stood open. I called out a greeting and snuck inside. I'd expected a group, but only Gresham occupied the office. His face snapped into a cheerful mask. He wore a starched shirt and red tie, his curly hair gelled. He sat behind a minimalist, metal-framed desk. He leaped up and crossed the room in a couple of short strides. After wrapping me in a snug, and overly familiar, hug, he stepped back and clutched my shoulders.

"Ready to make some of that real money?" he chirped. His chompers beamed. A cloud of musky cologne assailed me. "I promise your hand won't cramp too bad from the paperwork. At least, not so bad we can't lift a wineglass afterward!"

"What?" I twitched and broke from his touch. The words didn't compute. I wiped the rain from my face with a sleeve. Where was everyone else? Dad? Charlotte?

His head tilted back, and he chuckled, playing off my confusion. "Didn't Geraldine tell you? She's helping you get your groove back. What an amazing woman she is. The sale of your grandmother's land is all set up. Nothing more for you to worry about."

"So no one's been arrested?"

"Oh, darling." He reached out again for my shoulder. "You let your dad sort that out. Don't let it trouble you. You'll be off to medical school before you know it, with heavy pockets and maybe a sexy new ride. How sweet is that?"

"I'm not..." I froze, panicked. Addie's killer was still on the loose. I didn't have time for this. I hadn't even been accepted to a medical school. Moving forward with my life was not an option. At least, not in that direction. When I'd moved from San Diego, the idea of fulfilling old obligations had seemed simple. A return to my life before Mason. To restart where I'd gone wrong. But now the whole thing felt childish. I hadn't gone wrong by choosing Mason. I'd gone wrong by losing myself in the process. And I wasn't about to let that happen again.

"I'm not ready," I said. It was close enough to the truth.

"I'll be gentle, I promise." He winked. "It'll be easy." He waved for me to sit in one of the two client chairs in front of his desk. They looked like those stackable ones from a banquet hall but probably cost a thousand dollars for the set.

I perched on the chair's lip while he took his spot behind the desk. He had the paperwork out already, a thick stack of documents.

"Can we wait until Geraldine gets here?" I asked. But it dawned on me straightaway—she wasn't coming. She never had any intention of it. We were alone, without even his assistant nearby. *I should've checked his boots.* The thought came unbidden, and I shook it off. The boot prints at the trailhead had been Marvin's. *Simmer down, Charlie!* My leg started a nervous jiggle. I couldn't help it.

"Charlie, you're a riot." Gresham rubbed his hands together, fingers splayed. He reclined and eyed me. "I remember you and Addie running around town way back when, driving all the boys mad. Quite a few must've thought they'd wind up with you. Suckers, right?"

"Thanks?" I made sure the word sounded like a question.

He held up a hand. "No, what I mean is, you were never long for Harvest Falls. Not like Addie. She wanted to be the biggest fish in the smallest pond. You just wanted to escape, am I right?"

I stared at him, not knowing what he wanted. I'd witnessed this overly friendly side of him before—like the drunk uncle you didn't want at dinner—but it didn't make me feel any more comfortable. Addie had made fun of him for it. She knew how to play it off. It always made me clam up.

After an awkward silence, he put his hands up in surrender. "I know, not my place." Bouncing up, he rounded the desk and leaned against it an arm's length away. His cologne cloud enveloped me.

A low rumble gurgled from my throat. "Back up," I whispered.

His grin pulled wider. "What?"

"Back. Up. Please." The room blurred, becoming stuffy and choking. I clamped my eyes shut and clutched the bottom of the chair.

"Are you okay?" Gresham's mask dropped. He hopped off the desk and retreated a few steps. "Do you need water? Something stronger?"

I shook my head and swallowed. I wanted to bolt from the room, but I didn't think I could manage it without tumbling over. "I just need space," I said, wheezing.

"Got it," said Gresham. "It's a big decision. Not one to take lightly." He shuffled through some of the stack of papers. "I can give you a number. It might ease you a bit. It'll definitely make your knees weak."

Gulping in air, I lurched to my feet and grasped the desk for balance. "It's not the sale. It's you. I mean…everything. Addie's gone. My mother's gone. Grandmother's gone. And I'm still here trying to…trying to…" My mind went blank. Absolutely blank.

Gresham slumped in his chair. "Appease everyone?" he ventured. He donned the most honest and sympathetic grin I'd ever seen him wear.

"Yes!" I threw up my hands. The answer bowled me over with its simplicity. "I don't know why that's so hard for me to say." My hackles lowered, and with them most of my unease. If Gresham meant me any harm, he'd decided to smother me with wisdom first.

He no longer bothered with his salesman shtick. "I'll tell you something I've learned in my young years, Charlie. The big decisions—house, college, marriage—they're obvious to point out. You can feel the importance of them. They give you something tangible to sink your teeth into, to stake your claim that this is who you are. But it's all an illusion because it's the small decisions, day after day, that actually define your life. Whether to stay healthy and productive; whether to engage in your own present and in your future. These decisions add up. And the catch is that they're also the toughest to keep track of. Lose sight for just a little while, and you'll have squandered months, perhaps years."

"You should have children," I said, genuinely, but without thinking. Addie had been like a daughter to him for over twenty years. "Sorry," I chirped, wincing. "I meant that as a compliment." In all honesty, I'd never considered that Gresham had a past. That he'd moved to Harvest Falls and away from somewhere else.

He swallowed down something and glanced at his desk. He shuffled the stack of papers and set them aside. "Let's do this later," he said. "I'll tell Geraldine I didn't have my ducks in a row yet."

"You'll do that?" I breathed a sigh of relief. "Thank you."

I stared at the file he'd stuffed the stack into—my inheritance boiled down to a bunch of legal forms. My mother had spent my entire childhood plotting with her friends over the future of Harvest Falls. She, Geraldine, and Charlotte were determined to stem decades of gradual decline and turn the tide in the town's favor. And in their own favor, as well.

I paused, pondering. They must've done more than scratch out notes, if a solid plan existed. I was pretty certain those things had zoning considerations. Town meetings would need to be held and permits approved. That was unless they had schemed a way around such roadblocks. A scheme similar to the tale Sera told about Marc and Charlotte's surveyors.

"For this sale, does the land need to be surveyed?" I asked.

"A great question," said Gresham. "I can walk you through the process, if you like. What made you think of that?"

Reclaiming my perch, I leaned my elbows on the desk. There was no way to tactfully bring up Marc Newsome's death, so I jumped in headfirst. "Buckner's Folly. I heard a rumor that

Charlotte hired private surveyors to smudge the boundaries of the land she wanted to buy. Can that be done?"

Gresham's smug grin returned, like a defensive shield. "That was long before I moved to Harvest Falls. Charlotte used another broker then, but I can tell you in a word—no, she can't. More so, it's not uncommon when working on a deal that large to request a survey or challenge a boundary. But the recorder's office is involved. With the number of people and forms required, the paper trail is everywhere."

I chewed my lip. "Sounds like it would be easier to bribe someone."

"Perhaps." He glanced at the open door. "That is, if Charlotte was trying to buy the land near the folly. But she wasn't. It's unusable for development. I've heard the rumors, too, and I can tell you they're all wrong. The men who died near the folly weren't surveyors. They were prospectors."

I about launched into orbit. "Prospectors? Like with big hats and droopy red beards?"

He laughed. "The very ones. Gold isn't as common in this part of the state, but it's out there. The area around Harvest Falls has a wealth of mineral deposits. It's what brought the town its touristy reputation to begin with, back in its heyday."

"But how could prospectors be confused for surveyors?"

"Who knows? Charlotte says they were a pair of drifters trying to make a buck, nothing more. That's partly why their deaths never held much public notoriety. At least, not at the time. Their supposed connection to the Newsomes only surfaced after Marc's untimely passing months later."

"It made him look guilty for something that wasn't there?"

I wondered what busybody caused that to happen, though I imagined the Joyces and Seras of the day had something to do with it.

"Charlotte denies it, but there are some who say Marc's hands were by no means clean. They say he hired these guys to prospect on the sly. The land out there is so hard to reach, it'd be easy to go unnoticed and get away with it. But it's also impossible to get any machinery out there without building a road. It'd have to be done by hand, and that would've taken years." Gresham shrugged. "Of course, there's no proof of their association to the Newsomes, whatever was going on. It's all speculation, if you'll enjoy the pun."

"Maybe that's why the rumors had to change?" I imagined a game of drunken operator taking place at Hank's and The Oak Grove over the years. It wouldn't take much lubrication to flip the details.

"Makes sense." Gresham steepled his fingers. "Charlotte owns a substantial amount of land around here."

The phone rang. He checked the display screen, but he needn't have bothered. I knew exactly who it was. No crystal ball required. He snickered under his breath as I gestured for him to say I'd already left. I had too much to process. I'd face Geraldine some other time. His voice boomed a jovial greeting as I hurried to the stairs. Gold deposits, land theft, and a pair of unsavory goons—if these were the tales spun up after Marc's death, I wondered what tales would spawn from Addie's. And how far would they be from the truth?

CHAPTER 21

Mind awhirl with thoughts of Yosemite Sam, I dashed through a steady rain. I needed the library, Joyce or no Joyce. The local archives had to contain more about these prospectors. How did they connect to the Newsomes, if at all? And how had Dad wound up being dragged through the mud along with Marc and Charlotte?

The old library wasn't familiar anymore. Once a place for Dad to plop me when I was young, out from underfoot at the station, I'd spent hours reading among its cozy wooden aisles. But now plaster walls, fluorescent lighting, and metal shelving made the place a bit soulless. DVD rentals replaced slip-cased books. A bank of computers sat where I'd discovered Stephen King and Anne Rice. Other shelves stood half-empty and forgotten. Scheduled activities and special events ruled the day, rather than open reading.

I found the place quiet and headed straight for the aging microfiche catalog. Internet searches I could do on my own. Harvest Falls hadn't had its own paper in decades, and the archives of the *Harvest Bee* were lost to time. But I read what I could of the Portland and Coastal rags. Those someone had taken an effort to preserve.

Joyce avoided me at first. I couldn't tell if it was from embarrassment or spite. Probably a little of both. Yet after an hour had passed staring at the ancient machine, I felt her breathing over my shoulder. I'd found nothing so far.

"Finally ready for the truth?" she asked, when I glanced her way. She wore a smart blouse and slacks and had her hair pulled together loosely by a large barrette. The image of a helpful librarian, though she sounded like a zealot I'd cross the street to avoid.

"Book report," I snapped back. *Now who was embarrassed?* Reluctantly, I swiveled in my seat and told her what Gresham had said, and what I was looking for. There was no reason to hide it. If anything, having Joyce help me uncover the truth might convince her how far off she'd been.

"Can I help?" She sat and scanned the pages I was looking at, devouring them at a speed that made my vision blur.

My phone buzzed while I waited. Geraldine calling through. I ignored it, careful not to hit any buttons. The last thing I needed was her accusing me of sending her to voice mail.

"Family troubles?" Joyce asked. I wasn't sure how she'd managed to read my phone screen while shifting through gobs of text. I was a little impressed, but I made no response.

The microfiche text distorted as she scanned, teleporting from one day's paper to another a week later. There, an article held a photo of my mother and Charlotte Newsome, along with a dozen of their Women's League cohorts. They stood in summer dresses and wide-brimmed hats as if off to the horse races. "Women's League Champions Trail Revitalization," the headline read. The only evidence of a trail was the park bench sticking out from behind the group.

The Harvest Falls Women's League. My fists clenched unwillingly. My mother had been obsessed. Often, she'd placed the League above my childhood. Though taken a good ten years earlier, the photo threw me back to when I was a newly minted teenager. I'd tried lacrosse for a season. I'd loved it and had been good too. My mother had permitted it, if not with a smattering of disdain. Yet on the eve of a big game, she'd pronounced that my time was needed elsewhere. I was to serve and clear tables at a luncheon hosted by the Women's League. Something to do with town improvements. I'd been crushed. Devastated. I threw a fit. None of my teammates understood. I didn't understand.

A coldness invaded the house after my tantrum, slowly withering my resolve. The look of disapproval my mother wore. The short, clipped way she spoke. Everyone walked on eggshells. Even my dad, my biggest fan, turned stiff and quiet. It drained me, as if I'd been wrung out like a sponge. And I had the power to make my mother happy, to fix everything. All I had to do was give up on what I wanted. In the end, I'd done just that.

Joyce stared at me expectantly.

"I was too young to remember this, just a toddler at the time," I said, and added a little too defensively, "My mother did a lot of good for Harvest Falls."

"This is right after Marc Newsome's death," said Joyce. She pointed. "Don't you think its suspicious Charlotte's not in mourning?"

"I don't know, perhaps she needed a distraction? Something positive to take her away from everyone's finger-pointing and gossip? Is there anything else?"

"Nothing about prospectors, or surveyors, or even drifters. But I'll dig deeper, check a few other sources. There has to be a paper trail somewhere. Someone knows the truth." She turned back to the machine and made it zoom around.

A sense of foreboding came calling. Circling around the deaths of Marc Newsome and these prospectors was getting me nowhere. Worse, I was ignoring the obvious. Dad had the answers. I needed to ask him. Be direct and honest for a change. But that would mean coming clean about wanting to help with Addie's investigation. How else would I be able to explain why I was suddenly so curious about her father?

Geraldine buzzed my phone again.

"There's nothing here," I told Joyce, ignoring the call. "I was just wasting my time."

She didn't look convinced. But if she could find out anything more, the more power to her. I would leave her to it.

At least the rain had stopped by the time I emerged from the library. Low clouds floated through the treetops, and a damp scent hung thick in the air. I had every intention of marching straight to the police station. It stood a mere block away. But my feet refused to cooperate. The same desire I'd had as a child to make my parents happy had reared its head. It was suffocating, and I didn't know how to shed its thrall. I wasn't ready to see the disappointment in Dad's face.

Yet my small rush of courage continued to propel me forward. I gave it no resistance. It pulsed too sweetly to waste.

My feet wandered off the sidewalk and crossed to Second Street. The Oak Grove's brown door lay just ahead. It was time to act, to finally get off the proverbial pot and do something with the rest of my life.

The place was empty save for James. He stood near a table wiping down chairs. His blond locks, checkered shirt, and jeans stood out against a sea of dark wood and brass. *Crappity-crap-crap.* I stormed right for him, trying my best not to think. Not to consider a single repercussion. Not a single doubt. Dimples flashed as he caught sight of me.

"Hey there, Care Bear," he said. He grunted in surprise as I rammed into his chest, my head perfectly below his chin. His scent washed over me—stale yeast, hops, and citrus. The muscles of his back tightened. My hands roamed upward and cupped his cheeks. As I leaned back to watch his eyes, stubble scratched at my palms.

"Kiss me," I begged.

His fingers twirled through my shortened hair, lingering for a moment, before he shrank back. He snapped us apart with a straightening of his arms and studied me with concern. "What's happened?" he asked. "Is this about Addie?"

"Seriously?" The moment burst. I groaned and fell into a chair. Bracing for a wave of hurt, I oddly felt a bit proud. I'd done a thing—a real bona fide thing—even if it had backfired stupendously.

His cheeks reddened, and he glanced toward the door. "We haven't kissed since the eighth grade. I mean, I appreciate the offer and all—like, way more than appreciate it—but this isn't you." His head cocked to one side. "Is this because your dad is freezing you out? Case told me he suspended you."

"No, it's not...it's because..." I didn't know how to explain. There were way too many things. So I changed the subject. "I know about you and Madison."

"Me and who?" James looked thoroughly confused.

"Case said you were a hot item."

"What? No. Really? Is that what people are saying? We hung out like twice, months ago. Before you came home. But we don't work. She's always, like, not there, and she's not even into movies." He shook his head in disbelief. "How can someone not like movies?"

"So I'm not a slattern?" Relief flooded in on two accounts. Lost in my impulse, I hadn't considered how Madison might feel. Me trying to kiss her boyfriend in broad daylight. *Kissing James.* My head floated a little at the thought.

He pulled out a barstool and patted it. "Over here. Sit," he commanded. As I lurched to the bar, he went behind it, slapped down a pair of shot glasses, and filled them with scotch. "So, did you catch the game last night? I think it's the Mariners' year."

"Har-har." I chuckled all the same. James frequently argued the Timbers had a better chance of winning the World Series. It was one of his go-to bartender conversation topics.

"Shoot and spill," he said. "And be honest this time."

I gulped the scotch, felt the burn. He refilled and leaned on his hands.

My fingers played along the glass. "You ever feel like pretending is better than disappointing people with the truth? Like if you acted a certain way, they'd be happy, and that would make you happy?"

"Especially when those people are related to you?"

My eyes found the ceiling. "When did you get so wise?"

"That's what I do. I pour drinks, and I gain wisdom."

After throwing back the second shot, I waved off a third. The calming song of Tipsyville already called, and I didn't need the wail of toilet-hugging Drunkentown. "If I'd been accepted to medical school, I'd be there now without even considering another option. Dutiful Daughter Barbie playing her role, no questions asked, just like the teenaged me."

"Heh." Dimples flashed at my joke. "So where do you want to be?"

I tapped the side of my nose. "Bingo." I had no better answer.

He considered, plucking up a coaster and bouncing it against the bar. "You know the center of the earth can be anywhere you make it, even if it's here in Harvest Falls."

"Didn't you ever want to get out? Head to Portland or farther abroad?"

"Sure." He brought his arms wide to encompass the bar. "But I love this place. It keeps me out of trouble. It makes me happy." His arms dropped. "Will I do it for the next thirty years, day after day, until I retire? I'm not sure. We'll see. I just know there's no place I'd rather be right now. It's satisfying to commit to that and make this place my own."

I understood the sentiment in a way I might not have a couple of days ago. Case's words returned to me, what he'd said about seeing me happy for the first time all year. He'd spoken the truth. Every inch of me had woken up, fulfilled by a purpose I hadn't really ever considered an option. This obsession with finding Addie's killer, and uncovering what had happened with Marc Newsome—it wasn't something I wanted to give up. It felt a part of me, as surely as my arms and legs.

But did that make me more like my father, the chief of police, or more like Joyce, Gabby, and Ruth, a trio of bumbling nosy parkers?

James's gaze made me think my clothes had disappeared. His cheeks reddened once more, but this time he didn't look away. "Do you want to go for a walk sometime? Maybe find food? Like, walk to get food and eat it somewhere special?"

"Abso-freaking-lutely." I couldn't think of anything better, clothes or no clothes. It's funny how things worked out, when you didn't overthink them. "You can tell me all about your Twinkie."

He laughed as I stood. With all my racing around, late afternoon had snuck up on me. Outside, the sun was setting. Its rays painted the damp streets in gold and amber. I paused to take it all in, grinning like a lunatic, before hustling off. I had a hornet's nest to kick.

CHAPTER 22

The shops around The Oak Grove had started to close. It was nearly time for Gabby's vigil. *Catching everyone when they're hungry, just after work.* I shook my head and hoped Gabby hadn't timed the vigil that way on purpose. Yet I knew she had.

I'd wanted a chat with Sera before heading to Sweet Little Buttercup. But I realized I wasn't ready to speak with her again. I had no leverage. I could do nothing but beg another lie from her at this point. Besides, I was certain she had nothing to do with Addie's murder. If something had happened in the heat of their argument, it would be one thing. But to leave and come back later would take a callous mind, and I didn't see Sera as that coldhearted.

Confronting my dad would also have to wait. Not only had my nerve cooled, but I faced the same lack of leverage. It would be too easy for him, swamped by an active investigation, to blow me off. *Later, sweet pea.* Always later.

No, if I wanted to do some digging, I needed looser lips.

I barely stepped inside the café before Gabby pounced. She shoved a tray of cookies at me. Each was individually wrapped in clear plastic. A sticker displayed the price.

"Hiya! So glad you made it! I'm sure Addie would've loved

it, you being such a great friend, old school BFF and all. I've got more cookies coming. I bake when I'm nervous! It's like the worst thing for my thighs. Just take what you want and let Madison know. I trust you're good for it!"

I felt obliged and snatched a cinnamon oatmeal raisin. She winked and fluttered off. My guess was to go snort a line of pixie dust off a centaur's derriere. Her ponytail swished as she bounced away.

A dozen well-wishers had turned up. They held hushed conversations in little clumps. No one sat. I scanned the crowd and caught Darlene Devereux studying me from across the room. The florist wore a dark-green turtleneck with a swirling black pattern. Highlighted by tasteful gold jewelry, she looked like she'd stepped out of a London fashion shoot. She always did. Her smile beamed my way, and I did my best to return it.

Case popped up beside me. He clutched a cookie in each hand. "Gabby keeps shoving these things at me," he said, mouth half-full. "And, is it just me, or does she seem a little high strung, even for her? Do you think she's feeling guilty about something?"

"With what Darlene said, how could she not? Fighting with Addie, straying from her husband." But Gabby had been out of town the night Addie was killed. Wasn't she? I spotted her with Madison by the register. Gabby's mouth flapped as she buzzed around, a ball of energy. Madison tried her best not to slouch, but she didn't hide the terse reaction to whatever Gabby was saying.

Case leaned in and sniffed. "Where have you been? Day drinking without me? I'm appalled and wounded, Charlie

Goode. You may have just lost your chances at Employee of the Month!"

"Hold on." I waved at him to shush. "I want to hear what they're talking about." My curiosity had been piqued. Sliding forward a few steps, I barely made out Gabby's voice.

"I don't know why you won't tell me," she was saying. "It's not like I can't find out other ways. People open up to me all the time. They love spilling the beans my way. I can't help it. It's my personality that attracts them. You know that."

"It's none of your business." This, from a clearly irritated Madison.

"Ugh, you're never any fun. I bet James won't be so tight lipped. He'll tell me how hot and heavy you've gotten."

"They're not!" I shouted before I could help myself. My cheeks burned, and I had no choice but to step up to them. "James and Madison aren't a thing. The rumors aren't true," I said, a little too proudly. I wanted to save Madison from the interrogation. Yep, it had nothing to do with me. Nothing at all.

She glared daggers, melting my obvious joy.

Gabby swung her gaze between us. "Ooh, that's interesting. But I know you've been seeing someone, Madison. If not James, who is it? You have to spill."

The tiny bell rang, and Ruth Radford banged through the entrance of the café. Gabby's eyes lit up. She snatched her tray of cookies and hustled off, the prior drama clearly tabled. But I knew it would not be forgotten.

"Sorry," I said to Madison. A memory popped into my head, her preteen voice set against the beeping, dinging sounds of a video arcade. "I know you had dibs. Don't you remember? We were at the pizza counter in the arcade. Spring break my freshman year of college, I think. You said if anyone was going to have James Bryson, it was going to be you. He'd just started helping his uncle at The Oak Grove, and you had a crush." I tried a laugh, to lighten the mood. I'd forgotten all about the encounter—the cute way she'd played at an adult, the determination in her tone.

Madison's lips pulled into a smirk, half-amused but still a bit of a sourpuss. "Did you know that Gabby's stolen most of her so-called famous recipes? Robbed them from her own grandma without giving any of the credit. She barely knows how to bake. I have to come in and reset the ovens and check the timers every morning so she doesn't burn everything."

Ah, so it's Gabby you're still mad at. Madison seemed a bit more willing to share than earlier in the day, so I took her lead. "Addie told me about the recipes years ago. But I wonder, that kind of thing doesn't sound like someone who wilts from confrontation. Isn't that what you said earlier? I mean, her whole family must know she's a thief. Seems like she'd spend a lot of time fighting with them."

Madison shrugged. "She'll get a brick wall to chat with her. But it stresses her out to think anyone doesn't like her. It'll ruin her for days, until she finds some scheme to make herself come off smelling like roses. That's what all this vigil stuff is about, to make sure everyone knows how sad she is."

"You think it's all an act?"

"I've seen her frosty side. Back when she and Addie worked on that school fundraiser, it was Gabby who escalated things. Addie wanted to buy candy and granola bars in bulk because it would be cheaper. More money for the schools, right? But Gabby's whole plan was to sell stuff from the café. So instead of arguing with Addie directly, she drained their funds with a massive order of baking supplies—eggs, butter, and milk. Stuff you can't really return. It left Addie to pay for everything else herself."

"Which is why she went her own way and hosted her own event." She also got Gabby's permits pulled, but I didn't need to say that out loud.

"That was the start of it. If Gabby had learned of Addie's new scheme..." Madison trailed off and turned her head so I couldn't read her face.

"You mean the health spa?"

Her head whipped back. "Of course Addie had to go for the kill. Two frenemies vanquished in one stroke. Big money throwing its weight around. The whole thing reeks of Above the Falls snobbery."

"Two?" My pulse quickened. I ignored the passive insult.

Madison's eyes rolled skyward. "Darlene, as if you didn't know. The woman hated Addie, and apparently the feeling was mutual."

"But why? How did the health spa hurt her?" This was news to me. Sera and Gabby, and now Darlene? *Was there anyone in town Addie hadn't started a feud with?* It made me rethink Joyce's obsession with her death.

Gabby's voice rang out before Madison could answer, and she slunk away as a hush settled over the room. Cursing, I turned to watch the spectacle. I'd have to find out more about

Darlene's beef with Addie later.

"Everyone's here," said Gabby. She stood in the middle of the café, her hands tugging at her flour-dusted apron. "I wanted to say a few words about our dear Addie. Only a few of you knew her as well as I did, but I'm sure you'll all agree she could be the most determined woman in Harvest Falls. It takes one to know one, right?"

She giggled and continued blathering, as an uncomfortable heaviness grew in the air. I glanced around the room. Ruth Radford stood with her arms crossed, stout frame looking like a grumpy pumpkin. She became aware of her posture and dropped her hands to clasp lightly below her stomach. A practiced politician's pose. Joyce Townsend held a hint of mockery in her gaze. She studied Gabby like a science teacher about to dissect a frog.

Darlene Devereux wore an open scowl, letting the world know she doubted Gabby's sincerity.

"The feels," Gabby was saying. "If I only could chat with her one last time, the things I'd ask. The things I'd say."

Darlene grunted and muttered something under her breath.

"What's that?" Gabby faltered, rattled by the interruption.

"How many times did you practice this little speech?" asked Darlene. "It's very remorseful for someone who wished Addie a violent death not a week ago."

Gabby sucked in a sharp breath. Her eyes flared before narrowing into hardened slits. "I'm not the one without an alibi. The police have checked it. Just ask them! And motive, much? Oh yes, I've been taking notes!"

"Whoa!" Case's voice thrummed atop a chorus of startled

outcries. I jerked in surprise, along with half the café. Madison's story had legs, it seemed.

"What's this?" Ruth perked up. She stepped close to Gabby and rounded on Darlene.

Joyce hollered in an exasperated tone. "Well, anyone paying attention knows it's someone local. So of course they could be in this room."

"What about Sera Simmons?" Beckett asked. I hadn't seen him arrive. He stood at the back of the group, head bent as if he addressed one of the tables. "Isn't she the prime suspect?" A flurry of sniffles followed.

"Only the police would think that," answered Gabby. She waved her hands, trying to wrestle back control of the spotlight. "Sera's a possibility, of course, but not likely the killer. Why would she be? Addie was the best thing in her life. It's much more likely the murder was done by someone who had it out for Addie and the Newsomes. Someone with a financial motive, perhaps? Someone with a struggling business?"

She stared straight at Darlene, and the florist's nostrils flared.

Ouch. I felt a wave of sadness for Darlene to be singled out in front of everyone. I hadn't known the flower shop was in such dire straits either. Business was slow everywhere, in the offseason.

"Or someone who owns a lot of knives and is trained to use them?" Darlene snapped back. "Gabby Kemper, if I had a dime for every time I heard you say Addie Newsome should be put in her place, I'd be a rich woman."

Gabby's glare turned devilish. "But you're not, are you?"

"I've heard you say the same," said Ruth. She waggled a finger at Gabby. "In front of Vin D'Amato too. And everyone knows it was you who had Addie's car towed at the Strawberry Festival last year."

"She blocked two spots, and the police wouldn't give her a ticket!"

"Typical, but not unexpected from them," chirped Joyce. "Yet my money is on the one person in this room who hails from a family long associated with villainous acts. A family with blood on their hands and ties to dark rituals!"

Ruth recrossed her arms, optics be damned. Her voice boomed over Joyce's. "Fighting each other won't accomplish anything. We should comb the hills. Who knows what other vagrants are living out there? Just because one was dismissed doesn't mean it wasn't another. Our Addie deserves a full investigation!"

The mayor glared at me, punctuating the end of her declaration. I was dumbstruck by the sudden attack. Did she think Dad and Frank had to follow every notion that expelled from her backside?

"The police are doing everything they can," I said. The stares I received were a potpourri of skeptical, bemused, and downright hostile. Their weight knocked me back a step. I couldn't keep my mouth shut, and blurted, "They'll make an arrest soon, I'm sure of it."

"Yes, but will it be the right person?" Ruth asked. "No offense, but that state detective left today, and the case isn't solved. What are we to make of that? Have the police even checked where Addie's exes were? Ruled them out?" She stood firm, expecting a response. I could only shrug. I assumed they had. Wouldn't that be a basic thing to do?

Ruth turned and addressed the room, a practiced orator. "Do we all agree this case may be beyond the chief's ability? We have to face the possibility that it may never get solved if we don't lend our aid."

My gut clenched at sight of all the nodding heads.

Beckett's squeak came again. "These kinds of things happen in spates, especially in small towns. The killer will slip up at some point and leave a vital clue with the next victim." Sniffle. "They always do."

"Who else owns a giant dagger?" Gabby threw her arms wide.

"Or has access to one," added Case.

"Let me be clear," Joyce announced, her tone thick with condescension. "The proof I've uncovered cannot be overlooked—"

But I couldn't stand to hear any more, and I wasn't done with Ruth. "Perhaps if you didn't waste the police department's time butting in and sending them on wild goose chases, they'd have gotten somewhere by now," I hollered over everyone. "And as for my father's competence, you have no idea what he's capable of!"

Crap! I winced at the choice of words.

Ruth's expression turned smug. "I think I'm all too well aware. The chief of police may be an appointed position, but that does not mean I had a free choice in the matter."

Boom! Thunder rocked me. Everyone stared, stunned. I

grasped a chair for support, growing dizzy. I had no idea what Ruth meant, but the insinuation was clear enough. Once again, my family's name was being dragged through the mud, and I was in the dark.

Joyce shrieked. "Witches, people! I'm talking about witches!"

Case shuffled past Ruth and marched to my side. He folded his arms. His head bobbed as if he were trying to amp himself up for a rumble. "Charlie's the only person I know who couldn't have done it. Besides me, that is. We were at the game shop all evening with Beckett." He shifted his weight, cleared his throat. "Okay, Beckett, too, then. But everyone else is on the table." He blinked. "Er…and James, of course. He was working at the bar. But everyone else. Table."

He gave me a sharp nod. I gave him a tight smile and two thumbs up.

Beckett sniffled. "Th…thanks."

"That's fair," said Gabby. She stepped back and folded her arms to mimic Case. "Let's do this. My sources on the police force have confirmed Addie met her end sometime in the evening between seven and nine. You all know where I was, and you know how close Addie and I were. Like sisters, some have said. That makes it even more important that I get to the bottom of this. I haven't slept a wink since it happened. I've barely had time to try any new recipes."

Ruth snorted. "Well, I'm certainly above reproach. I'm a pillar of the community. You elected me as your mayor in order to clean up this town. If it takes shuffling funds, I'll do it. I hear with DNA you can track someone through their distant cousins these days. We should be doing that! No expense spared!"

"That's what I've been saying," Joyce whined.

Poor Addie. I couldn't believe how quickly the vigil had devolved into finger-pointing. My only solace was that she would've loved every second of it. I didn't know what to say. I'd barely kept myself functional over the past few months. But I knew I wanted better. Better for Addie. Better for Harvest Falls. Better for myself.

Tires squealed outside. Red and blue lights flashed through the windows. A car door slammed, and Vin D'Amato stormed into the café. The commotion drew everyone's attention and halted the bickering.

"Attention, folks. Time to break it up." Vin hooked his thumbs on his belt. He stood with his chest puffed out.

"A bit dramatic, don't you think?" muttered Darlene Devereux.

"It's my vigil, my café," said Gabby. She sounded meek all of a sudden, like a mouse who'd had its cheese stolen.

Vin stood his ground. "The chief sent me here to quiet things down."

"We have every right to assemble and discuss as we please," said Ruth. "Now run along, Officer D'Amato. Tell your boss I'll have words with him later."

"Madam Mayor." Vin bowed his head in deference, though he still didn't budge. Scanning the room, he addressed everyone else. "Obstruction is a crime. If anyone knows anything about Addie, no matter how trivial, you're to report it to the police immediately." His neck and shoulders swelled as he flexed. Meathead, full effect. I'm sure it was meant to look intimidating, but the pulsing sound effect of Mario turning into Super Mario played in my head. *Boing, boing, boing!* I half snorted, half giggled.

Vin fixed on me and sneered. "Of course you'd be at the center of this, *Little Goode*." He made Frank's moniker for me sound every bit as degrading as a sorority initiation.

"Shouldn't you be out petting bunnies?" I shot back. A dated *Of Mice and Men* reference. *Good one, Charlie!*

His lip twitched. "Shouldn't you be in medical school?"

I sucked in a breath. But I had nothing to say. No retort, biting, mocking, or otherwise. If I'd learned anything at all over the past two days, it was that I needed to stop denying the truth before my eyes. So I clammed up and took my medicine.

"Come along," he said, sneer dripping with sweet victory. "Your daddy wants to speak with you."

CHAPTER 23

Vin had overplayed his hand. The daddy comment drew a fierce glare from Darlene, and I made a gesture to Ruth to keep her from exploding. Case knew the score better. He waved in parting, mouth shoved full of chocolate and marshmallow. I stared past Vin as I wove my way through the press. I'd concede him the point, but there was no way I'd let him see me wilt. I had no fear of missing anything either. The vigil had been snuffed out as quickly as it had blazed. I pushed open the door, and Vin tried again to assert his authority, only to have Ruth dismantle his efforts. As the door swung shut, Gabby begged everyone to grab just one more cookie.

The night air bit against my arms and cheeks. The falls pounded behind me, cutting the silence of the streets. I covered the blocks to the police station in a shuffling gait and found Dad sitting behind his desk. He didn't stand, but his expression warmed at seeing me. He leaned back in his chair and stretched, resting his hands behind his head.

"I hear you've still been poking around, and I need you to stop," he said without preamble.

I half sat, thought better of it, and swung myself back to my feet. I wasn't sure who'd spilled to him, but it didn't matter.

It shouldn't matter. I had to stand firm.

"It's Addie—"

"It's making the case more difficult. I've got bakers and librarians, even our mayor, running around like the Scooby-Doo gang, barking out insane theories. I don't need you and Case joining them."

"They're not…we. We are trying to—"

He cut me off again. "Let the police handle it."

I threw my hands up. "Have you interviewed half the people at Gabby's vigil? Any of them? Do you know how many had a motive to do Addie harm? Or at least, wish her ill? Gabby herself threatened Addie only last week."

"I know!" The force of his reaction made me flinch. Dad rarely barked. When he did, it was a scary thing. Age had not taken that from him. Stress painted his face; his lips were tight and his forehead pinched. His hands found some papers on his desk, picked them up, and shuffled them. His face relaxed a bit at the distraction.

"The police are trained to handle this type of investigation," he continued. His voice returned to its calm cadence. "It's not just about collecting the facts. It's about how you collect them, and whether you can build a legal case in court. Leave any gaps, and the defense attorneys will eat you for breakfast."

I nodded. I understood. But there was no way I was stopping.

"Sweet—" He stopped himself. "Charlie. You have to trust me."

"I do. But I want to help. I'm going to help somehow."

"You can help by getting everyone to stop. Tell them if they know anything, they should report it. But snooping around, getting everyone all riled up, that's bordering on obstruction. Withholding information and hiding evidence, that is obstruction. It's a crime, and worse, it could hinder our ability to close the case."

"But it's more than closing the case," I mumbled.

He paused a beat. His nostrils flared as he sighed. "Explain."

"They...your reputation..." *Argh! Why can't I just say it?*

Regrouping, I folded my arms and stood defensively. "When is Frank coming back?" I asked. "His leaving didn't do you any favors. You should hear what they're saying, and it's not just at Gabby's vigil. The police were doubted from the second folks learned about Addie. You were doubted. They're saying you're incompetent. They're saying you'll bungle this whole thing. They say you always do."

I cringed, but Dad's eyes lit up with a measure of satisfaction, as if he reveled in the challenge to prove the town wrong. He'd always welcomed competition. He'd captained the football team and been a star wrestler in school. His easygoing "aw, shucks" manner only belied that part of him.

"Detective Nichols will be back tomorrow. I can't get into the details, but he's working the case as his top priority. We all are. Forensics takes time, and there were things better followed up on outside of Harvest Falls."

"Like where Addie's exes were the night of the murder?"

"Charlie." His tone warned, and I held up a hand in surrender.

"But how do you live with people dragging your name through the mud?" I asked instead. "Doesn't that bother you?" I landed hard in the chair opposite him. My body had turned into Jell-O. "Mom seemed to spend her whole life trying to cement our name in sainthood. I never realized how much work it took just to keep it clear of the muck."

"It can be exhausting. But it's part of the job. Everyone's going to have an opinion, especially in a case like this." He shrugged. "You have to let them. What matters is that we find justice for Addie, nothing else. The town will come around eventually. The truth has a tendency to out. Believe in that."

A part of me wanted to go along with Dad's fortune cookie wisdom. It'd be easier that way. Nod and appease—that's what I'd always done. That's what he expected. But I couldn't this time. Forty-year-old rumors tore holes in my conviction, and the doubts they exposed wore more comfortably than my old self.

"Speaking of, can I ask one more thing?" Another unresolved question had popped to mind, and I braced myself for the can of worms it was about to open.

"Shoot." He sounded tired again, rather than wary.

"Did Marc Newsome hire the gold prospectors who died near Buckner's Folly?"

For a fleeting moment, the life went out of his expression. Then he grinned. I went rigid at the unexpected reaction. I could tell it was genuine, but I didn't understand it.

"Well, Charlie Goode," he said, "have you been slow playing me? I'm impressed."

My gaze roamed his office as I tried to collect myself.

There was pride in his tone, and I hadn't the heart to tell him he was way off base. I'd done no such thing, at least not on purpose. Still, I noted he hadn't answered my question.

"Why is it such a secret?" I asked. "If you're protecting the Newsomes from something, just tell me. I want to be let in."

He checked the door to see if anyone had come into the station. But it was just the two of us. "There's nothing for you to know. It was all a long time ago, and you don't need to pick at Marc's memory, especially when Charlotte's dealing with the loss of Addie. How do you think she'll feel if she hears about that?"

"Then tell me, and I'll stop. Is it that bad? Your silence is making it worse. It's like I hadn't realized I grew up in the Corleone family, or something. Do you know what Joyce and Beckett and Sera all think?"

"Don't let the town get into your head." He sounded dismissive, but a hint of color traced up his neck and onto his cheeks. His eyes unfocused, looking my way but not really seeing me. He was hiding something, something that embarrassed him.

"Fine," I said. "Don't let the town take yours."

He snorted at that. As I marched out, he called after me. "Answer Geraldine's calls. It'll make life easier on us both."

I gave no response. Thinking about Geraldine would only crush my high. Rather than being mired in anger or sadness, my feet floated across the station. Everything felt right. Never mind that Dad had stonewalled me. Never mind that by all appearances, he harbored some worrisome secret. For now, I basked, pleased as a pig in porridge. I'd not backed down, and if I'd not directly gotten anywhere, at least I hadn't regressed.

I was moving forward in my life.

Outside, reality kicked in. I had no idea which way to turn. Spinning about, I considered my options. Though darkness had fallen, the evening remained young, and I didn't want to squander it. I started toward the game shop, only to have a half-baked thought about catching up with Gresham. Perhaps he'd know a better way to uncover what really happened with Marc Newsome. A paper trail, and all that.

But my enthusiasm for the plan petered out halfway to his office. It wasn't likely he'd be there this late, and besides, finding Addie's killer had to be a higher priority. Swinging back toward the café, I hoped to catch a few stragglers from the vigil. Gabby, at the least, could explain what she meant regarding Darlene's finances. What was all that business about, and how did it connect to Addie?

But Sweet Little Buttercup's lights were off. The vigil must've ended moments after Vin sent me away, and Gabby had raced to close shop. I tried the door just to be sure and found it locked.

The little bell rattled. As it did, a dim glow flickered along the back wall. It had a bluish tint, like that from a phone screen. The streetlights glaring against the windows made it difficult to make out anything more. I cupped my hands against the glass and squinted through them.

A figure moved. Too tall to be Gabby, I wondered why Madison would have the lights off, if she was still cleaning. But something in the figure's posture told me it wasn't her. It was too erect and graceful. Not slouchy and full of snark.

Which meant it shouldn't be there.

My breath caught. *Phone. Cops. Dad.* I couldn't race to the station and get him back here in time without risking the perpetrator escaping. I had to call. Slipping my phone out, I realized too late how my own shadow must've been illuminated by the streetlights. *Crud buckets!*

The figure darted into the kitchen. From there, I knew a back door spilled into a small delivery lot. Beyond was another street and a whole lot of darkness.

I didn't think. I reacted. Poorly.

Feet skittering along the concrete, I hustled around the block. My thumb swiped my phone screen, pulling up my camera. I bobbled it, trying to engage the video setting. It popped into the air, but I managed to catch it midstride. I had only a second to feel proud of myself before I rounded the back of the café. Footsteps slapped the pavement ahead of me. The red record button bounced in my grip. I couldn't hit it squarely. It wouldn't start recording.

My vision tunneled on the button. I jabbed again, and the counter started to move. *Yes!* Whipping the screen up, I strained to hold the shot steady. But my boot caught on a crack in the concrete. I lurched and sprawled.

When I smacked the sidewalk, my breath flew from my chest. My teeth rattled, and ribs were set alight. Wracking gasps tore through my throat, and I realized I'd screamed, a ghoulish sound that had somehow echoed against the stars and come back to me.

Ahead, half a block away, the figure slowed and turned around. A trickle of starlight outlined narrow shoulders and a lithe form. *A woman, just like the killer.* In her hand, a steel blade flashed. It looked absurdly large. I blinked to clear my watering vision, hoping my arms would start responding soon.

My phone was just out of reach.

CHAPTER 24

A car zipped along Bywater Street, back at the front of the café. The figure startled at the revving engine and took flight. Their footfalls faded into the distance, echoing for a time after they themselves had disappeared from view. I blinked, unsure how long had passed. My breathing had slowed, though my ribs still hurt. The scrapes along my palms burned, the skin raw and angry. *Not too long, then.*

I managed to phone Case. Thankfully, he'd gone to the game shop after the vigil. As I waited for him to show, I watched what I'd recorded. Steven Spielberg I was not. Only a few frames held the figure in focus, and those were so dark as to render them useless.

"What the freaking what?" Case called out when he arrived.

"Don't," I warned. "I'm going to hear enough when I call Dad."

"Already did. He's on his way along with Vin." Case stooped and glanced me over. Concern turned to relief as he saw I was unharmed.

"Yippee." I groaned.

"Maybe next time call them to begin with?"

"I tried. I didn't mean to go all Stephanie Plum. It just sort of happened." I told Case how it all went down, and showed him my footage. "What did they want in the café, anyway? They weren't anywhere near the register. Were they looking for Gabby? Searching for something in her possession?"

Case shrugged, ever so helpfully. "Did you see who it was?"

I shook my head. Big mistake. Wincing, I squeezed my eyes shut to stop the world from spinning. "No, but I'm pretty sure it was a woman."

Case took that in and came to the same conclusion I had. "Oh, crap! Do you, uh…think they recognized you? I mean, if they did, they might know where you—we—live."

Lovely. An iceberg shimmied down my spine. In a single act of insanity, I'd managed to injure myself and endanger us both.

"Another reason you should've called us to begin with, Doc." Vin D'Amato stomped along the sidewalk. His flashlight painted us in blinding white. I cursed at the insult. He must've overheard Sera's jab at me. He didn't have the brains to come up with it on his own.

Hovering over me, he swung his light down the empty street. A smirk passed his face. His shoulders and arms bulged. "I knew you'd wind up in the gutter. It was only a matter of time."

"Not tonight, man," said Case. But he backed off under Vin's glare.

"Where's your car?" I asked. I stretched my back and felt a bit better from the movement. "I can help search. Point out who I saw. We might still find them, if we're lucky."

"Or"—Vin made the word dramatic—"those of us with

badges will check out the café, determine who it was from the evidence, and go arrest them." He flashed the light back into my face. "Can I tell you where you should go?"

I fought the urge to snap back. "You can't let the perp go just to lord it over me. Swing your baton around another night. This is serious."

"Perp?" His chuckle came out like a snorting warthog. "That's good. As if you don't already know who did it. As if Daddy hasn't already told you. There's only one perp. It's just a matter of time until your friend goes down for everything. If she left her fingerprints this time, it'll be all over by sunrise."

Case swung his head my way, excited. He'd caught it too. Vin meant Sera Simmons. Frank hadn't interviewed anyone else at the station. And from what Madison said, he'd spent his last hours in town tracking down Sera's account of the Halloween party. She had to be their prime suspect. But Vin had let another fact slip. He'd confirmed there were no fingerprints left on Addie's car.

"Sera has an alibi," I said. I flared my eyes for Case, willing him to take the bait. I wanted to know what else Vin would spill.

Case squinted at me before understanding came. "Oh, you keep defending her," he exclaimed, throwing his arms up and shaking them. The performance was over the top by way of Mount Rainier, but Vin didn't take notice. "But the visitor's log at the elderly care home is handwritten. Tough to confirm. She could've come and left at any time."

Vin turned to study the café's back door, running the white beam over it. I slapped Case's arm and gave him the "tone it down" gesture.

"There were no traces of evidence on the sweatshirt," I prompted.

"None that you could see," Case replied. "Besides, maybe she took it off first. Simple answer. Right, Vin?"

Vin's attention returned to us. "Fits with what we saw on the porch camera. Makes the whole thing cold and calculated."

"If there's no direct evidence, it makes the case circumstantial, at best," I replied. Clearly whatever they'd collected from the car and boot prints hadn't been a smoking gun. What else was there?

"Whoa, save the big words for winners, Doc. Besides, whose side are you on? You know Sera's a criminal. Stolen goods, public unrest. Nothing to stop her from escalating. You really want to screw this up for your dad?"

I'm on Addie's side! I refrained from screaming the words. They weren't enough, not by a long shot. Worse, they would only land on deaf ears.

"That's exactly my point," I said, keeping my voice firm but pleasant. "She's stolen trivial things before, so why kill Addie over a stupid necklace? And then she breaks into the café? It makes no sense."

Vin shrugged. "Not my job to make sense of crazy. I just arrest the criminals." His radio squawked. Dad waited for us at the front of Sweet Little Buttercup. Time to face the music. I followed at Vin's heels like an anxious mutt. At least I'd learned a thing or two. The police still wanted to arrest Sera Simmons, and it didn't seem like they had anything on her.

CHAPTER 25

The rest of the night blurred. Dad greeted me with concern, but that waned once he'd seen to my scrapes and bruises. He became formal afterward, all by the book. That was fine by me. I was too tired to argue, and I hadn't done anything wrong. Not legally, anyway. Vin took my official statement before they shipped me off to an all-night urgent care. Dad wanted to make sure my head was okay, the irony not lost on either of us. A long wait and little rest followed, despite the place seeming deserted. Case kept me awake, rambling on about some new high level he'd reached on a game I actively tried to forget. Bandaged up and released under his observation, we made it home sometime after midnight.

Too much of the morning passed before I made it back to Bywater Street. I'd wanted an early start, eager to return to the café and find out what had happened. I still wanted to follow up with Gabby, too, about the accusations she'd made at the vigil.

Case gave me a lift into town, and I'd just left the game shop when Ruth Radford hollered. She hustled up to me, wearing a hand-knitted plum sweater and a delicate scarf of swirling earthen tones. I could tell straight away she meant business. She held herself with an authoritative air, chin high, shoulders squared.

"Charlie Goode," she said, after I returned her greeting. She wielded a pen and a spiral-bound notepad. "Who besides your cousin can confirm your alibi the night they found Addie Newsome? Anyone not related by blood?"

The earnestness of her tone shocked me. I sputtered something in between a laugh and a sneezing fit. Frank had been right. The people of Harvest Falls did have too much time on their hands. Once I recovered, I answered, "As Case said at the vigil, Beckett was there too."

"Hmm, well that hardly counts. He'd do anything for Case. And for you, I've heard." Pen tapped against paper. "So you deny you were with Gresham Forthwright?"

This time I couldn't hold back peals of laughter. The idea was so absurd. "Gresham and me?" I busted up again as she scowled. "Why would I be? How could I be? You know he was with Charlotte. A whole restaurant can confirm that."

Where was this coming from? The insinuation of an affair shocked me more than the passive accusation I'd been involved in Addie's murder. Sera said the man had a wandering eye. But was Ruth speculating based on that alone, or was there some wild rumor flying about?

I had to know. "Why are you asking about Gresham?"

"Just covering my bases," she said, a bit miffed. "Someone is lying, and I'm determined to catch them in the act." Her expression turned skeptical, and she scrawled on her notepad.

My hackles rose. I was still a bit salty about the things she'd said at the vigil, and the day was draining away. Time for an offensive. I sized her up and noticed a rosy flush to her cheeks. It could be from the cold, but I recalled the other morning at the police station. I'd thought she'd been drinking then. Had she hit the bottle early again this morning?

I leaned in and sniffed but only took in a wash of peppermint. When her eyes lit up in shock, I asked, "Where were you that night? What alibi do you claim to have?" I enunciated to make it clear I'd doubt any response she gave.

Ruth gasped. "How dare you! I am a pillar of this community!"

I folded my arms, satisfied by her outrage. "There's no reason you can't share the same information regarding your alibi. We're all striving for the greater good, are we not?"

Her lips snapped tight like she'd bit into a lemon. "Oh, all right. I was with my good friend Helen Tait, if you must know." She gave a quick, dismissive wave.

That caught me by surprise. I hadn't really been interested in Ruth's comings and goings, but now she had my full attention. "No, you weren't," I said. "Helen Tait was at The Oak Grove drinking wine and making complaints to the police."

A wounded expression crossed her gaze. She glanced at her notepad. Her words came in a rush. "That's right. I'd forgotten. I worked late in my office. This town never stops with its demands. Always needing my support. I'm sure my staff will vouch for me."

Of course they will. By her staff, she meant two overworked and underpaid assistants who knew better than to contradict her. I opened my mouth to pounce but stopped. Some things went better with honey, as the saying went, and I saw the lie had embarrassed her.

"Ruth, are you okay?"

"Oh, Charlie. You've caught me." Her shoulders slumped. The forcefulness left her voice. Her gaze wandered before finding mine again. "I was by myself the night Addie was killed. Just me and a bottle of Glenlivet. It's an old habit. Ridiculous, isn't it, that a taste for whisky abandoned so long ago can still drive such a thirst? Your father's probably told you all about it. He's fully aware of my past and knows the support I need when I fall off the wagon. He's a good man, despite my quibbles."

"He hasn't said a peep," I admitted. Yet I was happy in this instance he'd held his tongue. Ruth's personal issues were none of my business, as long as they didn't relate to Addie. "He is a good man, and a good police chief. And if you think that, maybe you should make less of your quibbles public. It's not doing him, or Harvest Falls, any favors."

"Oof, I know." She heaved an exaggerated sigh. "It's the stress of the past few months, and now with the murder. When you reach my age, you'll understand. You start to worry over your legacy." Her eyes pleaded. "Do you think I'll be remembered as the mayor who brought a murderer to Harvest Falls?"

I choked back a snort and kept my tone neutral. "How could it be your fault?"

"Because I have my hands in everything. Everyone knows me. Everyone relies on me. But even I find it difficult to be mayor and not make enemies."

I nodded. Charlotte Newsome certainly viewed Ruth as an adversary. The mayor's name had been on the tip of her tongue when Frank had asked. It made me wonder. "Why did you oppose Addie's health spa?"

"Oppose?" She flinched, as if finding the question odd. "No, you have it wrong. Who told you that? Addie and I discussed how the health spa was an opportunity for the town. She agreed to have an employee training program and discounts for locals like they do in Hawaii. Jobs and affordability, those have always been my goals."

She seemed sincere, but something didn't sit right with her bumper sticker declaration. "Would that include jobs for people like Marvin Shepard? You've been pretty vocal against him, despite having no evidence of wrongdoing."

"Oh, that." She rolled her eyes skyward, as if fate had put upon her a great burden. "It's the good I see in people. I refused to imagine one of our own could commit murder. My dogs found that giant knife, and, well, you saw it. But I've changed my stance since last night's vigil. The suspect is definitely someone we know."

"And you thought first of me and Gresham?"

"Not you, dear. Him." She leaned in and lowered her voice. "The man preens like a peacock. He flashes more money than he should. It isn't a proper image for our quaint town. Much too crass."

Oh, bother. I didn't need to hear anymore of Ruth's theories. But my thoughts hooked onto something. "The papers he brought to the Newsome house for Addie to sign," I mused. I paused to piece together where I was going. "They had to do with the health spa."

"Yes, that's right."

"Was there anything odd about that deal?"

Ruth folded her arms. "Other than Addie riling up a hornet's nest? I advised her to find a more suitable space, but she ignored me. That was Addie, always trying to assert herself as her mother's heir."

Riling up a hornet's nest? I tipped onto the balls of my feet. "Where was the spa going to be located?"

"Right where you would've guessed." She shook her head, disapproving. "Addie was taking over Darlene Devereux's struggling flower shop, right next door to Sweet Little Buttercup."

Two frenemies vanquished in one stroke. My throat constricted. That's what Madison had meant. Addie's attempt to rival Gabby's café was also going to put Darlene out of business. That gave Darlene some serious motive. Had she gone to confront Addie the night of the murder? Or to beg for her shop? Had things simply gotten out of hand?

Moreover, had anyone asked about her alibi? Was she even on Dad's radar?

With a polite word, we parted and headed in opposite directions. As I hurried to the café, the lithe figure I'd chased the previous night popped into my mind. It took on Darlene's features, sharpening into focus. A knife glinted in her hand. The pieces fit perfectly—her size and shape and grace. So why did my gut tell me I had it wrong?

Because when no one notices you shooting the moon, you don't draw attention to the tricks you've taken. You stay quiet until you've won the hand. It's basic Hearts. If Darlene were the killer, what reason would she have to break into Gabby's place now? I mean, if she meant to get away with murder, breaking into the café was as low key as wearing a bloody dagger as a necklace.

The thought made me sputter. If only solving murders were that easy.

Helen Tait, shuffling along with a bag of shopping, gave my outburst the stink-eye and crossed the street. I smiled and nodded her, wondering all the while if my favorite furry friend's owner had killed my onetime BFF.

CHAPTER 26

Stepping in from the cold, I basked in Sweet Little Buttercup's warm, buttery embrace. I'd caught the café during a midmorning lull, and the tables were mostly empty. Gabby trilled a greeting. Flour dusted her apron. Her ponytail danced as she scuttled behind the counter to pour me a coffee. Before I made a peep, she snatched a croissant with a pair of tongs.

"The uzh? Oh, you're so fun." She pawed the air with her free hand. "I've been meaning to tell you how glad I am that you were with Case the night Addie was killed. Seriously, right? When I heard the news, my first thought was of you. Not in a murdery sort of way, but like, maybe the jealousy finally got the best of you. You know, after the big breakup, fleeing home, and all these months of moping about. If I'd failed like that—"

"Moping?" Was that what she thought? Well, okay, maybe it wasn't far from the truth.

"I know, right? How stupid can I be? Of course you'd never do anything to our Addie. Besides, you're way too crafty for something so basic as a stabbing. Can you forgive me?" She wrapped the croissant in a brown paper sleeve and handed it over. The warmth melted into my fingers.

"Um, thanks. Sure?" It sounded like the correct response.

"Yay!" She bopped to an unheard tune, before her face took on the shocked emoji expression. "So I heard what you did last night, risking your life to save my little café. I can't tell you how much I love what that means for me, and you too! You're going to have to tell me all about it. It'll be great for advertising."

"I will." I seized the opening. "That's actually why I stopped by." We had the counter to ourselves, but I waved her to a table in the corner so we wouldn't be disturbed.

"Ooh, spicy." She followed and sat, leaning over her elbows. "Okay, spill. Why were you at the café last night? Start there."

"I came to ask you some things," I replied, amused. I didn't mind her taking the lead, as long as it kept her chatting. I was good at dealing with bossy. I tore off one end of the croissant before launching into the tale. Buttery flakes melted on my tongue as I spoke. When I got to the intruder, I didn't give any hint of my newfound suspicions.

Finishing with Case and Vin's arrival, I asked, "Who do you think it was? Have the police told you anything?"

"The police?" Gabby gave me a sideways grin and winked. "Like you wouldn't know already. Are you tricking me?"

"Humor me." I took a sip of coffee to hide my face.

"Oh, I see." Her eyes narrowed. "You're cut out of the loop. Bummer for both of us. The police aren't telling me anything, either, and it's my café! Seriously, totes lame. But it's okay. I know exactly who did it—Darlene Devereux."

Bam! A confirmation of sorts, if only by insinuation. But I kept still. I wasn't a good enough actor to play shocked. "Why her?" The question sounded strained, but Gabby didn't notice.

"Because she's the only person who has a key besides me. I gave it to her years ago and completely forgot about it. You know how I love to help people. It's a fault of mine. She used to store flowers in my refrigerator space. Ugh, that girl can never keep her own chillers running. Everything breaks all the time. It's like she's cursed."

"There was no forced entry?"

Gabby swung her head back and forth. "Nope. I overheard Vin tell your dad as much, and he was right. There aren't any scratch marks around the door. I checked. It was Darlene. No doubt about it."

I pushed the remains of the croissant aside. "But why would she do something so brazen?" I still struggled to come up with a reason. Had she intended to harm Gabby? Or plant evidence? Both seemed overly clumsy.

Gabby's shoulders scrunched. "She took some of my knives. I have bunches of them in the kitchen, just like she pointed out at the vigil. It's so lame. Didn't she realize it would be completely obvious? Not exactly subtle, but I guess obvi is as obvi does."

"She stole knives?" That was the *opposite* of planting evidence. "Why would she do that? If she wanted to borrow some, wouldn't she have asked?"

"I don't know. All these comments she's making, it's like she wants to pin Addie's death on me. But I have a thousand different ways to prove I was in Portland dropping my hubby at the airport. I even stopped for some ramen. You know I loves me some miso. And what? Like I'd stab Addie with one of my Wüsthofs, wipe the blade on my apron, and start chopping kale? That's so gross!"

My fingers tapped a little ditty. Gabby was right. It didn't add up. But so far nothing made any sense, and Darlene had other points against her. Time to dig into those. "At the vigil, you made it pretty clear Darlene's shop was having financial problems. Ruth Radford just mentioned something similar."

"The flower shop. OMG, yes! It's a mess. Between you and me, I don't think she'll last the winter." Gabby put on a sad puppy face. "Poor thing. It's so sad to see my fellow shop owners suffer like that." The face evaporated. "But that's business. It can be a cruel mistress. Or mister, in this case." She gave a big wink and giggled, lowering her head but watching my reaction.

"Whatever do you mean?" I asked, playing along with her pun.

Gabby's voice dropped to a whisper. "Darlene and Gresham, silly. Don't act like you don't know." I must've looked like a particularly dimwitted cow, because she exploded. "Are you serious? They've been an item for over a year. Harvest Falls' own little scandal, right? Though not unexpected of Gresham. It's not like she's his first mistress, and she certainly won't be the last."

My jaw dropped. The news wasn't as shocking as it would've been a few days earlier. With all that had happened, it stood in a rather lengthy line. But Gresham and Darlene? I wasn't sure I'd ever seen the pair together, or even in the same building.

"They must be well practiced at keeping things quiet." I

tried to slot in the new information. If Darlene's shop was already in trouble, how upset would she really be with Addie for taking it? Did the affair play a bigger role? Had Addie known about it? Or worse, suffered from Gresham's advances herself?

"Not as practiced as they think." Gabby couldn't contain her glee.

"A cruel mister," I mused, repeating Gabby's words. "Are you saying Gresham was cruel to Darlene?" *Not to mention Charlotte?*

Gabby's lips twitched before she spoke. "Nothing she didn't deserve."

I sputtered. "Gabby!"

"No, I don't mean physically. But he was, like, a karmic hammer. Boom!" She feigned an explosion with her hands. "I mean, look at this place. It's empty. Darlene scared away my customers with that nonsense she spouted, and that was before the break-in. Now she's a thief too. She should be in jail! Just because the men in this town have a soft spot for her doesn't mean she should get away with…well, everything!"

Gabby exhaled. She eyed the croissant, and I nudged it closer to her. "I shouldn't," she said, pinching off a healthy chunk of the remnants.

"So what did Gresham do to Darlene?" I asked, once she'd reset.

She tore another piece and licked her fingers. "He's a loyal customer. So as a friend, I warned him to stay away from Darlene. But she swindled her way into his pockets, and he was all too ready to play her rescuer. He planned on buying the building next door."

"Containing the flower shop."

"Exactly. Once he owned the building, he could offer Darlene a discount on rent. It'd keep her afloat, and he wouldn't have to give her any cash directly."

Sneaky, but it made sense. "That doesn't sound cruel, at least to Darlene. But then Addie came along?"

"Oh, you have been snooping! I knew it! Yes, Addie swooped in at the last minute and ruined Darlene's little coup. She wanted the space herself for her lame health spa. I knew all about that, of course. That's what the papers were for, the ones he took her the night of the murder."

I pressed my hands against the cool table to keep from fidgeting. "Addie assumed she could take what she wanted. It didn't matter what Gresham was going to do with the shop. To her, he was family. The move tied his hands too. He couldn't deny her without revealing his desire to help Darlene." *What a mess!* But I found it hard to feel sorry for Darlene. She'd made her bed, and so had Gresham.

"Who else knew about Addie's plans?" I asked, curious if there were any other players involved.

"It's public record, silly. She wanted to open this New Age healthy-living spa. She thought the town needed a healthier alternative to my Sweet Little Buttercup. As if that would ever fly. Just look at the folks around Harvest Falls. Did she think this was Eugene? I sell out of cinnamon rolls and maple bacon bars every day. Do you know what I throw out? Anything devoid of gobs of butter and sugar."

A sad, but truthful, point. I glanced at the brown paper

sleeve, now empty save for a few crumbs, and promised myself I'd hike to the top of the falls before the day was through.

"Okay." Gabby leaped on my silence. "Your turn again. What do the police think?" She stared with an intense curiosity I recognized. Ruth and Joyce had held the same expression. *A baker running around like Scooby-Doo,* Dad had called her. With the way she bounced in her chair, eager for my response, she was definitely more Scrappy-Doo.

"I don't know much," I answered honestly.

"Have they ruled out Addie's exes? Officially, I mean. I heard from my source the police have been making calls. But neither hubby was in town last weekend. It took me two seconds on Insta to figure that out." She leaned in. "That's Instagram to you boomers."

I sputtered. "I'm only six years older than you!"

"Aw, that's sweet. You're sweet." She wiggled her fingers. "Now spill."

After an audible grumble voicing my grievance, I gave Gabby some brief highlights of my morning with Frank, including how tight-lipped he'd been, and how I'd waited on Addie's front drive while evidence collection was performed. Then I shut my trap.

The cheeriness on her face plummeted. "Wait, are you telling me the police don't know about the flower shop, or about Darlene and Gresham? What have they been doing all this time? It's the first thing I thought of!"

I thought I was the first thing you thought of. I gave a smarmy shrug. I had nothing to add and no reason to speculate. Especially not in front of Gabby.

Her gaze dropped to the floor beside the table, as miserable as a caged puppy's. For a moment, I thought I'd broken her. But a wave of giddiness took root. No doubt, the croissant's sugar was kicking into gear. Her face lit up.

"Do you know what I did?" she squealed. "I saved everyone's cup from last night, and I'm going to keep saving something from everyone who comes through the door. You know, for the DNA. Wouldn't that make an amazing news story? Baker nabs murderer by serving the best latte in the state!"

"Gabby." Dad's familiar tone crept into my voice. "That can be very dangerous." I stopped short of adding, *And most likely useless to the police.*

She huffed, making sure I heard the sorrow in it. "Well, I have to do something for all the years Addie and I were BFFs. I know you and Addie had a falling-out, but you still have to understand. You get it, right?"

My face scrunched before I could contain it. "Addie and I didn't have a falling-out. We just didn't speak as often as we used to."

"Uh-huh, I gotcha." She gave an exaggerated wink. "Same camp, different tent. But honestly, don't let it get to you. I never did, that's how we remained so close. I couldn't care less what that girl thought. Not one bit. But I mean, all the hate she spewed, we all knew it was going to come back to bite her at some point."

I reached for my coffee. I needed to have something to hold. The cup started to crumple in my grip, but I kept a pleasant smile. "Speaking of, I heard you and Addie got into quite the shouting match just last week."

"Ugh, that. Much ado about nothing. Part of the Addie show."

"It wasn't personal?"

"You know what I mean. She liked to needle, and she always knew where to jab. I got hot. But come on, do you see me putting my hands on anyone? I've built way too successful a business to let something that basic tear it all down. Besides, it would totally mess up my vibes."

"So you didn't threaten to stab her for flirting with your husband?" Despite my irritation, I made the question sound trivial rather than accusatory. I wanted to know if Case's rumor had any legs.

Her response left little doubt.

Her eyes narrowed. Venom cut through her voice. "Darlene should keep her trap shut. Telling everyone she runs into about a trivial spat, making it seem bigger than it was." Rising, she tugged at her ponytail. "All her finger-pointing and blaming, it's nothing but a distraction. She's manipulating everyone. Wait until the truth comes out. You'll see I'm right."

"Do you really think she had something to do with Addie's murder?"

"At this point, I wouldn't put it past her! Addie must've found out about her and Gresham, and you know what she would do with that information. Nothing good. So Darlene has her back up against it, and Addie's acting like a terrier with a bone. Two women fighting because of Gresham's wandering eye. That's how it all went down."

Gabby stomped her way behind the counter, not allowing

me a chance to challenge her theory. I slurped my coffee, considering it. I wondered if Gresham knew about the rumors concerning him, and whether Gabby had firsthand knowledge of his playbook. But confronting him about his affairs would have to wait. I wanted to hear from Darlene first. What had driven her to steal Gabby's knives, and how much ill will did she really hold against Addie?

An itch at the back of my neck also begged to know: If it was so obvious she was guilty of the theft, why hadn't Dad arrested her for breaking into the café?

CHAPTER 27

I hit the sidewalk and strode to the flower shop next door. Leaves danced at my legs, picked up by a blustery wind. The steel sky had brightened a bit, yet I kept both hands clasped around my coffee, sucking up its remaining warmth. I told myself I had nothing to fear from Darlene Devereux. The woman had never showed me anything but kindness, no matter her actions the previous evening. I just hoped my gut wasn't blinded by our history.

I couldn't see her harming Addie either. Even if she blamed Addie for the loss of her shop—a stretch, since it was hurting anyway—the woman I knew went out of her way to help any bird, toad, or butterfly that crossed her path. She wouldn't hurt anybody. Besides, Addie's takeover gave Gabby as much motive as Darlene. Both had their businesses at stake.

Branson raised his head when I entered the shop. The black Labrador was late in his whiskers and liked to sleep on a giant pillow bed near the front windows. I gave him a hello scratch. He seemed content to sniff my hand and lie back down. His eyes closed to slits, in a sleepy watchfulness.

Bouquets, vases, and porcelain trinkets perched on shelves lining the walls and on a few wooden tables at the front of the shop. A long counter for trimming and arranging flowers divided the back of the shop from the front. The chillers along the back wall were barely half-full. The bouquets at the front were largely of dried thistle and autumn leaves, with a few carnations and the odd rose.

Incense burned from near the register. Its scent carried above the sweet floral aroma, along with one of Darlene's spicy teas. She stood behind the trimming counter holding a rose in one hand and a curved pruning knife in the other. A steaming mug sat an arm's reach away. Her face fell when I smiled at her. Her posture melted, as if my presence alone had deflated whatever cheer she'd clung to throughout the morning.

"Why?" I blurted, marching right past pleasantries. There was no sense denying what we both knew was true. There was no one else in the shop to overhear us.

Darlene shook her head. She might've been holding back tears as she swiped the knife along the rose stem. "That woman. If she didn't have the best chai in town, I wouldn't have anything to do with her."

"But why the café knives?" I stepped farther into the shop. "Do you think Gabby's been lying about her alibi?"

The scrape of the knife came harder. "I wasn't aiming on Gabby being found guilty. I just wanted folks looking at her like she was. Like y'all were looking at me last night."

A bit of understanding came. "You wanted the gossip to be about her," I said. The behavior was shameful, but I tried to sound supportive. The woman was obviously having a rough time, and her moment of insanity had only made things worse.

"You know how she is, treating me like I don't belong.

Like my shop isn't good enough to share a wall with her café. She got my blood up during the vigil. All those accusations she cooked up against me. I thought it'd be nice to bring her down a peg, so she wasn't looking down on me from so high a perch."

"Is that why you don't get along?"

The blade scraped. Thorns flew. "Huh, as if she'd stay in business herself without her husband's money. She tries to fool everyone, but anyone paying attention can see there's no profit in half her schemes."

I glanced at the empty chillers, wondering how much of that was sour grapes. From what I could tell, Gabby's café always turned over a healthy number of customers. Tourists queued out the door in the summer months.

"You had a key," I said, steering her back to the break-in.

Darlene shrugged. "I didn't think there'd be much risk. I'd just sneak in and swipe a knife or two, put them in a bag, and drop them off at the station. Vin D'Amato, with those loose lips of his, would get folks talking about her, even if there was nothing to it."

I blew out a deep breath. "Using your key, folks would've thought the theft happened during the vigil," I said. "There'd be no signs of a break-in." I leaned against the far side of the counter. The plan had a certain logic to it, despite its spiteful conception.

Branson rose up, stretched, and yawned. The tags on his collar jingled. He slowly padded to a water bowl. Darlene set the paring knife down and watched him. The tears and sorrowful expression returned.

"Then you came along and scared the bejesus out of me," she said. "It screwed the whole thing up. I should've just played it off, like I was there putting flowers in the refrigerator like I used to. But I didn't know what you wanted. I didn't know if I could trust you. Now there's no chance. The shop's gone for good, and I'm like to be arrested."

I gripped the counter's lip. Ruth, Gabby, and now Darlene. All had thought I couldn't be trusted, that I could somehow be involved in Addie's murder. The lens they viewed me with had mighty sharp edges.

"Maybe Gabby won't press charges," I offered, shaking off the hurt. I didn't have time to wallow. That could come later, with ice cream. "She gave you the key. We can say it was all an innocent mistake. I'll back you."

"Huh, she'd love that. She'd get to tell me and everyone else all about it every time I graced her presence." Her eyes narrowed. She picked up the knife and a fresh rose. The scrape sent bits of pulpy green stem flying.

There was no doubt Darlene had it right. Gabby would never let such a juicy tidbit go, especially since it featured her as the star. Yet the thought reminded me of something else. "You said Gabby had it out for me. Why?"

"Oh, I don't know. I haven't been right in days. These reckless things keep overtaking me, making me act a fool. I'm sorry if it did any harm."

Reckless from guilt? I summoned Frank's deadpan stare, knowing I had to ask a tough question. "Sorry, but uh...where you were the night Addie was found?"

Darlene twitched. She let out a soft huff and flourished the knife. "Right here with Branson. We had a nice walk to the falls and ate some smoked salmon. No one around to see us but the park squirrels, who love to tease the old fellow."

I gnawed the inside of my cheek, listened to the knife whisk down a stem. So she had no alibi. The knowledge didn't sway my thinking, but she'd have to remain on the list of suspects, especially with what I knew about her affair. *Time to play that card.* The route she described was short, and I knew from experience that Branson liked to stretch his legs, especially when it meant sniffing the evening air along Second Street.

"You didn't walk the long way? A route past the restaurant where Charlotte and Gresham were having a late dinner?" I asked, as coyly as I could muster.

"Why would I...?" Her gaze rose to mine, and she stopped herself. "Oh, all right. I suppose everyone knows by now."

"You and Gresham. Kind of an open secret, huh?"

She shook her head. "It wasn't. Not until Gabby caught me hanging around his office with Branson. I played it off, but then Gresham comes out and tries to give me a sneaky peck without seeing she's just down the way. Honestly, the man is thick as mud sometimes."

Not thick, just full of hubris. The man thought he could talk his way out of anything, and apparently, into anything. "It's been a year?"

"More or less. I wasn't looking for it. I knew his reputation. But we took to talking a bit too long one evening, and feelings sprang from there." She gazed out the window. "It was nice to have someone doting on me all the time. You know what I mean. Boyfriends add a sense of comfort, like a cozy winter coat, even if they don't fit quite right."

Oh, yes. I knew exactly that. My entire life with Mason had never completely fit, and that had taken years to shrug off.

"He was going to buy this place, help you out of a jam."

Her gaze flicked away, annoyed. "Seems you know everything already."

I held my ground. "I only mean saving your flower shop is a bit more than doting. It'd be more like moving into together, wouldn't it? A financial tie?"

"No, not at all." Darlene shook her head. "That's just his way. He likes to play the savior, all flash and charm. He'd promise a trip to the moon if it'd solve my problems. If not, he'd say we could go away, escape our lives here and start over somewhere else. Anywhere I wanted. I knew it was foolishness, just sweet little lies to make what we were doing seem romantic. But saving the shop, somehow I bought into the reality of that promise. It felt real, something I could almost touch."

"It must've made you angry to have Addie swoop in and unravel all your plans. The hope you'd built. What happened between you two, anyway? I thought you'd been friendly."

"Friendly, yes. Friends, no. I don't know if that was really possible, not with Addie, and I have no idea what set her against me. But I'm not surprised by it. I'm not surprised by anything in this town anymore."

Darlene took a moment to sort her roses. I could tell she wanted to say more—a whole conversation spun behind her eyes—so I stayed quiet.

"Addie was always snooping into everyone's business," she finally said, "and creeping on Gresham. She wouldn't let things go. If she couldn't assert her superior airs, she'd destroy your world just because she could. I'd seen her do it to Gabby countless times. She'd bully Ruth too. Treated the woman like a servant. And Madison and Sera, who were almost too beneath her to ridicule."

Her eyes found mine again. "Do you think Sera Simmons really did it?"

"I don't know," I replied, honestly. "It's possible. There is so much truth in her account, and yet she's lied about a few things that don't make sense. They don't seem important."

"We all have our reasons."

I glanced around the shop. The lights in one of the chillers flickered. A thickness clung to the air, as if Addie's memory haunted the place, even by the proxy of a dream that never was. "It must be weird having Gresham buy the shop now."

"Oh, that's over. I can't trust him anymore." Her voice caught. I searched for a tissue box, but she waved me away. "It has nothing to do with Addie. I've made a mess of this place all my own. It leaks money like a rusted-out bucket. No amount of bailing is going to fix that."

"But you still feel betrayed?"

"I'm in real trouble, and I'm not going to make it through the winter. I needed Gresham's help. I needed one darn thing from him, for him to support me. But he chose Addie and showed his true allegiance to the Newsomes. He ain't the man I thought he was."

The man you knew had a reputation. People lied to themselves for all kinds of reasons, but especially when it came to hope. Hope and the future. I knew that song and dance. I'd lied to myself ever since I could remember.

"How many other women is Gresham sleeping with?" The thought popped from my mouth before I could send it through my brain's Tact Department. "What I mean is…do you think he made the same promises to other women recently?"

Darlene's tittering answered the question clear as day. "Girl, you are a trip. I forced myself not to worry over that. Closed my eyes to it. But seeing as the man flirts with every woman in town, I'd be surprised if his dalliances ended with me."

"Do you think he was seeing Sera?" Again, the random thought sprang to mind. This time, a familiar flush washed through me, like I'd just drawn the key card in a board game.

"No," Darlene answered without pause. "Those two stared daggers at each other, the last I saw." She waved the curved knife absently, pulling at some thought. "But tell you what I did see. Joyce Townsend leaving his office early this morning. I was out giving Branson his morning saunter. She looked real distracted, too, like she'd forgotten where she was. Made me wonder what business she might have with Gresham. She doesn't have the kind of money needed for his services, not as far as I'm aware. They don't pay librarians like they do drug reps. The whole thing played as strange."

Joyce and Gresham. Could that be a thing? Her having used Beckett's dagger, cleaned it, and concocted an elaborate tale as a means of misdirection no longer seemed so outlandish. Beckett had certainly been frightened of her, and I'd thought those two thick as thieves. She had found the body, too, without any reason to be by that part of the highway.

"Have you seen them together before?" I asked. "Has he ever mentioned her?"

Darlene didn't respond. Stepping back a step, she swallowed hard. The pruning knife clattered to the table. I spun and saw Dad through the front windows. He marched toward the door with purpose. *So he did know.* Guilt fizzled through me for doubting him, but I choked it back.

Branson padded to the middle of the shop as Dad entered. He gave a single swish of his tail, uncertain. Dad's gaze trained on me for a moment, before turning on Darlene. She sunk farther down, folding and unfolding her arms. But she kept her head raised.

"Chief Goode," she said, then to me, "You'll take care of Branson, won't you?"

"For the afternoon," I replied, firmly. "You'll be back by the evening, free as a bird." I ignored the stern warning in Dad's gaze. Still angry from our last discussion, I wanted to shout at him. Besides, he needed to know the truth. "You had a key—"

"Charlie, I need to speak with Miss Devereux alone."

I drew back my shoulders and addressed Darlene. "You had a key that Gabby gave you for the purpose of entering the café when she wasn't there. You never threatened me, nor attacked me. It was a misunderstanding. There's nothing more to it than that."

Standing firm, I readied myself for Dad's fury. But his lips tugged into an amused smile. His brow rose. He didn't say a word.

I was confused by his reaction; my posture lightened. Had he seen how I was helping and conceded defeat? I wasn't sure but decided to claim a small victory. Leaping into motion, I found Branson's leash on its hook and called to him. He checked with Darlene.

"Go on, then," she told him. "I'll be good."

He obeyed, aware something was amiss but wanting a walk all the same. I nodded encouragement to Darlene as I clipped on the leash and led him outside. Branson took the lead at a plodding pace. He sniffed around the sidewalk, unperturbed by the wind. I shivered but barely noticed the cold. Joyce Townsend. It kept coming back to her. Could she have been playing us all along? I needed to know what she'd been doing at Gresham's office, and whether he made promises to her, the same as he'd done Darlene Devereux.

Perhaps she hadn't taken those promises as romantic fancy. Perhaps the whole thing boiled down to a woman obsessed with a cheating man who'd never leave Charlotte Newsome. But what did that have to do with Addie? Despite all I'd uncovered, I was still missing something vital.

CHAPTER 28

As I guided Branson up the street, I replayed my conversation with Darlene. Her remorse seemed genuine enough, and convincing. She hadn't sugar-coated her account either. But, all the same, I wished none of it were true. Had everyone gone insane? Ruth, with Marvin's hunting knife; Darlene, with Gabby's chef's knife; and not to mention Joyce, with Beckett's Sting. It was no wonder Dad had a short fuse.

My phone vibrated. I fished it out and came to a full stop. Geraldine's face flashed on the screen. She wore a surly expression, giving me the stink eye. I'd snapped the picture earlier in the summer, just after telling her I was moving in with Case. Normally, it made me laugh.

But not today.

Blowing a raspberry at the wind, I considered shoving the phone back into my pocket. But I couldn't keep putting her off. Putting things off only caused more problems. Over the summer, I'd collected a mountain of evidence to attest to that fact. Tapping the phone, I answered the call.

"Sorry, my phone's been dead." The lie stung. It came a bit too naturally. "I'm fine, though. You know, still breathing and eating vegetables."

"Charlie, you must grow up." Geraldine's voice sounded impatient. "Your father told me all about last night. Cavorting with those scandalmongers in the café. Your impertinence. The reckless behavior afterward for something so trivial. By the time I was your age—"

"I'm fine," I repeated. Branson gave up on me. He sat and craned his neck my way. His dark eyes carried a mark of skepticism. I patted his head to block them out.

"And refusing to sign the escrow papers. Don't think I didn't pull the truth out of Gresham. You are not fine. You are being willful and not acting like yourself. Your father told you to stay away from his work, and now I am too." A heavy sigh came through the line. "But no matter, you can sign the papers today."

"I'm heading to Gresham's right now," I said, to cut her off. I winced. *Crap.* I hadn't even remembered the signing. I'd had too many other thoughts whirling around in my head. "But I want to read through everything first. I should know what's in the documents I'm signing."

I held my breath.

After a short clucking sound, she said, "Wonderful. Reading legal documents is a very wise and grown-up thing to do." She barely paused before rattling on. "Now that that's settled, I have other news. Charlotte's friend from Miley University is in town. Lunch is set for tomorrow afternoon. You can impress her then, and everything will be nice and tidy."

"Oh. Yay. Great." My soul shriveled to ash, just a little bit.

"Charlie, you know this is an important step. Your

mother's dream was to bring a health center to Harvest Falls, and you and I have to take up that dream. Around it, we'll build clinics for holistic healing, for the reduction of stress and pollutants in the body. It'll be just like a hundred years ago when they used the minerals of the falls. Our ancestors were far smarter in these things. They knew the land provides."

"Uh-huh." I'd heard the speech before. It was better to let the train pass than step in front of it. I wanted to get her off the phone. I was losing daylight.

"I'm talking about jobs too. A revitalization of the town. Not just health care workers, but all the shops and restaurants needed to support patients' families and employees. It'll put Harvest Falls back on the map as a tourist destination."

Pointing out that the town was already overrun with tourists each summer would do little good. Geraldine wouldn't entertain any facts that interrupted her narrative. My mother hadn't either. Two peas in a pod. Dad had a type.

She paused to breathe, and I butted in.

"What if I don't want…?" I almost said it—the truth, finally—but I didn't have time for the fallout. Geraldine would lose it, and I'd have to go into witness protection. Pivoting, I asked, "What if I don't feel right about taking someone else's spot at Miley?"

Geraldine trilled like a warbler. "They always leave a couple spots open for these sorts of things. Connections, you know. It won't be a problem. Charlotte would love to help you. She sees you as family, just as I do."

Charlotte. Family. A weight fell on me as the two words collided. The lunch meeting was forgotten. Shamefully, I hadn't yet considered what I should tell Addie's mother about Gresham's affair. Anything at all? Or would holding my tongue be a sort of betrayal? Yet for her to find out now, after Addie's death, wouldn't that make it worse? I had to admit I needed Geraldine's advice.

"Listen," I said. "I found out a horrible thing. Gresham has been cheating on Charlotte with Darlene Devereux."

A long silence followed before Geraldine spoke. "Don't talk about unpleasant business. It's not how your mother raised you."

"You knew? Does Charlotte know?"

"Yes, of course she does." Geraldine's voice sounded pleasant but clipped, as if she spoke about the weather to a passing neighbor. "There are so many gold diggers in this town, all after his fortunes." She chuckled. "It gives Charlotte a good laugh to think of it."

"Why laugh? I'm by no means an expert, but it seems an odd reaction to infidelity."

A belabored sigh. "Because Gresham has no money of his own. He's up to his eyeballs in debt."

I took a step back and blinked. Branson's eyebrow rose. "Really? Since when?"

"Since before he came to Harvest Falls. He made bad investments and had a messy divorce, and it's only gotten worse from there. A few weeks ago, he let go of his admin girl. Her before that car of his! Only Charlotte keeps him afloat, and she keeps him well under her thumb. It's a shame his diddling has become common knowledge, though I suppose it was only a matter of time. I warned Charlotte about him, but she's very headstrong."

I barely registered the last part. If Gresham had no money of his own, who exactly was buying my grandmother's land? I'd been led to assume he was making a private purchase. That he was acting as broker and buyer. No one ever mentioned another party.

Another thought staggered me. If he had no money, how was he buying the building that held Darlene's shop? The shop Addie had planned on taking for her own. The answer came as quickly as the question: Charlotte Newsome. Who else could afford it? And who else could Addie persuade to hand over the keys so easily? Certainly not some outsider.

But had Charlotte really meant to help Darlene, like Gresham promised, before Addie's plans for a spa materialized? I wasn't sure. Nor did I know why Geraldine was so interested I sell my land through Gresham. What did she stand to gain? Or was I to believe her heart was as altruistic as she claimed?

Nope. No way. I'd believe that when I believed Madison flew on a broomstick.

"We want to make a strong impression tomorrow," said Geraldine. "Come to dinner tonight, and we'll strategize. We can celebrate too."

"Sure." I clicked off the phone. Celebrate. As if Addie hadn't existed at all. As if closing my eyes would make everything fine. As if she wasn't trying to control me on the same strings my mother had used.

Dance, Charlie, dance.

CHAPTER 29

Gresham's office was dark. Midafternoon, the sun hung just above the buildings of Bywater Street. The trees along the sidewalk rustled. Leaves shook free and fluttered to the ground. A heavy dampness clung to the air, promising rain before long.

Branson and I made a lap around the block. I hoped Gresham wasn't done for the day. I dismissed calling him. He was too good a salesman. I needed to see his face, and I wanted to get my hands on the escrow papers. Read them for myself. Confirm it was Charlotte's name on them, or an entity she controlled. I also wanted to confirm my suspicions she'd allowed Addie to swoop into the flower shop deal. That it'd been her money all along. But if both were true, did that make her actions sinister? If she'd known about Darlene's involvement with Gresham, had she purposefully set out to ruin the woman's livelihood? How much had Addie known, and did any of it matter at all? I couldn't see a clear connection to murder, especially not Addie's, unless my gut was wrong about Darlene.

Gresham hadn't returned by the time Branson and I finished our fifth lap. Darlene's adorable pooch had slowed.

His eyes pleaded for a change of direction.

"Ok, big boy," I told him. "Let's see if Case has some of those bacon treats."

His ears perked up. He'd knock into a door sometimes, forgetting to check if it was open, but bacon he always remembered.

I'd have to check on Gresham later. Maybe I could arrange a meeting. *No*, I reconsidered. Such a request would give him time to prepare, and I wanted to catch him unaware, like Frank had done with Sera.

The notion gave me an idea. Gresham wasn't the only one I could surprise. It took two to make a thing go right, after all. And apparently Gresham's math didn't stop at two. Just because Darlene couldn't see him flirting with Sera Simmons didn't mean it hadn't happened, and she'd been the one to first mention his wandering eye.

"Just one more stop," I told Branson. "Promise."

A couple short blocks brought me to the apparel shop where Sera worked. The shop had changed names and owners a couple of times, in recent years. It was a hard business. The tourists ate up the tacky sweatshirts and loud T-shirts during the summer months, but during the offseason the racks of winter wear only gathered dust. The locals had no need for a "Harvest Falls Gathers Memories" bandana.

I was in luck. I caught sight of Sera's pink-and-green hair and told Branson to rest near the entrance. He whined, reminding me of my promise, but plopped down after a short stretch. I scratched his jowl and dropped his leash next to him. An electronic bell tolled as I entered. Sera's head rose. Her eyes narrowed.

"If you're creeping for your father, you can turn right around," she said. "I've got nothing to say to you."

"Hardly," I sputtered. "I mean, I'm not creeping. My father..." *Grr!* I charged forward. "Look, I just have a quick question."

Sera's eye roll would've put Geraldine to shame. "Because you're on my side?"

I stopped short. Two days ago I'd shouted that very thing and begged her to believe me. We were friends, or so I'd thought. But now I didn't want to make any promises. I'd come to see if she'd cheated with Gresham behind Charlotte's back. Or in front of, if Charlotte had known about it. Either way, if she had, that could've been what set her and Addie off.

"She's on everyone's side. That's always been her shtick. Make sure to appease everyone. If everyone plays nice, there'll be no hurt feelings. Am I right?" Madison stepped from behind a rack of floral dresses. She held one in her hands, fingering the material.

I yelped and sprang back, knocking over a stack of shirts. "Madison! I did...didn't see..." I took a breath to stop my stammering. I wasn't sure if she'd meant the words to sting, but what was wrong with making sure no one's feelings were hurt? I glanced at the dress she held—a ditsy print, dark green with scattered white petals. She'd look amazing in it, no doubt.

Sera smirked. "So what is it? You working for the old man, or have you gone nutty like half the town?"

I straightened the shirts I'd upset, taking the moment to catch my breath. Madison worked her way over to Sera, and the pair watched me. Clearly, I'd interrupted something. Gossip about Gabby and Darlene? Or maybe Sera venting to a friend? Whatever it was, there was little chance I'd be able to wheedle my way into their confidence. They were as tight as Case and I. As tight as Addie and I had once been.

"Those things you told me about Gresham," I said. "I should've believed you. I just found out about him and Darlene Devereux."

"Seriously?" Madison gave me one of her looks. "Just now?"

I shrugged. What else could I do? "I guess I had my eyes closed, like you've both rightly pointed out." Turning to Sera, I asked, "But I wondered, whom else he might've…I mean, did you ever take him up on his advances?"

"No way!" Sera snickered. "I'm not that hard up." Her gaze swung to Madison. Mine followed, inquisitively.

"Ew." Madison flinched in revulsion. Her upper lip sought refuge in her nose.

"But he did try?" I asked.

She turned back to the dress. "Yeah, of course. Just like he did Gabby and Sera and everyone else. So gross. I feel sorry for Darlene that she doesn't have better options. She could do so much better."

Everyone else. I strained once again not to feel offended. Had Gresham thought I didn't need to be whisked away? That my life was perfect, without need of rescue? Or had he just not liked what he saw?

I glanced over my shoulder to ensure we were still alone. "What about Joyce Townsend? Do you think he ever turned his charms on her?"

The pair exchanged a glance that landed somewhere between curiosity and mockery.

"No doubt," answered Sera. "Not that I've heard anything. But she seems just his type."

"Why the questions?" asked Madison. "No longer sure your father can handle the pressure? Doesn't have a lead, does he?"

"He's fine," I answered, a little too quickly. "Don't you worry."

"Color me pessimistic." Sera slumped onto a counter. "Any bets, if he doesn't find the killer soon, I'll be the one in cuffs?"

My jaw worked, but I couldn't think of what to say. If I were Sera, I'd be worried too.

Branson raised his head as I left the shop. A scratch behind the ears garnered a prolonged yawn. He stood and stretched his back legs, while I pulled out my phone. I rang Charlotte as we started toward Roll For It. I felt so close to the truth that my earlier trepidations were cast aside. I wanted to learn about Gresham's other conquests and hear her reaction to his infidelities being made public. Charlotte would forgive my lack of tact, if it meant catching Addie's murderer.

At least, that's what I told myself.

"Hi Charlie, I was just thinking about you." She made it sound like I'd made her day.

"Geraldine told me about the lunch tomorrow," I replied. "Thank you for even thinking about me."

"Of course. You're family."

Huh, is this how families are really meant to act? All secrets and smiles?

"That's why I'm calling." Time to leap in with both feet. "I don't know how to say this, but I've learned something, and I think you should know about it. I would want to know, if I were you. Even if it upset me."

"What is it, dear?" Her tone was more intrigued than concerned.

"Gresham and Darlene are having an affair. They have been for a year." I jammed the phone closer against my ear, desperate to read her reaction through the connection.

Charlotte's peal of laughter sounded hollow. "Is that all? But of course he's told me all about that. We have an open and honest relationship."

I grinned at the small victory. Charlotte could've feigned distress over the news, or denied my claim as vile gossip. But I knew she would never play the victim. She wanted me to see her in complete control.

"Oh, open. I didn't know. I don't think I could…" I broke off. *Stay on target, Charlie!* I summoned my most innocent, nothing-to-see-here tone. "Does he always tell you about the other women he's with?"

A brief pause. "I like to think so. But he's his own man and doesn't think things through all the time. You know how men can be."

"What about Joyce Townsend?"

"The librarian? I would hope not. She's a bit extravagant, and he's meant to behave himself." Her tone became harder, not as carefree. "But I wouldn't necessarily know. I don't ask for details."

So much for open and honest. I'd definitely stuck a nerve. I wondered how much Addie knew about Gresham's transgressions, but I couldn't bring myself to ask Charlotte. I was treading past delicate ground already.

"Why do you stay with him?" I asked instead. "Don't you worry it will...like, look bad?"

"What? To the town?" A trill of laughter. "I've never much bothered with what the clucking hens thought. That was your mother's purview. I've no patience for it. I've always been more the romantic. So you see, when Marc passed the way he did, I felt this enormous betrayal. I suffered so much from it, I never wanted to get that close to another man again."

"You keep Gresham at a distance?" I asked. I didn't think I could ever be in an open relationship, much less one stilted in such a way.

"We have fun, and of course we care for one another. But yes, my relationship with Gresham is how I want it. When he moved into town, all flash, and no account, I knew that's how it would be. And I made it so. I let him have his dalliances. Things that don't cause a fuss. Something on the Coast, away from prying eyes. Though he has gotten sloppy of late."

That's because the man literally promises the moon to get what he wants. I couldn't fathom how Charlotte lived with such an arrangement. But I couldn't imagine living through Marc's death either. And now Addie. It must be a lonely house Above the Falls, and Gresham could, at least, charm the paint off the walls.

"One more thing," I said. *As long as she was talking openly.* I twirled my fingers through Branson's leash. I was tempted to ask about my grandmother's land, but thought it better to broach that topic already knowing the answer. So I pivoted to the other mystery swirling around my head. "It's about Marc, if you don't mind my asking."

"What is it, dear?"

"How true are the rumors about Marc and a gold-prospecting venture?"

As glass clinked as it was set down. "That's a rather odd question, Charlie."

"Is it?" I tried to sound surprised. "It seems so ridiculous, I thought you'd deny he had any association with the prospectors."

But of course Charlotte wouldn't. Control. Always in control.

"There was some involvement, but it was a mistake. Marc liked to flirt with fanciful notions of the past. Your father helped Marc out of a tight spot, and that was it. You can ask him, if you need the details. It's been so long I don't remember anymore. But nothing came of it; that much I can say."

Nothing except for two dead men, and a third, if Marc's actions were from guilt.

After thanking her once more, I hung up. Branson studied me with an intense silence, no doubt eager for an updated status on the bacon front. I stared down an empty street, listening for a hint of the falls behind the wind. I needed its comfort. Between Charlotte's rationalizations and Dad shutting me out, I'd lost what sense of home I'd had at the start of summer.

Your father helped Marc out of a tight spot. What more was there to say? Dad had known everything right from the start. They all had, and they'd chosen not to trust me. Meanwhile, I'd lived years for everyone else's happiness, and I didn't even get a stupid T-shirt.

Swallowing, I shoved my emotions aside. The only thing to do now was follow Addie's playbook and go on the offensive. No matter whom it upset. Not even her killer.

CHAPTER 30

"This town is going to you-know-where in a handbasket!" Helen Tait's purple-haired hobbit form leaned into Case. Her sourpuss expression defied him to interrupt. "Trash flying in the wind, gum on the sidewalk. It's all these youngsters roving around like hyenas. No parenting. No responsibility."

At least the game shop had a customer. Helen came in twice a month to buy jigsaw puzzles. Case kept a rotating selection just for her. I slipped into the shop quietly and dodged to the side, hoping not to draw the woman's attention. Branson pattered at my heels. He knew the drill.

"That Gabby Kemper raised her prices again." Helen took no notice of me and continued her tirade. "Three dollars for coffee and cream. How am I supposed to afford that? This isn't the city."

I stopped short. The shop had a second customer. James grinned sheepishly at me. He stooped along the farthest aisle, keeping his head bent. He pretended to be enthralled by some brain teaser. I sidled over, and he knelt to ruffle Branson's ears, getting licked in return.

"I heard about Darlene," he said, in a hushed tone. "News of her arrest is traveling fast. Your dad walked her from the flower shop to the station."

"I came to talk to Case about that," I said. "It's a big misunderstanding. She had a key Gabby lent her." For James's sake, I didn't elaborate. If I went any further, I wouldn't stop rambling for an hour. He seemed to recognize this; I could see the hint of knowing humor behind his eyes.

Full-on flushing, a part of me loved that he read me so well.

Okay, a large part. A majority interest, even. And after the afternoon I'd had, I needed it. Our banter felt comfortable. *Like a cozy winter coat.* Darlene's comparison sprang to mind.

"Is town gossip why you're here, or is there something else you'd like?" I asked, none too subtly.

His dimples flashed. "I had a few hours before work tonight. How about that walk?"

I glanced at Case. He was going to be busy for a while.

"Kathy Wilkes was hit by a skateboarder the other day, just minding herself at the park," Helen was telling him. "And Madeline Parker almost ran me down with her car Sunday night." She shook her head. "No one looks where they're going anymore."

"Yes," I told James. "Now is perfect." I'd hunt down Gresham later, and maybe get Case to join me. I snuck Branson to the back of the shop, pulled out the blanket we used for him, and got him some water and a couple of bacon treats. He devoured the treats and curled up for a long pre-dinner nap. Case watched me but kept quiet. The saint. He knew I wanted no part of being drawn into his conversation. I gave a wave of apology and gestured that I was leaving

Branson with him. He nodded. All the while, Helen never stopped talking.

James held the door for me. "This isn't crazy, is it?" he asked, once outside.

"Walking?" I replied. But I knew what he meant. There'd been a barrier between us ever since the start of high school. Other relationships, family pressure, Addie. Life being life. Then I'd moved, and the years had grown us apart. Folding my arms to keep my coat closed, I walked at his shoulder. The distant rumble of the falls filled a span of silence.

As we headed that way, he studied me. His arms crossed to mimic mine. "After my parents split, my mom pulled me from baseball. She didn't want to spend money on something that wasn't taking me anywhere. Money was tight, and I needed to get my head out of the clouds. At twelve years old, she told me I wasn't good enough for the pros. Basketball was free. I should just go down to the park and find some other boys to play." He laughed at himself. "Thus, the legend was never born."

I shared his humor for a brief flash, but a dark sedan crawled past us and caught my eye. Detective Frank Nichols had returned to Harvest Falls. He slouched in his seat. One arm hung out the window. The other sat loosely on the steering wheel. He didn't turn my way. He seemed lost in his own thoughts. Had he worked out who'd killed Addie? Was he here to make an arrest? I caught myself before calling out. I fought an urge to rush to the police station. He headed away from it, anyway, and probably wouldn't tell me a thing. The way he'd teased me along should've pissed me off, but I was past caring at this point. Frank could be a loathsome prick all he wanted, as long as he'd uncovered the truth.

"What I'm trying to say is," James continued, "I might've been at the opposite end of the scales, but I know about expectations. I get it. No one in my family thought I'd keep The Oak Grove open a year. Even now, they think it's some fluke."

Frank's car grew smaller in the distance, and a hint of disappointment blossomed. If the murderer had been identified, it meant I'd failed in catching them. Guilt and shame quickly jabbed back. *What did it matter who solved the murder, as along as Addie found justice?* As long as it was justice. My gut pulled tight.

James followed my gaze. He nodded, his lips compressing. "We can do this some other time."

His wounded tone about broke me. I whirled and snatched his arm, mortified by my behavior. "Sorry, I am listening. I heard everything. Basketball. Expectations."

He chuckled with uncertainty, a defensive gesture. He plucked my hand from his arm but held on to it. His palm was warm. The touch sent vibrations streaking through my body. "What's got you all bottled up? Spill the beans, Dairy Queen."

He'd donned his bartender schtick like armor. *Real great, Charlie Goode.*

"I'm so sorry. I want this. I do. But the timing..." I wasn't sure what I wanted to say—that the timing conflicted with my playing at Miss Marple? That I didn't trust my father's abilities as a police chief? Or that I'd peeled back a mask I hadn't realized I'd worn for over forty years, and I found the thing disgusting?

"It's okay." James gave a quick squeeze of my hand. "Ask."

"Ask what?"

He directed us forward. "The next question. Just be you."

Something in me released. I'd never before understood how women could swoon like they did in the old movies. It seemed such a demoralizing act. But having James truly understand me almost brought me to my knees. They weakened, and I willed myself to remain upright.

"Have you heard anything about Gresham and Joyce Townsend?"

James pulled a face. "Darlene, and now Joyce? Wow. Busy man, that Gresham. I need to get out more. Go somewhere to socialize. To one of them, what do you call it? With the drinks and stale air?"

"Har-har." I rolled my eyes playfully and told him what I'd learned from Gabby and Darlene. "Sera said there were others as well. She made it sound like he went after every woman in town. Charlotte claims to know everything, but I can't see how it all fits, or whether it matters at all. I mean, how would knowing about an affair get Addie killed?"

"Sounds like someone's lying to you." James spoke louder. We'd reached the park and continued on a path toward the base of the falls, away from the switchbacks climbing higher above. The water's thundering reverberated off the mountainside, coming at us from all directions. The air grew damper. The tree canopy made it darker.

"Gresham didn't say anything about him and Darlene to the police," I pointed out.

James shrugged. "Probably wanted to keep it a secret, and maybe he didn't think it mattered. Omitting something isn't the same as lying, especially if not done deliberately. I'm sure there's all kinds of things I haven't told you about."

"Like what?"

His face turned sheepish. "Like how much I wanted to kiss you at the sixth grade Halloween dance. You were dressed as Inigo from *The Princess Bride*. But I hadn't his courage. It took me two years to muster it."

"I had a mustache." I remembered the dance. The principal had taken my plastic sword away at the door, and I'd spent the night explaining to everyone I wasn't dressed as one of the Village People. James had recognized Inigo straightaway, though. He'd come as Marty McFly, complete with orange vest and white kicks.

"It highlighted your lips." He swung me so we faced each other. The falls crashed next to us, broad and violent, with a full-throated roar, showering us in an icy spray. I thought the damp on my cheeks might turn to steam as it met the heat racing up my neck. My fingers twirled through his. Our gazes melded together. We silently dared the other to lean in and make a move. To break the seal. To make it real.

I cracked first. My hands found his shoulders and pulled him closer.

But as our lips brushed, a loud sniffle and hacking snort blasted from a few paces away. James jerked and craned his head. I squeezed my eyes shut and cursed. I'd recognized the nasal symphony. The falls had hidden Beckett's approach. He stood behind us staring at the ground. He was anxious but too embarrassed to speak.

"What is it?" I sighed. I didn't want to let go of James, but he stepped back. My arms fell slack. The moment was gone.

Beckett didn't look up. "I f-found it."

"You're going to have to narrow that down." I glared at the top of his downturned head. I wasn't ready to give him a pass. He clearly knew what he was interrupting.

He sniffled. His voice barely raised above the falls. "The murder weapon."

My nails dug gashes into my palms. "Listen, Beckett. I can't deal with another lame goose chase right now, okay? We're kind of busy."

His head shook like it was trapped in a paint mixer. His eyes finally raised to meet mine. "No, honest. I found the real one this time. Look!" He thrust his phone under my nose. On the screen was a grainy image I couldn't make out. It looked like underbrush and maybe some scattered stones.

"Zoom's not very good on this thing," he said. "But you can see it there." He tapped at one of the shapes. "It's a garden trowel. Not a dagger at all!"

I squinted. James did too. He leaned in, and his stubble scratched along my cheek.

"Sorry, I can't make anything of this," I said.

Beckett sniffled, defeated. "Charlie, I swear. I was out walking, trying to think it all through, and the blade caught against the sun. I stopped to check it out, and…and there was blood. Dried blood." He jabbed his finger at the image once more. "Don't you see? The killer tried to hide it. They threw it into the bushes as they fled from Addie's car."

That got my attention. I stiffened, snatched the phone from him, and peered closer. "Wait, where did you find this?"

"That's what I'm trying to tell you!" Sniffle. "It's just a couple miles or so from the trailhead, down toward Buckner Falls." Beckett pantomimed as he spoke. "Think about it. The killer stashes Addie's car, so now they're on foot. They take the murder weapon with them and chuck it off the trail hoping it won't ever be found. They must've carried on down the trail and looped back toward town at the next intersection."

James eyed me. He ran a hand through his spray-soaked hair.

I was already reaching for my own phone. "I hate to admit it, Beckett, but that makes a whole lot of sense." Away from the highway, a network of trails crisscrossed. If the killer knew them, they could've found their way back into town with ease, without needing to return to the trailhead. No one would've been the wiser.

"I'm texting Case," I said. Sadly, James and my seven minutes in heaven would have to wait. As I punched in the message, I thought of Frank's sudden return and wondered if he and my dad had already made a big mistake.

CHAPTER 31

To fit us all, we took The Oak Grove's panel van. It had an oak tree painted on both sides, along with the bar's name in golden letters. The insides stank of beer and motor oil. Their fumes warred for supremacy as we tutted along. I'd claimed the passenger seat, with Branson hunkered between my legs. Case and Beckett sat on the bare metal floor of the rear compartment. My cousin had folded himself into a defensive ball. Beckett splayed out like a stick insect, arms braced. But they were both jostled by every bump and turn.

"Why aren't we going to the police?" James asked as he drove. He glanced at me askance. "You could call that one guy, the chief."

"We need to offer something better than a grainy picture," I stated. The reasoning sounded way better than, *Because I want to see it.* And it was certainly better than explaining why my father might not jump at my claim of finding crucial evidence.

James was dubious but let me slide. He pulled into the trailhead and parked. As we all crawled out, he pulled a flashlight from the center console. Case fed Branson something from his pocket. Beckett sniffled and wiped his nose.

"Jeepers," I muttered, taking in our motley crew. My dad's premonition had come to life. "Well, at least I'm Daphne," I added, louder. I could live with that.

James scanned the group and chuckled. Case frowned. He used a finger to count through our number. "Wait. Who's Velma?" He pointed at himself. "Am I Velma?"

Snorting with laughter, I motioned for Beckett to lead the way. We took the main trail this time, skirting wide of the path to Marvin Shepard's clearing. We had an hour of light left in the day, maybe less where the trees became denser. My feet didn't have the foreboding tread I thought they might. I'd convinced myself finding the murder weapon held more than morbid curiosity. The evidence, with its likelihood of fingerprints and other trace elements, might very well be the key to not only finding Addie's killer but to locking them away for good.

Joyce Townsend popped to mind. It wasn't hard to imagine her stomping down the same trail, a sneer of malice on her face. But had she and Gresham really been a thing? That, I couldn't quite picture, and not for superficial reasons. The pair were an odd match as friends, let alone as romantic partners. Their worlds seemed miles apart.

And if they weren't together, what motive did she have? That I could see her as a jealous lover didn't mean I thought her capable of random violence.

"What you said before about someone lying to me, I think you're right." I spoke over my shoulder to James.

"I'm telling you, we need a board," droned Case.

Beckett's ears perked up. He walked sideways so we could

hear his excited yammering. "We can use sheep meeples to denote the innocent, and like, Cthulhu as the murderer."

My whimper was heard round the world. Why did everything in my life turn into game pieces and Lovecraftian monsters?

"But we don't know the murderer," Case pointed out. "We'd need a dozen Cthulhus as suspects, and who would be the sheep? Everyone else in town? That's a lot of sheep."

"Hey, I'm no sheep," said James. "You take that baaaaah—ck!" He shrugged when we didn't laugh, and added, "Besides, Cthulhu's overplayed. Why not zombies?"

Shaking my fists at the sky, I growled. "Oh, yes, much underplayed. And don't you start with the meeple twins. I'm being serious."

James put his hand up. "Okay, sorry. Serious now. But where do we start?"

"At the beginning, McFly. Always at the beginning." Heads nodded. The answer seemed correct. But I realized quickly we didn't know when that was. So I pivoted. "What do we really know? The facts."

We tramped in silence a few feet before Case spoke up. "The murderer is most likely a woman. They know Addie's house and avoided the camera."

"That could be sheer luck," said James. "It's only one camera."

"They had a fit of rage against Addie," offered Beckett. He pawed at his nose, kicked against an exposed root, and stumbled a few paces.

"That hardly narrows it down," Case replied. "Half the

town cursed her name at one point or another."

"They're fit," I said. "I don't know about you, but my quads are starting to burn. They hiked this trail in the dark of night. They probably knew the trail and had been out here before. Else, they might've gotten lost." I pinched my lip, considering the thought further. "They were able to lift Addie, too, and they were able to carry out the murder to begin with. All of it takes strength as well as endurance."

"That rules out Ruth Radford," said Case. "You ever see her on a trail? I've seen her drive from the café to town hall, and that's only a couple blocks. There's no way she hiked up here. She would've hidden the evidence somewhere else."

"So who does that leave?" asked James.

"Of Addie's close associations? Gabby and Madison used to hike with her all the time, and Darlene would join them sometimes. They're all fit, I've observed." Case's grin became puckish. "Though our boy James might've had a better vantage."

James chewed his lips but held his tongue. I didn't know what the reaction meant, nor what Case had implied. But neither mattered. The past was the past, and I needed to keep my thoughts focused for Addie's sake.

"What about Addie's exes?" Beckett asked.

"Not women," Case replied. "You can tell by their pelvic bones."

"Not in town the night of the murder either," said James. "At least, that's what Darlene was saying at the bar the other night." At my quizzical look, he shrugged with a "you never asked" sheepishness.

"Gabby told me the same," I added, after pointedly clearing my throat and ignoring the hypocrisy of my disgruntlement.

After a few moments contemplating what else we knew, I said, "Sera Simmons lied. She doesn't have a strong alibi either."

"I thought you were defending her." Case again. He'd started to breathe hard and fall behind. Heavy shadows fell across his pink cheeks.

"I was. Am." I slowed my pace, threw my hands up. "I don't think she did it, but we can't exclude her, can we? We have no proof that she's innocent." It would've served her better to be honest about why she and Addie had fought on the night of the murder. Her ever-changing story about that, and her theft of Addie's necklace, only hampered disproving her as a suspect.

"Welp, that narrows it. The police have checked Gabby and Madison's alibis. Darlene and Sera's are weak." Case patted Branson's head. "Sorry, old boy."

"There's also Joyce," I said. I couldn't hold my tongue any longer, despite Beckett's presence.

"Wh…what!" He stiffened like he'd jammed his toe into an electrical outlet. His eyes pulled wide.

"Think about it," I returned. "Joyce knows Addie's house, at least well enough to know the porch has a camera. She found the body and admitted to lying to the police about what she saw at the scene."

"To get their attention, she said," Case added.

"Exactly. And she doesn't have a good reason for being

out by the trailhead that night. Beckett, you told me that yourself. The trailhead doesn't go anywhere near the route she'd take home from work." His head bobbled soundlessly. I let it all sink in before continuing. "She's definitely physically capable. You were scared enough of her the other night. That business with the hobbit dagger."

"Sting," Case and Beckett corrected in unison.

"That still leaves motive," said James.

"Joyce is into some, ah, interesting pastimes," said Case. "But yeah, I can't see her randomly snapping." The way he paused to choose his words was odd, and I remembered how Joyce had fancied him years ago. Maybe there'd been more than awkward flirting, yet it wasn't like Case to keep anything a secret. I'd have to ask him to spill the details later.

"I have a theory that revolves around Gresham." Speaking the words aloud made my convictions steadier. "We know he was having an affair with Darlene, but something Gabby said got me thinking. If Darlene and Addie were at odds over Gresham, and he had a wandering eye—"

Case took my meaning. "There could be another woman, someone like Joyce?"

"Yes. The man apparently has a formula. He promises the world and gets his flings' hopes up, wrapping them around his little finger. But it's all a show. He doesn't have any money of his own and will never leave Charlotte."

"But how does that make Joyce—or anyone else—mad at Addie?" James asked. "You said the same before. It seems like Darlene still has the strongest motive. Her shop is going under, and Addie ripped away her hopes of rescue."

I'd given that some thought as well, but it treaded on weak ground. "What if it was a mistake? What if Joyce found out about Gresham's lies and went to confront him, only to track him down at Addie's that night? Maybe Joyce felt like she was being mocked, toyed with by Above the Falls snobbery. She wouldn't take too well to that."

"And so she attacked Addie? We know nothing happened while Gresham was there. It's all on the tape."

"Addie either found out, or perhaps tried to interfere. She can get under anyone's skin. Joyce is upset. She feels betrayed, and Addie turns the screw."

"Turns the screw?" Case snorted. "Your petticoats are showing, Charlie. The nineteenth century wants its metaphor back. It's worn out like the dickens. A tuppence—"

"Got it." I glared him quiet.

"Yeah," James mused. "It's a bit of a stretch. Maybe something's there, but hasn't Joyce been snooping around trying to play detective on her own?"

"Like half the town," said Case. "I could've made a windfall on deerstalkers, if I'd only known."

James laughed. "Who's a dated reference now?"

"That's a point against her," I said, taking the high ground. "Think about it. All her playing at solving the murder is doing one thing: keeping her in the loop with all the gossip. You have to admit, she's been acting a bit unhinged, even for her."

Case couldn't hide his tittering. James turned his face away and studied something off the trail. Even Branson made a noise.

I groaned. "Yes, fully aware of the irony. Thanks."

"I don't think she'd like you accusing her." Beckett's voice came low but firm. He didn't mean it as a threat. He was trying to be a friend to us both.

"I know." I sighed. "Trust me. I'm not pointing a finger lightly." The same sting had jabbed me over the past few days. Ruth had all but accused me, and Gabby had not been far behind. Even Sera and Joyce had called me out for no other crime than being born a Goode.

Beckett stared blankly, sniffled, and gave a slight nod. "Oh, okay."

"It still could be a random stranger," said James. He ducked under a branch that reached over the trail. "That, or a slender man with small feet. Or a woman in town we haven't yet considered."

Case piped up. "Not likely. Random killings are rarer than you think. Plus, they didn't take anything from Addie's house, so why move her? If they were a stranger, they would've fled the scene and hightailed it out of town."

James shook his head. "Doesn't mean the killer's on our list. Maybe someone had a relationship with Addie in secret. If you're going by statistics, the killer's much more likely to be a man, small feet or not. And if Gresham's the key, I'd argue Sera a stronger suspect than Joyce. Do we know if either of those two hooked up with him?"

He turned to me, and I shook my head. I didn't trust Sera's denial but conceded his point. Even if I didn't like it. We lived in Oregon, where trees fell on the roads and a few seconds driving before or after could mean life or death. The likelihood of being crushed by a branch at forty miles an hour was almost nonexistent, but tell that to those it happened to each year. All the same, until Joyce was ruled out, I saw no reason to start hunting for shadows.

As for Sera, we'd have to keep digging.

We trudged on for a few minutes. The air thinned, growing colder as the last warmth of the day fled. My legs passed the burning stage and started to go numb. Sweat took up residence down my back. Shadows caught my eye deeper in the trees. I wasn't about to let fear of a maniac prowling the woods get to me, but all the same, I was glad I wasn't alone.

A cold tension built in the silence between us. Case must've felt it too. "Beckett has small feet," he proclaimed, out of the blue.

Beckett flinched as if struck. He rounded, shocked and defensive. "I was with you all evening! I couldn't have done it!"

"Correction, you were with us," I said, gesturing. "Team Goode. Like Captain Marvel and that puking cat." Had he forgotten we were on a date? I didn't know whether I should be offended, but I let it go either way.

"Hey!" Case chuckled gleefully.

Beckett's face twitched into something of a smirk. He relaxed, though I couldn't tell whether he'd been hurt. Back in high school, kids used to joke about him summoning water demons from the pools near the upper falls. He never denied it. Never once let on that it wasn't a normal thing to do, or something to be embarrassed about. Perhaps I needed to give him a little more credit for his own brand of courage.

"Are we there yet?" droned James. He checked his watch. "I need to get back to the bar before it gets too late."

"It's up just over there," Beckett answered. He hurried his pace as if to prove he was telling the truth, and we labored to keep up.

At a bend in the trail, where the slope of the hill fell away, he pointed. Silently, we piled around and followed the track of his arm. I grew antsy standing still, unable to focus. My limbs wanted to move. Perhaps it was from excitement, but I couldn't shake a sense of warning that crawled through me. Not of danger, but of a boundary being passed. Some next step along the game board of Life.

I sidestepped Case and shuffled closer to the trail's edge. Then I saw it. The trowel lay against a boulder half-covered in moss, about twenty paces down the slope. In the dark of night, the killer must've thrown it without being able to see where it would land. If they'd aimed a foot to either side, the towel would've plummeted farther down the slope and been lost from sight under a sea of leaves and grass.

Dark stains traced along the blade and handle. I swallowed hard and shoved its significance from my thoughts. Shirking away would do Addie little good.

"Wow," Case breathed. He stepped back and squatted onto his haunches. Branson pressed against him, confused as to why we'd stopped but grasping that something was going on above his paygrade.

"Don't touch anything." I checked my phone and tried dialing Dad, but the signal dropped. "Does anyone have reception?"

"On it," said James. He had his phone out too. Raising it high, he strode around until he found a signal. A ringing tone came through the speaker. Vin D'Amato's garbled voice came next. I bit my tongue as James explained the situation.

"We'll look into it," Vin said, once James had finished.

James tried to be polite, but I'd run out of patience. Pulling his arm closer, I shouted into the phone. "Being lazy is not an option, Vin. You can be the hero. Take all the credit yourself. I don't care. But this isn't a joke."

Silence came through the line, and I imagined him fuming like a stomping bull. But when he finally responded, he sounded remarkably human. "Okay."

"Just tell Frank, and get out here." I glanced at the darkening sky. "Bring some floodlights." I didn't know what else to say. Launching into the theories we'd been discussing—Gresham's affairs, Sera's lies, and Joyce's odd behavior—would only derail our credibility. We needed the connection to Addie first, even if it meant hunting Gresham down and yanking it out of him.

CHAPTER 32

Our excitement quickly waned. Unlike in the movies, a cold trowel lying in the dark far out of reach wasn't a smoking gun. It'd be weeks before we found out anything forensically from the murder weapon, if the techies recovered anything at all. And if it was relevant to the case. And if the police decided to share. Big ifs, all around; none were promising.

We stood in a huddle, cold and slightly deflated, knowing the night had just begun. Thankfully, Vin D'Amato took us seriously and soon arrived. We traded a few snide remarks, but none of us had our hearts in it. He squawked into his radio, and I got to hear the strain in my dad's voice followed by an exasperated groan from Frank. The next hour blurred: a trudge back to the trailhead, Frank's arrival along with some pointed questions, and more childish digs from Vin.

After they finally released us, Case and I rushed to Gresham's office only to find it locked and dark. Cursing, I tried Gresham's phone but had no luck. I texted Charlotte, but she hadn't a clue of his whereabouts. Neither did Darlene. We found the florist in her shop, closing up for the day. She'd been released after Gabby refused to press charges, yet the cost of the friendly gesture was already evident. Darlene's whole body slumped like a pudding left to melt in the sun. We exchanged nods with tight-lipped smiles. There wasn't much else to say. Branson yawned mightily, received a giant hug from his owner, and fell asleep before I'd handed over his leash. Exhausted from all the running around, I left the shop with only a vague notion to keep going. To do something. Yet that's where my plan hit the proverbial brick wall.

"What's next?" Case asked, after I'd stared aimlessly at the street for a few minutes. When I had no better answer, he convinced me to make a quick stop at the apartment.

"For supplies," he explained. "We can make a plan and head back out."

Yet the second we arrived home, he headed straight for a frozen pizza. I went the other direction—to my bedroom and a hot shower. My shoulders had twisted into knots, and I wanted to wash away sweat from the trail. That, and a slight stink of fear. Well, apprehension really. At the trailhead, Frank's anger had been palpable. He'd kept his questions professional but didn't hide the acid in his tone. He'd directed us to come into the station in the morning. From his razor-sharp gaze, I planned on wearing a Kevlar vest.

So much for a thankful pat on the back.

Steam coated the glass of the shower door. My neck and back hummed in perfect numbness under the heated spray. Case had been right to suggest regrouping. But as I sluiced off the last of the soap, a muffled rustling came through the bathroom door. Someone had entered my bedroom. They rummaged around, floorboards creaking.

"Case?" I called. I shut off the water. No response came.

It wasn't like Case not to respond, nor would he enter my room without permission. I called out a second time. Crickets answered. By the time I grabbed a towel, my heart raced.

Slowly, I cracked open the door. Geraldine stood at my dresser, swathed in a designer princess coat. A checkered silk scarf popped with color at her neck. She clutched the letter from Miley University. I spotted the opened envelope on the floor as the warmth from the shower drained from my body. My shoulders balled into stone nuggets once more. But I had no one to blame but myself. Wrapped in the towel, I shuffled into the room.

"You scared me," I said, sidestepping Dumbo by instinct. But that'd been my problem all along, hadn't it? Hoping the elephant lodged in my periphery would magically fly away.

"You've had this for days," she said. She waved the letter, and I caught a waft of lilac. Her eyes held firm, but I knew she was wounded from the silence that followed. It was thicker than soup.

"A couple weeks," I admitted, and a realization clicked into place. "But you knew that, didn't you?" Charlotte's friend was going to ensure I got accepted, no matter what the letter said. The woman had to know I'd already been rejected, and that meant Charlotte and Geraldine did too. I should've seen it earlier, but my thoughts had been elsewhere. They'd played along and let me hang myself. My honesty to Geraldine had been a test, and I'd failed.

"You didn't trust me?" She stared at the paper as if willing the ink to dissolve. "I should never have allowed your father to drag you into the station. When you first came home, I thought it was just a little bump in the road. Nothing disgraceful. A boon for us. More time to spend together as a family—you hardly ever visited. Now, I don't know what to think. You seem excited to throw away any chance of happiness."

I pulled the towel tighter. "I wanted to help. For Addie. I couldn't do nothing." No, that wasn't right. That wasn't why. Not fully. "Case and I—"

"Uff!" Geraldine threw her head back. "Always that boy. Head in the clouds, worse than Addie. Board games. Chutes and Ladders, that's a career? I knew he was a bad influence. He has too much of his father in him—a flippant man with flippant ideas. It's landed your poor aunt Jane in who-knows-where California, life draining away, so far from her brother and son." She shook her head. "No, this nonsense has gone on long enough."

"What does that mean?" I folded my arms defensively. Pointing out that Case's dad had run a successful pizza parlor in Harvest Falls for years, had chosen to sell it, and was happy in California would get me nowhere.

Her gaze narrowed. She read something on my face. "Oh, not you too."

I glared back, wanting to explode. "You think I'm throwing my life away? That I always have been? Well, I'm not. I'm just not my mother."

"Your father told you to stay away. No more meddling."

"So, what? I'm supposed to listen to that but ignore everyone else in town? Do you know what they're saying? How little trust there is? I thought I was protecting him. I thought we were on the same side. You want me to listen to you, yet neither of you can answer simple questions. You won't let me in unless it's part of the script I'm meant follow. Dutiful Daughter Barbie, still in its original packaging. Only I'm not your daughter, am I?"

"You're being childish. I can't talk to you when you're childish."

My voice dropped a thousand octaves until I barely recognized it. "Charlotte's buying my grandmother's land, isn't she? Just like she was going to buy Darlene's flower shop for Addie. Gresham is just pushing papers for her. But you didn't want me to know that. Why? What is there to hide? Or did you think I'd never bother to check?"

Geraldine clamped her mouth shut and turned away, but not before I saw the truth on her face. I'd hit the nail on the head. She didn't think I cared. She took me for a frivolous woman, an ornamental pawn she could brag about to the Women's League. A trophy she could pick up and wave about while invoking my mother's legacy.

And the worst part was, I'd let her.

Her hand strayed to her lips. Her head shook in disbelief. All drama. She wanted an apology, for me to chase after her, seeking approval. To fix the problem I caused. But there was no way that was happening. Instead, I went for the can of gasoline.

"Did Marc Newsome kill himself out of guilt?" I demanded. "Why won't Dad tell me anything? Is he hiding something? Is he ashamed?" The force of the words hurt, as did their intent. *Take it back! Take it back!* My gut reacted in terror. But I didn't take back the words. I'd had enough of being coddled.

"What!" Geraldine's expression turned to horror. Her feigned anguish vanished, and she collapsed onto edge of the bed.

"Well, what am I supposed to believe?" I calmed my voice but held it firm. "None of you will talk to me, so all I have is the rumors flying around."

"Oh, what do they know? What would any of them know?" As she gathered herself, I sensed she dug at memories she'd long kept at bay. "Well, if it's what's needed to put you at ease: Marc had a history of depression. He'd seen doctors for years, but all they did was push pill after pill on him. I tried to warn Charlotte those last few months. The signs were there. The dangers of it all. I'd been through the same with my aunt Eloise, when I was young."

"I'm s-sorry." I sat on the bed next to Geraldine. She had never spoken of her aunt to me before. "Tell me about her."

"When I was a little girl, Eloise kept mostly at home. She was taken to long spells of confinement. But I would bring her things from my mother—cakes, magazines, that sort of thing. Sometimes we would read the articles together, when she was in the mood. Often, she wouldn't want me to stay. Her place those days would have this heaviness. It's hard to describe, but I had the sense that if I took one breath too many, the entire house would crumble down around us."

"The health center," I said, regretting that I'd never asked about Eloise before. The relationship clearly meant a great deal to Geraldine, for all her hiding it. "Is that why it's so important to you?"

"In part, I suppose. For Marc and Eloise both. But for the town, as well. It's needed. Something to revitalize its heart." She patted my hand. "Someone has to ensure the whole place doesn't fall to ruin. Your mother and I talked about that all the time. And Charlotte, with her Addie too. You were such a blessing, the next generation. We were going to set things in motion, but you two were going to make it happen."

"As what, puppets?" I said it softly, but it was enough.

She snapped to her feet. "What are you saying? You blame me for your choices? For what happened to Addie? You blame your mother? If we put pressure on you to do the right thing, it was because you needed it."

To get what you wanted! I groaned. Our moment of reconciliation was lost. But we'd taken a small step forward together. That was something, at least.

A floorboard creaked. Case coughed and started pacing outside the bedroom door. It wasn't like him to snoop on my conversations, and I wondered if he'd found Gresham.

Geraldine's gaze tracked mine, furious I hadn't responded to her. "We are meeting for lunch tomorrow. You are expected to be there on time, Charlie Goode," she barked. "Charlotte has gone out of her way to help you, at such a horrible time, and you will not stand her up the way you did me tonight."

Oh, crap. I'd completely forgotten about her dinner invitation to strategize for the lunch meeting. "Sorry, I—" I tried to explain, but she talked over me.

"You will be presentable, and you will make a case for yourself. For your mother's sake, you will not go the rest of your life never having lived up to your potential. She wouldn't have allowed it, and neither will I!"

"That's…" The urge to defend myself withered as the floorboard creaked again. *What harm could a single meal bring?* I wouldn't commit to anything I couldn't undo. Charlotte would understand. As for Geraldine, Dumbo could stick around one more day. It would give me time to organize my argument. To find a compromise that would appease her.

"I'll be there," I said. "I promise." Case and I were close. Another couple hours could make all the difference. If we couldn't find Gresham, we'd go to Frank, spell everything out, and make him listen.

Geraldine looked less than convinced, but she let it slide. As she smoothed her coat, her gaze slid to the Miley letter. It had fallen to the carpet. "Things can't remain as they are," she said. Her eyes held mine as she opened the bedroom door.

"I know." We agreed on that, at least.

She strode out in silence. The apartment door had barely closed behind her before Case crashed into me. He shoved his phone at my face. His eyes bulged. "Beckett texted. It's all going down! The police are there now!"

I pushed the phone aside and snatched him by the shirt. "What? Slow down."

"Joyce broke into Sera Simmons's house. They're hunting for her! They're going to arrest her!"

"Joyce?" Goose bumps danced along my arms. Had we actually solved it?

"No." He gasped, thudding against the wall. "Sera! They're arresting Sera!"

CHAPTER 33

"Arrest Sera? But that makes no sense!" I slapped my forehead. "Unless they don't know about Joyce breaking into the house." Clutching my towel, I snatched up some clothes and retreated into the bathroom. Wet hair clung to the top of my neck. The last of the steam coated the large mirror above the sink, damp droplets streaking down.

Case hollered through the door. "Or they found something at Sera's place. Something bad."

"Frank was there days ago. Why search her house now?" And for what? We'd found the murder weapon. It didn't add up. "Wait," I said, coming back into the bedroom. I'd thrown on jeans and a mostly clean sweater. "Who told Beckett about Joyce breaking in?"

Case shrugged. "You think Joyce planted evidence?"

Blessed stars, that had to be it!

"Absolutely," I agreed. "Planted it, and probably called the police herself. My dad is about to make a huge mistake!"

I grabbed my phone, but he didn't answer. Driving to Sera's house was out of the question. It would only enrage Frank, and I'd likely be in handcuffs before he'd listen to me. I started texting Dad, but my thumbs froze over the screen.

What would I tell him? What did we really know? Suspicions about Joyce? But that didn't prove Sera was innocent. Even if I thought she was, the last thing I wanted to do was be a distraction.

Or the reason Dad's case fell apart.

I sank onto my bed and groaned. Case hovered over me, full of nervous energy. He bit his thumb and started to pace.

"He won't understand." I tossed the phone aside. "We don't have enough solid facts. There are too many open questions to make an accusation."

I drummed my knee. If this were a board game, how would I tackle it? "Let's do the opposites," I ventured. "Besides planting something, why else would Joyce break into Sera's house? And if she didn't make the call, or get caught, how else would the police get involved?"

Case wore treads in the carpet. "They can't be unrelated."

I had to agree. The timing of the police's arrival was too close to be a coincidence. "Maybe Sera found evidence of a break-in and called the police herself?"

"This is Sera," Case reminded. "Sera Simmons. She doesn't call the police."

"Oi, you're right." Sera trusted the police as much as Branson trusted a bathtub.

Case flopped onto the far side of the bed and heaved a sigh. "So we're stuck. We can't prove anything. Sera doesn't trust us, and Joyce won't tell us the truth. We're out of moves. Checkmate."

"Not yet." I sprang up, refusing defeat. "We find Gresham, like we planned. He's the link, the reason Joyce has motive. If we're wrong about their affair, we're wrong about everything. But checking won't do anyone any harm. The knot unravels, and no one gets mud on their face."

"Except for us."

I snorted. "Too late for that." I scooped up the Miley rejection letter, wadded it, and threw it in the wastebasket. It'd be easy to turn in for the night, to click off the lights and forget about solving anything except what I should wear to lunch. Dutiful Daughter Barbie. But screw that. If my family wanted a vapid doll, they should've bought one.

"Get your keys, Elmer," I told Case. "We're hunting wabbits."

Case pulled his Scion to the curb and killed the engine. The night had turned frigid, and I spread a blanket over my legs. It'd been folded on the back seat along with a stash of almonds. I'd forgotten to eat at the apartment and munched the nuts greedily. Case was a great squirrel companion. He had stashes everywhere.

Gresham, we couldn't find. We'd tried his office again to no result. Charlotte still had no idea where he was, though I'd caught a whiff of acidity when she spoke, as if the man's name no longer shone so bright.

After driving around for a time, looping through the streets, we'd parked outside his house. A modest affair for a man full of flash, the single-story Craftsman was all but hidden by a pair of sprawling cherry trees. The house sat as dark as his office. *No luck here.* I started to wonder whether he'd skipped town. But would that mean he was involved, or just scared?

Good Lord, Charlie Goode. How about he's clueless to the whole thing? Probably eating at a restaurant or meeting with another client?

"We can't report him missing," I mused aloud, between crunching almonds. "But there are two of us. We should watch his office as well."

"We're not splitting up." Case eyed the blanket and nuts. "You'd starve, and freeze."

I shrugged deeper under the blanket. Point taken. Splitting up wasn't the best idea, anyway. The later it got, the more confronting Gresham alone sounded like a bad idea. Settling in, I leaned the passenger seat back a few clicks. I'd just brought up a text from James, him checking in on me, when Case broke the silence.

"Can I ask you something?" He stared straight ahead. He sounded a bit hesitant. "Where are you going?"

"What do you mean?"

"Where. Are. You. Going?" He poked my shoulder between each word.

I glanced at the door handle, the still of night outside the window. "I'm not going anywhere."

He clicked his tongue and pointed at me, his hand shaped like a gun. The gleam in his eye couldn't be removed with a jackhammer. "See what I did there?"

"Ugh. Please, not you too." He must've overheard some of my argument with Geraldine. "I'm fine. Nothing to see here. I'm handling it."

He offered a smug grin in response. I didn't blame him for not believing me, but nor did I have the energy to elaborate.

"As a wise snow princess once said, 'Let it go.'" He chuckled at his own wit. "And if you don't like that one, I know decades of other cartoon icons, all with family issues, and I've got all night to quote them."

I grunted and shifted the other way, mumbling something about turning him to ice. But of course he was right. I'd mucked about in the woods long enough, and no amount of guilt would set me free. To truly thrive, I needed to create my own happiness. To blaze my own path.

The irony was deafening. Blazing her own path had been Addie's greatest strength, and look where it had gotten her.

◆ ◆ ◆

Sunlight lit the horizon in a dim glow. The blanket was warm and soft, but my backside ached from sitting too long. I snapped awake, suddenly alert, and glanced about. Case rested his head on his palm. He leaned against the driver's-side door. The windows had fogged up, but I could still see through them. A few birds chirped away. Everything else was still and encased in deep shadows.

"Nothing?" I asked.

Case leveled a weary gaze at me. "There'd better be donuts coming my way. And coffee. Lots of coffee. With sprinkles."

Crud buckets. I studied Gresham's house. Beyond the cherry trees, a slew of giant cedars cast a web of branches that drooped over the side yards. The garden borders verged on wild, like an English cottage's. The windows remained dark. Nothing looked out of place.

"I'm going for a closer look." I threw open the door and instantly regretted it. Biting cold prickled my flesh. My muscles railed against me, refusing to respond. But at least I had no reason to skulk. I strode up the driveway like I owned the place, albeit a little stiff.

Reaching the porch windows, I peered inside. A sitting area held a collection of antique furniture. The room was tidy, and perhaps rarely used. The pieces looked like they came from an upscale boutique. But I knew Gresham's budget wouldn't allow him such a shop. No doubt he'd found them at an estate sale, or elsewhere as cheap, so he could keep up appearances.

I retreated up the drive until Case could see me and made a looping gesture. I'd spotted windows along the side of the house. But snooping along each of those provided nothing of interest either. No signs anyone was home. Nothing disturbed. By the time I returned to the Scion, mud caked my shoes, and spiderwebs clung to my arms. My bladder screamed. It reminded me how long it'd been since I'd given it relief.

"Let's head into town. We can provision up and learn what happened at Sera's last night. Swing by Gresham's office first, though."

"Then a donut?" Case cranked the ignition.

I nodded. "Then a donut."

Barely past sunrise, we turned onto Bywater Street and found Harvest Falls in the sleepy throes of morning. A truck rumbled past. The lights from a few shops glowed, and I checked the time. Too early for Sweet Little Buttercup, but it would open in an hour. I inhaled, imagining the sweet scents spilling from the ovens. I didn't know how Gabby and Madison withstood the temptation, day after day. If I worked in a bakery, I'd be balloon-size within the first week.

Case parked outside Gresham's office building. Focusing on my bladder, I pointed at the doors and launched myself from the car. The lobby had a public restroom. Two birds, one stone.

"Be right back," I hollered. But as I crossed the sidewalk, my Spidey senses tingled. I craned my neck and stared. A light shone in Gresham's office. The higher windows were tinted, but I could make out the soft hue. My head whipped around, and the tingling exploded. Gresham's sports car sat against the curb, farther down the block. He'd parked slightly cock-eyed, like he'd done it in a hurry.

I blew through the front door, bathroom forgotten in the excitement. My legs thundered up the stairs. It wasn't until I reached the reception area that self-preservation tolled in my brain. My pace slowed. I caught my breath. *But Gresham knows me.* He won't find it odd, my showing up at his office in the wee hours. Not once I explained everything.

Unless he was involved. I grabbed a stapler from the admin's desk and hefted its weight. *Idiot, he's not a stack of disorderly papers.* I set it back down. Case's footsteps thumped up the stairs. When he appeared, I gestured for him to remain quiet while I padded to the door leading to Gresham's inner office. Pressing my ear against the cherry-stained wood, I listened.

No sounds came through. I caught Case's eye and raised a knuckle to rap against the door. He snatched the stapler I'd discarded and tucked against the wall, ready to pounce. I punched him in the arm.

"Hello, Gresham?" I called, rapping away.

Crickets. I called out again before trying the doorknob. The door slid open, and my tingling melted into icy sweat. Something was wrong. A tornado had hit the place. Papers were scattered everywhere. Drawers were yanked from the cabinets, the client chairs upended. It was obvious they'd been thrown against the wall. Coffee pooled on the desk from an overturned mug. My gaze tracked to where it dripped to the carpet. Case must've done the same. He yipped and pointed. A shoe peeked out from behind the desk.

Polished leather. Gresham's shoe.

"Hello?" I called again. I didn't know why. Perhaps to avoid the truth. We'd arrived too late, a step too slow to help poor Gresham. *No*, I corrected as I pushed my way closer to the desk. If we'd arrived any earlier, we might be just as dead. The selfish thought tasted bitter, like a mouthful of brussels sprouts dusted in iron.

But I was wrong on both accounts. We hadn't arrived too late or too soon. We'd arrived just in time. Gresham sprawled on his back, his legs and arms at awkward angles. Blood spread from a darkened wound near his temple. His face appeared waxen. He had his eyes closed. But his chest rose and fell with the slightest vibration.

"Holy crap!" If my meddling did nothing else but save Gresham, it'd be well worth the fallout. Dad and Geraldine would have to see the truth in that. I yelled at Case to hold pressure on the wound and call an ambulance. I was already bolting for the door. I'd reach the police station fastest on foot. I just hoped I didn't run into Joyce Townsend along the way.

CHAPTER 34

I burst into the police station, heaving and flushed. My throat cracked as I yelled. Betsy D'Amato's cheery greeting wilted on her tongue. She'd clearly just arrived at work and still wore her coat. Sinking into her chair, she took in my panicked state and clutched her desk. I bent in half, hands on knees.

"Gresham. Hospital. Fix," I wheezed. I really needed to up my cardio.

Vin D'Amato appeared from the rear of the station, a steaming mug in hand. His smirk disappeared as he caught sight of me. A scowl quickly formed in its place.

"What's this about Gresham?" he barked. I managed to spit out what had happened, and the scowl deepened. He set the mug down for his mother. He made no move for the door.

"Where is everyone?" I panted the question.

"In the boiler," Vin replied. That's what he liked to call the interview room at the back of the station. To him, it was tough-guy speak. Yet the table there had seen more birthday cakes than interrogations. "We arrested your friend Sera last night. Detective Nichols and the chief are back with her right now."

"You searched her house? What'd you find?" I straightened

on wobbly legs.

"None of your concern, Little Goode. This is for the real police." The radio on his shoulder squawked a rambling set of codes. He squawked back and hit the door at a jogging pace. I was grateful to see him hustle past, even if he'd hesitated taking my word. The call had to be about Gresham, maybe the EMTs Case had contacted.

The door barely closed before Dad's voice filled the station. Frank's tenor followed, softer, almost a low hum. Both sounded tired. They emerged from the back with glazed eyes and rumpled clothes. They'd been at it all night—searching Sera's house and interrogating her. Dad glanced me over and judged me unharmed before frowning.

"Charlie," he said. My name hung thick in the air, a loaded question seasoned with notes of displeasure.

"Gresham," I replied, confirming what he suspected. I saw it on his face. He'd heard the call come in, the same as Vin. "Case and I went there to—"

He exploded. "I gave you your last warning! If you've interfered in any way…" He slowed and wiped a hand over his eyes. When he spoke again, it was at a lower volume. "You could've been seriously hurt. You—"

"Dad, stop! Listen to me!" There was no turning back. I had to tell them everything and suffer the consequences. "It's Joyce Townsend. Beckett says she snuck into Sera's house last night before you arrived. Whatever you found, it's tainted evidence."

Frank moaned like a moose stuck in a bog. He flipped his notebook into the air. It whirled, smacked onto a desk, and clattered to the floor. He shook his hands at the ceiling and bellowed. "What is it with this town?"

"Besides, we know now it obviously can't be Sera," I continued. Both men glared at me, but I plowed ahead. "I don't think Gresham was attacked that long ago, and if you've had Sera in custody all this time, she couldn't have done it."

"Are you a medical expert yet?" Dad punctuated the inference with a sharp uptick at the end of the question. "And if memory serves, you're no wizard with a clock either."

Ugh, ouch! He was beyond mad to let them rip like that. I stood tall, allowing the attacks to hurt. I deserved them, but it didn't mean I was giving up easily. "You can't ignore me on this. Punish me all you want. For failing you. For failing Mom's grand plans. Lock me up! But don't let the real killer slip away while you're wasting time with Sera. The town will never forgive you."

I won't forgive you.

Dad turned to stone. He'd read my final thought. But rather than shattering, he hardened further. We studied each other in a crippling silence, until I grew dizzy.

Thankfully, Frank's patience ended. "Joyce Townsend? The librarian who reported Addie's car abandoned?"

Dad grunted and gave a nod. I exhaled.

"Well, that makes sense." The way Frank's tone rose and fell, I couldn't tell whether he was being sarcastic. He shared a look with Dad.

"It's your investigation," Dad said, conceding some point but making his position clear.

Frank leaned against one of the desks and spoke to me.

"We found a second hoodie at the Simmons residence. Same logo as the first: Rosie's Tasty Cones. Except this one has blood on it. We've sent it to be processed, but it's not a big leap to what they'll find."

"Addie's blood," I said.

Frank nodded. "An anonymous call came in last night. Told us just where to look, very detailed. It smelled suspicious from the start. Like a setup." He hooked a thumb over his shoulder, as if an imaginary group stood behind him. "Our guys went over that house with a comb. Nothing else to find besides the smoking gun—or hoodie, as it were."

"Joyce," I said, lighting up like a Christmas tree. "She broke in, planted the hoodie, and made the anonymous call. It all fits! She's trying to frame Sera!"

A twinkle of humor came to Frank's face. "Don't get too excited. We still have a long way to go."

"Like motive." Chief Grumpy Pants folded his arms.

My lips pulled wide. "I may have that covered." *Ha!*

As I started to explain about Gresham, and Addie's possible turning of the screw, Dad made a noise—half growl, half wounded bear. "I'll get Vin to pick up Joyce Townsend," he said to Frank. Without a word to me, he marched from the station.

"You have proof of any of this?" Frank asked. He fetched his notepad from the floor and brushed it off.

The question tugged on my sails, but I wouldn't let them go slack. "That's why we went to see Gresham," I admitted.

"Then I hope he pulls through." Frank strode after my dad. Pausing at the door, he spun his head around. "Stick around,

Little Goode. I'll need another statement from you. And keep all this to yourself. I don't need half the town playing along this time." He punched the door open like a gunslinger blowing out of a saloon.

I stepped to follow but knew to stop while I was ahead. Between the paramedics and the police, Gresham was in good hands. Frank and Dad didn't need me stomping around the scene any more than I already had.

My bladder tapped me on the shoulder, reminding me I'd never stopped at the restroom. I gave a friendly nod to Betsy and headed for the rear of the station.

Joyce Townsend. I shook my head as a grin stretched across my face. I'd done it. I'd helped. Dad and Frank could be as mad as they wanted. Geraldine, too, for that matter. Case had had it right. Despite the tragedy of it all, this was the happiest I'd been since returning home.

No, I checked myself. Longer than that. Much longer.

I was washing my hands in the station's single-stall restroom when the grin faded. A nagging question kept rattling through my head. Who told Beckett about Joyce breaking into Sera's house? In the earlier excitement, I'd forgotten about that simple detail. But it blared louder than a trumpet now. Beckett had found the murder weapon. Beckett had inserted himself into the investigation as much as Joyce had. Could he have played Case and me all along? I shook my head. Beckett was no Keyser Söze, no mastermind fooling us usual suspects.

But who else would've known besides Joyce herself?

Another odd thought barreled into me. Joyce Townsend

never worked at Rosie's Tasty Cones. So where did she get the hoodie to plant on Sera? My gut wiggled in discomfort. I texted Beckett and paced the length of the single stall staring at my screen.

If she was framing Sera, why would Joyce tell Beckett about sneaking into her house? She was possibly unhinged, but she wasn't stupid. And why plant something now? If she wanted to set Sera up, she could've done so earlier. She could've done so the night she found Addie. It didn't make sense for Joyce to tell Beckett anything at this point.

Except she had. I stared at my phone. Beckett's affirmation was short; I asked him to elaborate. My gaze locked on the little flashing dots letting me know he was typing a response. When it finally came through, I choked on my own breath.

Joyce told me she went to Sera's looking for proof. She didn't find anything. A couple hours later the police showed up anyway. She says she didn't call them.

I reread the last line, and then again, until the truth sunk in. We'd been wrong. I'd been wrong. Joyce wasn't the killer. She was merely on the hunt, the same as us! My head sank to the counter. Its cool kiss was slightly moist. I ignored the unpleasant significance of that sensation and moaned. How could I be so certain, and yet so blind?

Better question: If Joyce hadn't called the police, who had? Backing up, I considered the whole picture. Frank said the caller knew exactly where to find the hoodie, so they had to be the one who planted it. Gresham was attacked later, sometime after Case and I had last checked his office. His office light hadn't been on then, I was sure of it.

My head jerked up. Gresham attacked. Not robbed. A target. He had to be involved, at least as far as motive, even if he wasn't aware of it himself. And the means had always screamed of overwhelming emotion. Raw fury. Nothing planned. Both attacks reflected that. I eyed myself in the mirror and was encouraged to see a measure of confidence return. Case and I might've been wrong on the who, but we weren't far off on the why. We'd missed only by inches.

I left the restroom and entered the short hallway at the back of the station. Linoleum tiles squeaked under my shoes. A corkboard on the wall was plastered with ordinances and safety posters. I'd have to face the music and let Dad know about Joyce. With any luck, she'd never know how far I'd besmirched her name.

I groaned at the irony. I'd been trying to protect Dad from making the same mistake!

The door to the interview room stood closed. Its eggshell paint was chipped, its little window dusty. I stopped short as I caught a flash of movement within the room.

Bad idea, Charlie. Bad! But someone was framing Sera. When he woke, Gresham would point the finger at whom. An arrest would follow, Dad and Frank would have their glory, and Sera would be cleared. What did it matter if I talked to her now or then?

I ignored the thousand reasons that sprang to mind—my own arrest and disownment chief among them—and turned the knob. I couldn't help myself. Dutiful Daughter Barbie had come out of her packaging. There was no going back in.

CHAPTER 35

Sera's head rose as I slipped into the interview room. She sat on a metal folding chair pushed up against a blank wall. Her feet were propped on the barren table. Her colored hair was a mess. Penguins dotted her stretchy pajama bottoms. A black zip-up jacket had a bee logo from some coffee shop. Her hands were shoved in its front pockets. At least she wasn't in cuffs.

Her face scrunched. "Why are you here, Doc?"

"They wanted to know…um, food?" I plastered a smile on my face, like I was working a bake sale. But I wasn't even fooling myself. I landed on the chair opposite her and planted my palms on the table. "Forget it. There's no time. I need to know some things. It'll help."

Her eyes rolled. "Great, I'm rescued already."

"Trust me or not, but I don't think you're guilty. So here's the deal: I'm not a cop, and if you don't want to tell me why you stole Addie's necklace, or about the fight you two had, that's fine. But you lied about hooking up with Gresham, didn't you?"

I rolled the dice, but the accusation explained why she'd been so adamant about his philandering. Besides, I wanted to catch her off guard.

She shifted, uncertain. "So what if I did? A drunken night. It's embarrassing. Why do you keep on about him, anyway?"

"Let's start with what he promised you. The moon, I'm guessing? To take you away and start a new life?"

She pulled a face. "Total prick move. He came on simple and sweet, all while flashing his watch and car, those ridiculous shoes of his. Like I needed a billboard to know what he was after. He buys me a couple of drinks at Hank's, and I made it easy for him. He's not bad on the eyes." She shrugged. "I have nothing against a good time."

"Did it happen more than once? When was this?"

"About a year ago. Once was enough. We went back to his place. It's done up like Pottery Barn, rustic chic, which looks expensive but isn't. Nothing but cheap crap from an old barn all polished up. I played along like I need him, wowed by his steady control. And he's telling me that he dreams of heading off somewhere, of spending the rest of his days trekking the planet. He can take me away. We can go together."

"What'd you say?"

She snorted. "Whatever I needed to, just to play along. I needed cash. If he wanted to take me away, sure. I said I'd let him. We were both adults."

"But you knew it was a line?"

"The talk, yes. The rest…" She shook her head. "Not until the next morning. I woke before he did and sniffed around a bit. He had ten bucks in his wallet, a single bottle of wine in the cupboard, and no signs of anything more valuable than I'd already received. The dude's as broke as I am."

I relaxed in my chair. My phone buzzed—Case telling me he was heading to Sweet Little Buttercup without me. Donuts called. I spooled up my next move and decided it was best to give a little back.

"Look," I said. "You're being framed, and I'm trying to figure out by whom. I think Gresham promised other women the same things as you, and maybe Addie found out. Maybe she dug a bit too deep. Or maybe the killer came looking for Gresham and trailed him to Addie's place. Either way, it has to point back to him."

Sera sneered. Her eyes flashed with fury. "Oh, I'm being framed, Doc, and I can tell you exactly who's doing it—your dad. This new evidence they happened to find, all based on a bogus call. Give me a break. He's always had it out for me."

"And Detective Nichols too?" I lost it. "He's also determined to ruin your life? He hasn't known you a week!"

"Typical." She folded her arms and glared.

Crap! I bolted to my feet. The door seemed to crush inward and throb, draining the room of air with each pulse. The hallway outside was silent, but I knew time had run out. I had to play all my cards.

"You stole Addie's necklace. That's what the fight was about." I didn't wait for Sera to respond. "You thought she wouldn't notice the thing was missing. Maybe you'd stolen from her before. Small things. Trivial things. But the necklace was special, a gift from her mother. It meant something to her."

Sera sighed, exasperated. "She always had new clothes, new shoes, new jewelry. She had so much she couldn't keep track of it all. She'd try on a shirt and toss it away without even wearing it outside. She gave me things without looking at them—a watch, a pair of sunglasses, more lotion than I could use in a lifetime."

"So you started helping yourself."

Sera nodded. "How was I to know she'd flip out over the necklace?"

"Why not just give it back?"

"I couldn't. Not after..." She studied the table. "When Addie asked, I told her I didn't have it. I don't know why; it just came out. Not a big deal, I thought. But she looked at me with such disdain, like I wasn't anything. Not fit to lick the soil from her shoes. It pissed me off. I couldn't bow down to her after that."

"You kept it even though she suspected you?"

"I thought I'd sell it the next time I was in Portland. She'd never be able to prove anything. What's the harm? No one would know, except for Gabby and Madison."

I flinched. "Wait. Madison knew? She told me she'd never seen it."

Sera's face scrunched. "She knew damn well I had it. We laughed about it, something to hang over Addie's head."

With a slight wobble, I struggled to slot in the new information. "When was this? At the Halloween party, after you took it?"

"No, later. Madison bailed early that night. Had a date or something."

"Then why lie?" My pacing turned frantic. "It wasn't to protect you. If anything, she made things worse for you. She could've said you borrowed it, or at least confirmed you had it before Addie was killed. Either would've helped. Denying everything left you—"

The door banged open. My dad filled the opening, arms akimbo. Traces of red ran up his neck. But his gaze was distant, as if he stared at nothing at all.

"Charlie Goode," he said. "My office." He pivoted on a heel and stormed away before I had a chance to utter a word.

♦ ♦ ♦

I trailed at his heels, a sad puppy who'd lost her stick. The fluorescent lighting buzzed overhead, the only sound besides the clack of our footfalls. But I deserved what was coming. I'd gone too far this time. Was there such a thing as suspect tampering?

As we rounded the end of the hallway, Ruth Radford perked up from where she huddled with Betsy D'Amato. She was flustered, planting her hands on her hips and marching forward at the same time. It made her look like a crazed chicken.

"Chief Goode!" she called.

Dad didn't slow. "It will wait."

Ruth started at his clipped tone. Her eyes widened, jaw worked. "You can't speak to me…I deserve to know what is going on. I…"

She trailed off. He wasn't paying any attention. He waited for me to clear his office door and slammed it shut behind me. Through the glass walls, I watched her chest heave, shoulders rising in outrage. But she came no closer. After a moment to collect herself, she rushed from the station.

Dad gestured for me to sit. He towered over me, arms folded, one hand gripping at his chin. His gaze locked in my direction, but it still had that distant focus, as if I sat a million miles away. He didn't want to connect. Didn't want to see his daughter before him. He was too furious. Too disappointed.

"I was wrong," I said, when he didn't speak. "It's not Joyce. I'm sorry. But—"

"Who now?" he asked. I winced at how defeated his voice sounded.

"Madison," I mumbled. I'd lost the threads I'd had before, but I still wanted to know why she'd lied.

"Great. We checked her alibi. She was at the Coast. Didn't check out of her hotel until after Addie was found. Made it to the café to start her shift the next morning just in time. Gabby said she had to change in the back room."

Ouch. I squirmed in the chair. I had nothing else to add. The game had ended, and I'd lost.

Game. That's what it'd been after all. I wasn't a professional. I didn't know what I was doing. How had I ever thought I was helping? My hands trembled. A rolling tide of sadness bubbled up through my chest. Deep sobs would follow, but I sucked it all back down. I'd let it out later, when I wasn't in the way.

Dad clutched my shoulders, warm and firm. "You're not going to the lunch with Charlotte's Miley friend, are you?"

"Oh, crap!" I smacked myself in the face. "What time is it? No wait—that can't be happening still, right? Isn't Charlotte at the hospital with Gresham?"

"She is. Geraldine is waiting with Charlotte's friend, but

that's not what I meant." He leaned against his desk. "And you know it. Time to confess."

"I…" My throat cracked. My gaze drifted from his face, but I forced it back. He watched me, clever and knowing. *Time to choose, Charlie Goode.* I could either be the woman my family expected, or the one I could live with. I couldn't be both.

"I don't want to go to medical school," I said. "I'm not sure I ever did. When I came home…it was just easier to play along. But really, I was running away from the start, just like I did before." The words floated between us for a moment, and I gripped the chair hard enough I felt the edges gouging my finger.

Dad nodded, letting the words sink in. "You pretended for your mother, when you were younger? And now, for me? For Geraldine and Charlotte?"

"I wanted to make you proud. I couldn't let you down."

"That would never happen."

"But the plan—"

He held up a hand to cut me off. "Let me talk for a moment. I have something to confess, and I best do it now." He glanced away at a picture of the two of us that sat on the corner of his desk. In it, I was still in pigtails, with round sunglasses making me look bug-eyed. "I've had a long and mostly successful career, but no one goes through life without wishing they'd done a few things different."

He took a deep breath, and I caught in his expression something I'd only seen once before: shame. It'd been just after Mom had died, and he'd had to face the town's question as to what had happened, and who'd been at fault.

"Marc Newsome's death had nothing to do with Addie's murder. Nor did the deaths of those prospectors. I know this for a fact. But there is something else. Something I should've told you. You were right about that. I didn't out of...well, embarrassment, I guess." He shrugged sheepishly. "I didn't want you to think any less of me."

"You wanted me to be proud of you?" I offered.

"Sound familiar?" He shook his head. "Anyway, the Newsomes were involved with the land near Buckner's Folly, just like you found out. Marc was trying a Hail Mary to get the legal boundary of the land changed, but there was an old survey document standing in his way. Your mother got ahold of it through one of her Women's League friends and burned it."

I shot upright. "She destroyed it?"

His lips pulled tight. "When she told me, I didn't know what to say. She was trying to help Charlotte, of course. She argued that the land was just sitting there anyway, being no use to anyone. But that didn't make her actions right. They didn't even make a difference in the end. The Hail Mary failed. Still, I looked the other way. I convinced myself I had to for our family, and maybe I was right about that, but I've regretted it ever since. Sometimes, it hangs over me like a cloud, tarnishing everything good thing I've done."

I leaped into his arms and squeezed. He'd faced all the town's doubts, all the challenges to his integrity, knowing deep down he'd earned their mistrust. The hurt oozed out of him, a weight and pressure I understood. I'd carried my own lie, for the sake of the family. It'd done neither of us any good, in the long run.

"I should have been honest with you," he said.

I pulled back and considered that. "It actually helped that you weren't. In an odd way, it gave me the strength to finally be honest with myself."

"I'm sorry, sweet—" He cleared his throat. "I'm sorry you couldn't tell me about what you've been going through. I haven't been there for you lately. That needs to change."

"I'm a Goode. I compartmentalized."

He chuckled, and the tension broke. "We'll talk more later."

"Yeah, just the two of us?"

He nodded. "I'll have time. Ruth's probably drafting my termination notice as we speak. I'd better go see what she wanted."

"This mean I'm off the hook regarding Sera?"

"Nope. Not at all. But you still have to tell Geraldine about your decision. Let's call that even for now." He winked and strode for the door. "By the way, Frank's got someone posted with Gresham. We'll find out what happened as soon as he wakes. But there might be something to Joyce Townsend's involvement." He hollered over his shoulder as he crossed the station. "We can't find her anywhere."

CHAPTER 36

I tried Case. I had to let him in on the bad news regarding Joyce. Or maybe it was good news. He was tight with Beckett, who was clearly tight with Joyce. Her being innocent of murder would certainly make things less awkward. Case didn't respond, so I tried Beckett next. Maybe he was with Joyce somewhere, probably plotting their next investigative move with a giant map and little painted figures. But I got no answer there either.

Chuckling at the memory of those thorny green monsters, I slumped back into the chair in my dad's office. Some old photos sat in frames on his desk. One caught my eye, the same he'd studied minutes earlier. The two of us Goodes were dressed for a summer hike, me with my enormous sunglasses. I knew it and the others by heart. They hadn't changed since I was six, as if he wanted to preserve the memory of what our lives had been before that year.

Tapping my phone, I brought up Geraldine's number. Time to face the music.

Tick, tick, tick. My hand wavered, and my phone clattered to the desk. The timing of things. That had to be significant.

I imagined a giant game board, made it a clear picture in my head. The board displayed the town, Above the Falls and

Below, with all the details in between. Then I rotated it and saw myself, and Joyce, and Sera as the other players. And everything clicked into place. A series of moves, not in isolation, but made to counter and maneuver.

The lies. The feints. A trap. Some planned. Some only reactions.

A couple hours later the police showed up anyway. Not an hour, but a couple.

Joyce hadn't framed Sera. No one had. The frame-up had been for Joyce. A beautiful snare. It'd only needed a dupe to trigger it, a real rube—enter me.

Two frenemies, one stroke.

But then, why had Joyce broken into Sera's at all? My hands shook as I snatched my phone and sprang from the office. Little figures—some painted like elegant Victorian ladies, others like dockside wenches—swirled and danced across my imaged board as I retreated to the beginning. The start of it all. The night Addie was killed.

There had to be a trick, a missing move hidden in plain sight.

Voices broke my concentration. Helen Tait had come to conspire with Betsy D'Amato. The pair leaned on the front counter, the one woman griping about frozen mushrooms, the other praising the forecast for a break in the rain. Helen eyed me suspiciously as I came closer.

"I'm off the clock," I said, attempting to hurry past.

She sneered and made a noise like a coughing wombat. "But I have a complaint! I've almost just been killed!"

I stopped short at that and glanced the woman over. Not a

speck of dirt was on her clothes, nor a strand of purplish hair out of place. But the appraisal triggered a memory from the day before, what seemed like eons ago.

Oh, crap! Crippity, crippity, crap! I felt the blood drain from my face to pool heavily at my feet.

"Did you say you saw Madeline on Sunday night? Madeline Parker?" I demanded. I'd overheard her say exactly that to Case, I was sure of it. It hadn't registered as important then, just the nattering of a confused old woman. And I'd completely missed the connection.

She chomped her gums. "Yes! And that daughter of hers is a pea from the pod. She ran me down not twenty minutes ago, squealing away from the Buttertramp Café!"

"What?" I grasped the counter for balance.

Helen relished the attention, as Betsy gasped. "The place is closed too. Lights off and everything. They run out of beans, or what?" She made a sourpuss expression. "Figures. No one has any sense these days. No one wants to work."

"Where did you see Madeline?" I demanded.

"I told you, the café."

"No, not Madison. Madeline!" I resisted the urge to shake Helen until the answer fell out. "On Sunday night. This is very important."

"Oh, Madeline?" Helen looked at me like I was crazy, and probably had the right of it. "She's been dead for fifteen years."

"I know!" Madison's mother passed a few years after my own. She'd been a source of town gossip, always stirring up trouble at the bars. My dad had spent a few late nights sorting out her messes, and I remembered her clearly. She and

Madison could've been twins.

I scoured my phone. No response yet from Case. The last text he'd sent said he was headed for the café. About twenty minutes ago. Freaking donuts!

I put up a finger, silencing Helen.

"Get the chief," I told Betsy. *And tell him what?* That Helen Tait saw a dead woman? That Gabby might've closed up early? I needed better proof than that. I wouldn't send Dad on another wild goose chase.

"No." I changed course. "Call Geraldine, please. Tell her I won't make lunch!" I yelled the last as I bolted through the station door.

CHAPTER 37

As I sprinted the short blocks across town, my feet barely kissed the pavement. A sunlit morning free of clouds had arrived while I was in the station. It warmed the sky, one last gasp before the winter chill set in for good. A great day for a hike, or a picnic. Not so much for accusing one friend of murdering another.

I mis-stepped and bounced off a brick wall. *Don't think about that!* Slowing to a walk, I rubbed at my bruised shoulder. I had one more block to go. Daisies from outside Darlene's flower shop fragranced the air, sweet and earthy. A few cars parked along the street, but the sidewalks were clear. Not a peep to be heard, only the falls spoiling the hush.

Sweet Little Buttercup was dark, just like Helen had said. The "Closed" sign hung in the window. My heart thudded, but if Madison had already fled, what did I have to fear? *Best not to think about that either!* I pushed on the door, and it swung open. The little bell chimed, shrieking like an alarm. I straddled the entrance, one foot holding the door ajar, and called out.

"Hello?"

Nothing but silence. The tables were cleared, the floors clean. No chairs were overturned or glass broken. I braved a few paces, edging toward the counter. A half-filled coffeepot sat atop the display case. A pair of dirty mugs sat next to the register. Gabby wouldn't have left them like that for all the Gummiberry Juice in the world. But was it enough evidence to warrant calling the police? My hand wavered over my phone. I needed a sanity check. I punched a few buttons, and James's soothing voice answered.

"Hey there, Honey Bear. I've been thinking about you—"

"I'm at the café. Case isn't answering. It's closed, and Madison—"

"Whoa, Charlie. Slow down! What are you talking about?"

Clattering sounded from the kitchen. A pot toppling? A spoon clanking against a pan? Or a knife? My heart pummeled my throat with gusto.

"Charlie?"

Phone forgotten, I crept toward the kitchen door. Its darkened plexiglass window told me the lights beyond were off. I hoped that meant some rat had come looking for food, or perhaps to whip up a Michelin-starred stew.

The clattering sounded again. A bowl being kicked across the floor? Cracking the door, I slipped my hand through, held my breath, and flipped on the lights.

Three voices squealed in unison. Case, Gabby, and Joyce, bound hand and foot with kitchen twine and gagged with dishrags, squirmed against the sudden brightness. My phone slipped, cracked against the counter, and skittered away.

The kitchen hadn't been cleaned since the morning's baking. Flour dusted the surfaces. Batter-crusted bowls sat in stacks. Blueberry muffins perched on a central island near racks of maple scones set out to cool. The only other exit, the door to the back alley, was blocked by a large trash can half-full of recyclables.

Lurching into motion, I tripped over a pot and stumbled into Case. He looked unharmed, if not a little panicked.

"It's not Joyce!" he gasped, as I yanked off his gag.

"I know!" I shook his shoulders. "Madison worked at Rosie's Tasty Cones!"

"Mad—what?"

I struggled to free his wrists. The knots were insane. "She worked at Rosie's, remember? For a hot minute, until Helen Tait claimed she hadn't cleaned the scoop properly. Madison told Helen where to shove it and was fired on the spot." He stared blankly at me, as if I were insane. "It means she has a Rosie's sweatshirt!"

I rested back on my heels and sighed. "Or at least she had one years ago. It's not that convincing, now that I say it out loud. Anyway, I started piecing it together when I imagined her position on the board."

"Ha!" Case barked. "I knew that was your sleuthing hobby! But anyway, I guess we don't need the sweatshirt now." He held up his still-bound hands. "She kind of outed herself."

Gabby screamed through her gag, toppling from the strain. Her eyes lit up in dismay.

"Oh, sorry." I reached over, pulled her upright, and removed her gag.

"I solved it!" She beamed, gasping and thrusting out her chest.

Case made a noise. "Running blindly into the killer is called being a victim."

Gabby's face contorted. Even her ponytail looked in disarray. "She was on my radar." Turning to me, she asked with a bit of vinegar, "How did you solve it, then? Some tip from that detective, I bet. Insider information is cheating."

"A confused Helen Tait," I replied, feeling my chest puff a little in return. "She thought she saw Madeline Parker the night Addie was killed."

Case whistled. "And Madison looks just like her mother."

"Not only that," I said, "Helen saw Madison tear out of the café a little while ago, and the place has been dark since."

"We heard her race off," said Case. "She already had Joyce and Gabby tied up by the time I came in. She threatened to kill them if I didn't do what she asked. She's totally lost it!"

"But you thought it was Joyce," said Gabby, pouting. "Beckett told me as much."

I shook my head, regarded Joyce, and pulled her gag out too. Her eyes narrowed, lines pulled tight.

"No. I mean, yes. For a bit. Sorry," I stammered. "It was a total frame job. I just had its target wrong. I thought Joyce was framing Sera, but it was Madison framing Joyce." I spun to Case. "Think about it. The timing never worked. The police found the sweatshirt right where the caller said it was. But that was hours after Joyce left, and she told Beckett she didn't find anything."

"I didn't," Joyce confirmed, justifiably miffed. "And I only broke into Sera's to prove her innocent, for the record. I mean, someone had to."

I let her insanity slide and stayed aboard my own crazy

train. "I bet Madison didn't just stumble across you this morning either. She wanted to…" What? Complete the frame job? I struggled to see how. And why at the café?

Joyce nodded. "She told me she knew something about the murder. She knew I'd been looking into it and asked to meet me here. But when I showed up, she pulled a knife and ordered me into the kitchen. The place was empty after the morning rush. If Case hadn't come looking for a donut…" She shivered and trailed off.

"I really need to get cameras installed," Gabby wailed. "My hubby is totally fired!"

"Best not dwell on ifs," I said. I'd heard Dad say that before. It seemed more than appropriate now. If Madison had lured Joyce to the café, she'd planned on doing more than knocking the woman unconscious. But I wasn't about to say that out loud.

"So the police find the Rosie's sweatshirt with Addie's blood on it, and we all point the finger at Joyce?" Case asked. "Because we know she broke into Sera's before they arrived?"

"I was investigating." Joyce spat the words.

"Exactly." My gut twinged in alarm. My gaze drifted to the blocked alley door.

"But how did Madison know Joyce had broken into Sera's, and how did she know we thought Joyce was Addie's killer?"

"Witchcraft, obviously," Joyce answered.

Case's binds weren't loosening, and my increasing unease wasn't helping my concentration. My fingers twitched. My palms became moist. Why had Madison tied Joyce up before Case arrived? It didn't make sense. Had she suddenly lost her nerve? I cast about for something sharp and found a long butcher's knife.

The blade would've been perfect to cut the twine. But unfortunately, it gleamed in Madison's hand. She slouched in the kitchen doorway, eyes wild and lips smirking. The black jogging suit and trucker hat she wore made her nondescript, just another shadow in the background. They hid her athletic frame and caramel-colored locks. I gasped, as Case and Gabby shrieked. Joyce groaned and knocked her head back against the wall.

"I watched Joyce sneak in and out of Sera's house, if you want to know," Madison said. "I knew you thought she was guilty. Blame Beckett for that. He was so eager to be involved. So eager to spill every bit of gossip to me. I'd been following her, waiting for an opportunity to enact my little plan."

I slapped my forehead. "You came back. Ugh, of course you came back. You made sure Helen Tait saw you peel out of here on purpose, as an alibi. You almost ran her down. Then, what? You parked and circled back on foot? That's why you tied Joyce and Gabby up to begin with; you wanted the police to keep thinking Joyce had done it all. That you couldn't have. Addie, Gresham, and then a final crime gone wrong—with Gabby taking down her supposed killer. That's quite the spree."

Madison's manic tittering was all the confirmation I needed that I was right.

"Fooling the police was easy enough, especially with you and the other cows trampling through their investigation. Thanks for that, by the way. Now, I just needed to set the stage one last time to seal the deal." Madison waved the knife about the kitchen. "Gabby would've put up a valiant fight, Joyce a frantic attack. The police would've found them both in here, all wrapped up with a bow. Any evidence of my involvement would've been easily explained: I worked here, cut myself prepping food all the time. Left fingerprints and hair. The lot."

"But we're friends." Gabby had turned ashen.

"Sorry Case and I spoiled the party." I tried to keep my voice firm. My eyes roamed the kitchen for a weapon and caught sight of my phone lying next to the sink. So far away, so close to certain death. Bugger.

Madison's face lit up like a wicked jack-o'-lantern. "Oh, I have room for plus-ones, Doc. Always room for Little Goode." Raising the knife, she stalked forward.

CHAPTER 38

Doc. Well, at least now I knew who'd poisoned Sera's ear, and probably egged Vin D'Amato on as well. But my ego aside, I had to keep her talking. Delay and evade. It was our only hope to survive. I backed against a pair of oversize refrigerators. *Think, Charlie, think!*

"Did you know about Darlene and Gresham's affair? Did Addie? Is that why she had it out for Darlene?" My hands groped behind me for anything I could use but came up empty. My gaze darted to the door to the back alley, judging the time it would take to clear the way and what would happen if Madison chased me. Or if she *didn't*. Neither of those options was stellar.

A pile of dirty utensils sat on the counter above Case. But he'd turned into a opossum. I wasn't sure he was breathing. Joyce flared her eyes and jerked her head. But what she meant by the gesture, I had no clue.

Madison stopped, hovering over a squirming Gabby. "Everyone knew about those two. But Addie didn't care. She laughed, thought it served her mother right for slumming it with a man like Gresham. So beneath them, the great Above the Falls Newsomes. No, that was one of my little fibs. Addie didn't have it out for Darlene. She didn't think about Darlene at all."

"And you? You didn't care about hurting Darlene?"

"I didn't want—" Madison's expression hardened.

"The flower shop," I said. "You thought he was buying Darlene's place with his own money? Choosing her over you?"

"No! I knew he didn't have money. I'm not a fool. Oh, he promised to take me away. Kept saying we'd live on a warm beach someday. But I never believed that. I knew it was a fantasy."

"But it was your fantasy." I thought I understood that.

Madison shook her head. "A worthless dream from a clown of a man, but it was the only thing I had." A titter escaped her lips. "The prime of my life is gone. All I do is wake up, head to the café, force on a plastic smile, and go home. Life is meant to be better! I thought something would come along, if I was patient. Something I'd stumble into. A better job. A family. An opportunity. But it hasn't, and all my dreams have disappeared. You have to know what that's like—years wasted! And for what?"

"Oh, boo-fucking-hoo," muttered Joyce. Gabby squeaked in shock. Madison whirled. She slammed her fist against the island counter. Muffins and scones jumped, a few spilling to the floor.

I stretched for the pile of utensils, shuffling a cautious step forward. I thought I saw a paring knife among them.

"Don't!" Madison whipped the butcher's knife my direction, and I clunked back into the refrigerators.

"But why kill Addie?" asked Case, suddenly returning to

life. "Why not Gresham? Why kill anyone at all?" The question cut through the kitchen, freezing us all. Precious seconds continued to tick by. I exhaled, never wanting to hug my cousin so much. It was an added bonus that I thought I'd figured out the answer.

"Because she didn't mean to kill anyone," I replied. "But Addie was Addie. She mocked everything, and everyone, that wasn't her." My gaze locked onto Madison's. "She pushed you and wouldn't let go. That's right, isn't it? And what stung worse that night is that you weren't even supposed to be there."

Gabby perked up. "She was supposed to be at the Coast with Gresham! I knew it!"

Madison's brow pulled tight. "I'd already checked into the hotel on Friday, but he canceled at the last minute. He did that a lot, but this was meant to be special. Our first long weekend away from Harvest Falls. I spent it alone, stewing. By Sunday, he'd stopped responding to my texts, so I came back early. It was dark when I reached town, but I had to find him. Had to confront him for abandoning me. I spotted his car leaving his office and followed it to Addie's house. She answered the door and put on her fake smile."

Her gaze drifted, remembering. "The excitement on her face, the way he kissed her cheek, the way she hugged him back…they were so happy. He was so proud just to be near her. I felt so small and insignificant."

"They left you in the cold," I prompted, holding my breath she'd continue.

"I drove into the woods and parked. I needed some air, some time to think. But my feet kept forcing me back the way

I'd come, and I found myself at Addie's house again. Higher up the street, staring down at her backyard. Staring in through the windows at her perfect life."

"You never saw Sera?" Case asked.

"I wish I had. I might've talked to her instead of…" Madison swallowed. "I tapped on the back door and confronted Addie. Just nonsense. Stupid accusations about her stealing my weekend, of plotting against me." Her body stiffened. "She could've let it go, could've tried to console me—we were supposed to be friends. But she laughed! Just laughed…she found my life one big joke. So I shoved her, and a switch flipped in us both. Suddenly, she was screaming that I was scum, that I was a leech, a parasite who fed off her. How I didn't deserve to grace her shadow. The trowel was sitting there on a stone bench. Left out by a careless gardener. I don't know when I picked it up; it just appeared in my hand."

Joyce made a face. She opened her mouth, but I shook her off. "You moved her to confuse the police. That was clever."

Madison smirked, gave a small grunt of gratitude. "My car was too far away. Surely, I'd be seen running from the house, leaving a trail of evidence. I saw her Audi and remembered the porch camera. I thought if I hunkered in the seat, maybe they'd believe she'd gone out and ran into trouble along the highway. A trailhead at night—who knows who passed through? I knew it wouldn't fool them forever, but I only needed to sow doubt. Muddle the evidence."

"You chucked the trowel along the trail, working your way back to your own car." The trails crossed a network of forest roads. I was certain one of them connected, even if I couldn't picture it. "It almost worked, you know. Except for the scene left at the house. Too bad for you rain didn't wash that away before they found it."

"It was good enough!" cried Madison. "Enough to delay your daddy. To confuse the timing of things."

The phrase unlocked something in my thoughts. "The timing, ugh! We should've known, should've considered the possibility!" I threw my hands toward Case, in disgust. "She drove back to the Coast and made sure to be seen there in the morning." The trip would've only taken a couple of hours. It gave her plenty of time to arrive in the dark, wait to check out, and return once more to Harvest Falls. How had we not considered that? I wondered if my dad or Frank had; I'd have to ask them later…assuming there was a later.

"Men are so simple." Madison traced her fingers along the knife's edge. "I only had to lean over the front desk and smile a little, and I knew the guy at the hotel would remember when I checked out. To him, I'd been there all weekend. I had plenty of receipts to prove it too."

"But Helen Tait saw you driving in town," I pointed out. "It must've been when you were tailing Gresham. She was at The Oak Grove later, whining away."

Madison jerked in surprise. "She didn't."

"She did," I replied. "The police know it too." My voice strained at the half truth. I hoped Betsy D'Amato had paid attention, had told Dad or Frank, or even Vin, about what Helen had said. The questions I'd asked. Perhaps they'd be searching for us now.

"The police don't know anything," Joyce declared. "They

have Sera in custody. They don't care about the truth."

"That's not...that's..." I stammered, furious. I should've left the woman's gag in place. Was she trying to get us killed? Madison scraped the tip of the knife along the counter. The metallic scratching made my knees wobble, my neck pinch. I clamped my mouth shut.

"Doc, Doc, Doc." Madison shook her head in mock pity. "Joyce is right. You will never understand this town. How easy it was to throw everyone off the scent. A few lies, a gentle nudge, and the town was eating from my hand. And do you know why?"

"Because everyone hated Addie," said Joyce.

"Because everyone wants to believe the worst of their friends," corrected Madison. "Everyone relishes in the drama. How gleeful you all were to point fingers at one another, to pull out dark secrets and splay them in the open. Because the truth is your lives have little meaning. You're all stuck here, spinning your wheels, and going nowhere. The same as me."

"That's..." I shook my head, snorting with laughter. "That's pathetic." Madison's gaze turned to steel, but I wasn't done. I'd picked up on something, another loose thread. Switching strategies, I went for the proverbial jugular. "Really, you are Addie's equal, looking down your nose at us the way she did at you. Did you care about Gresham, at all? Or did you only use him from the start?"

Case squirmed. "Come on, Charlie."

"If I did, it was only fair." Madison spat, defensively. "First it was the drama with Darlene. Then he was so sad about his little Addie. He had no time for me anymore. He deserved what he got."

"Joyce, Gabby, Case, me—that's an awful lot of bodies." I rolled onto the balls of my feet, ready to spring. "And for nothing. The police are on to you. You've made too many mistakes. No one will believe it was Joyce."

"Yes, they will!" screamed Madison. "She was seen at his office! I made sure to spread word of that!"

Time for the hammer. "But what will Gresham say, when he wakes?" I asked. "He won't back your story. The truth will all come out then; it's only a matter of time."

Madison's face drained of color. "You're lying."

"You didn't know he survived," I said, convinced I had it right. "That's why you went ahead with your plan to frame Joyce. But Case and I got to him in time. Another witness left behind." I shrugged, sheepishly. "Oops." Thank Jupiter we'd been searching for him.

Madison's cold fury ripped through the kitchen. No one moved. No one spoke. No one dared. The buzz of the refrigerators rattled against the walls.

"I did it!" Gabby broke first, bursting into sobs. "I cheated! I had an affair with Gresham too!" Her shoulders shook. Tears streamed down her cheeks. "I can't believe I held that in for so long. It's given me wrinkles."

Snarling, Madison surged toward me. As she charged, a soft ringing reached my ears. One door closing, another opening. Lunging forward, I snatched a tray and pelted her with scones.

"Feast on my Valkyrie ass!" I bellowed. She raised an arm to shield herself as I continued my maple-glazed onslaught. But she didn't slow. The knife lashed out, blindly slicing the air. I leaped aside and tumbled over Case. Gabby squeaked. Joyce growled. I scrambled upright, knocking everything I could off the countertop. It rained whisks and spoons. Bowls clattered and spun.

"Run!" Case hollered. He rolled onto his back and tucked his knees to his chin. As Madison stumbled closer, he drove his feet into her gut, knocking her back.

The distance between us spread. I could make the kitchen door, maybe even the back alley door. Clear it and get out. I could do as my cousin bade. But I wouldn't. We'd win as a team, or we'd...*Stop thinking, Charlie! Act!*

I grabbed a metal cooking sheet and a pair of tongs. My breath came in labored pants. In the background, a heavy tread of boots scuffed.

"Give it up, Madison!" I cried. "It's over!"

She jerked to a halt and swayed, punch-drunk, as if my words had struck her. Her gaze rolled over me, eyes blinking, before settling on the kitchen door. Then the fight drained from her. The butcher's knife fell from her fingers, and she raised her hands.

"Magic," said Case. His jaw went slack in awe.

"Police," said Detective Frank Nichols. He rushed through the kitchen door with his service revolver drawn. His gaze swept over the scene and locked onto Madison. Vin D'Amato stalked at his heels. I'd never been so happy to see Vin. If I thought he wouldn't lord it over me until the end of days, I'd have kissed him.

CHAPTER 39

Rain cascaded down in sheets. Rivulets streamed over the sidewalk and filled the gutters. Even the rush of the falls couldn't be heard. I buried myself into James's warmth, tucked underneath the shelter of his height. We scrambled the last block, splashing through puddles and giggling like schoolchildren.

"Here we are, the Pit of Despair," he said, once we'd reached the safety of the police station's front canopy. He pulled down his jacket hood and ran a hand through his hair. Water puddled beneath us both.

I stared at his dimples and the soft lips in between. "I'm so glad I called you," I repeated for the thousandth time. A week had passed, but Madison's arrest still dominated the town psyche. "I owe you. We all do. Dad should give you a medal. There should be a parade, a statue—"

"He should be giving you a medal, instead of this." James waved at the station door.

"Believe me, I deserve what I'm getting. Probably more." I sighed. "I guess I'll be out in five to ten."

"Minutes or hours?"

"Depends on the chief." I shrugged. "I serve at his will.

Literally. But one last thing…" I wrapped my arms around James's neck and pulled him close. He leaned into the kiss, and we held it until I could no longer hear the rain.

"Wait for me?" I begged, once we'd parted.

His face scrunched. "Don't know, we'll see. The clink can change a person. I got to keep my options open. Lots of fish in the sea, and all that."

I nudged him, laughing. "As you wish. I'll be here either way."

He leaned in for a final peck before I turned to face the music. After Madison's arrest, Dad and Frank had needed to re-interview everyone involved, and it'd taken them a few days to get the paperwork in order. But afterward, Dad had turned his eye to the group of us who'd been most active in…let's say alternative investigation techniques.

"Charlie!" Betsy's face beamed as I shoved through the station door. Her greeting caught Dad's attention, and he waved me into his office.

"Chief," I said, giving him a short nod. But he jumped from his desk and squeezed me in a smothering embrace.

"Just got off the phone with Charlotte," he said, perching on the edge of his desk. "They released Gresham from the hospital. He's made a full recovery. He wants to thank you too. You and Case. Maybe you can swing by a little later?"

"That mean I'm off the hook?" I feigned a clownish grin.

"No. But I'm proud of you. You stuck to your convictions, even when I told you not to. That showed a lot of strength."

"Proud enough to tell me why Madison attacked Gresham to begin with? Was it all to set up Joyce?"

"You're like a dog with a bone." He rubbed at his forehead. "Madison knew Gresham didn't have his own money, but she still believed he had enough for her to run away. She thought he owed her that much. But, of course, he refused. He had no idea Madison had killed Addie, and when she told him, he threatened to turn her in."

"But why confess to Gresham? No one was looking at her."

Dad's eyebrow rose, but he let the comment go. "She panicked when Beckett found the murder weapon. Up until then, she thought she'd gotten away with it. She'd kept that sweatshirt in her car to use as a rag and used it the night of the murder to clean up after she hiked through the woods."

"She should've gotten rid of it."

"She was going to destroy it, but when she heard we were looking at Sera, she kept it just in case. She says to protect her friend, but I'm not sold on that. To me, she was always looking to hang Addie's death on someone else." He folded his arms. "Anyway, she had it ready when she saw the opportunity to frame Joyce."

"The joke would be on her, though, right?" I asked. "Her trace DNA all over the sweatshirt, along with Addie's. None of Joyce's."

He snorted. "So you were paying attention, watching all those crime shows?"

I studied my hands as heat rushed to my cheeks. I still couldn't believe Madison thought she could get away with so much. Maybe she really thought Dad that incompetent. But at least Harvest Falls stood behind him now. I'd watched more than one person congratulate him on a job well done. Even Helen Tait had grunted a kind word. That was something.

I wanted the praise to go his way too. His and Frank's. They'd done their jobs, protected the town, and made the arrest. I'd never wanted anything but to help. Discovering I really enjoyed the work was just sprinkles on the donut. And a big freaking donut, it was.

"Has Geraldine cooled off?" I asked. We'd come to an agreement. I'd pursue my own dreams, whatever they may be, but promised to help her continue my mother's plans. One sticking point remained, and it was a doozy: What to do with my grandmother's land? I'd decided to keep it for now, and she'd decided that was rather selfish of me. We hadn't spoken since.

Charlotte had been accommodating, but I could sense I'd ruffled her feathers. I wondered how long ago my mother had promised her the land, and how much she had riding on obtaining it. I'd have to pry that out of her, once things settled with Gresham.

"We'll get Geraldine onboard," Dad said. "And I'll support you no matter what."

"I know." The reassurance made me smile. I'd held on to my parent's expectations for so long they'd crippled me. But I'd been wrong. I'd never make them ashamed, as long as I lived my life with conviction.

He stood. "It's time to pay the piper." He ushered me out of his office and to the back hallway. I spiraled through joy, pride, and satisfaction as I marched along. I'd done a thing, a real thing.

One last question flitted through my head as we reached the iron door of the station's small holding cell. "How did those prospectors die? You know, the ones involved with Marc Newsome."

"Accident." Dad's hand paused on the door. "Land slipped, and they fell. The state police made the determination. None of us yokels were involved."

I chewed my gums. "But there's nothing in the papers. That would've been big news at the time, right?"

"Your mother had friends. Same with Charlotte. One of them must've asked the paper not to print anything."

And they complied, just like that?

"Huh," I grunted, noncommittally.

"Remember, lunch tomorrow. Just us. I'll see you're out in time."

Dad pulled the heavy door open. He struggled to keep the grin from his face as a chorus of protests erupted. Ruth, Gabby, Darlene, Joyce, Beckett, and Case were already crammed into the cell's tight space. Only James had gotten a pass, since we'd only dragged him along unwittingly—that and the fact that he'd saved some of our lives by actually calling the police in a timely manner. I pressed inside and found a spot next to Case on a long wooden bench.

"Chief," hollered Ruth. "You can't get away with this. I am a pillar—"

The door clanked shut, cutting her off, though I noted it didn't lock. Legally, we were here voluntarily and not being detained. That Dad failed to mention that to the others was our little secret.

"Is your dad really going to arrest us?" Joyce asked. She sounded halfway between pleased and enraged.

"He's just giving us time to reflect on how we might've acted differently," I replied.

Ruth scoffed. "Well, I shouldn't be here. I did nothing but help!"

"I knew from the start Madison had too much to hide," said Gabby. "I mean, I pegged her as guilty at one point, for sure, and my intuition is never wrong about these things."

Darlene chuckled and muttered something under her breath.

"We could've solved it faster if we'd worked together," said Beckett. He sniffed. His head bobbled. "We got in each other's way. That was the problem."

"We should form a club," said Ruth. "I'll volunteer my time to lead it."

"Ooh, we should totally form a club." Gabby bounced with excitement.

"I'm in, sounds fun," said Case. "What do you think, Charlie?"

"I think you're all missing the chief's point," I replied. "You should leave sleuthing to the professionals." Leaning against the stone wall of the cell, I hid the grin spreading across my lips. It was easy to be smug. My application to the academy was already being processed. It took all my willpower not to pull out my phone and check its status.

Come summer, things were definitely going to change.

Thank you for reading! Find more about Harvest Falls and other works by Craig Comer at: www.craigcomer.com!

ACKNOWLEDGEMENTS

First off, thank you readers for finding my book and giving it a try. I hope you enjoyed the mystery and all of Harvest Falls' antics. I certainly enjoyed writing about Charlie and am looking forward to her stumbling into future mischief.

Thank you to my early readers. Your notes and feedback were invaluable and helped me focus on what was working, and trim the rest. Likewise to my Beta readers, those final comments provided much clarity on the final draft.

Thank you to my editors, Shannon Cave and Stephanie Chou. You both improved the book immensely while providing much encouragement and enthusiasm.

And last, Charlie and Harvest Falls would not exist without my wife, Martina. Our long walks in the woods led to the town's creation, many of its denizens, and certainly several of its murders (both in this book and the future series.) I would not want to plot these "crimes" with anyone else, and I'm incredibly lucky to have you in my life. Thank you, as always, for telling me to go write, for reviewing and editing every draft, and for putting up with my writer's brain.

ABOUT THE AUTHOR

Craig Comer is the author of the Gaslamp fantasy series A Fey Matter and the amateur sleuth mystery novel A DAGGER AMONG FRIENDS. He is also co-author of the mosaic fantasy novel THE ROADS TO BALDAIRN MOTTE. Craig earned a Master's Degree in Writing from the University of Southern California. He enjoys tramping across countries in his spare time, preferably those strewn with pubs and castles.

Find out more at: www.craigcomer.com

THE LAIRD OF DUNCAIRN
The Fey Matter, Book I

City Owl Press, ISBN: 978-1944728168

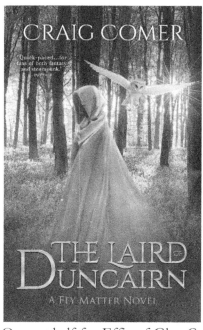

A war is brewing between the worlds of fey and man...

When Sir Walter Conrad discovers a new energy source, one that could topple nations and revolutionize society, the race to dominate its ownership begins. But the excavation of this energy will have dire consequences for both humans and fey. For an ancient enemy stirs, awakened by Sir Walter's discovery.

Outcast half-fey Effie of Glen Coe is the empire's only hope at averting the oncoming disaster. But she finds herself embroiled in the conflict, investigating the eldritch evil spreading throughout the Highlands.

As she struggles against the greed of mighty lords and to escape the clutches of the queen's minions, her comfortable world is shattered. Racing to thwart the growing menace, she realizes the only thing that can save them all is a truce no one wants.

OAK SEER
The Fey Matter, Book II

City Owl Press, ISBN: 978-1944728885

Thrust into the public eye as the "Green Lady," Effie of Glen Coe has become a living legend, the fey woman who saved Scotland from devastation. But can she do it again?

Determined more than ever to forge a peace between fey and humans, Effie finds herself navigating a realm increasingly divided.

The lords of London have other plans, and once again Effie is pulled into a quagmire of politics and greed. She must stand against plots to remove her kind from the shores of the empire and madmen who murder fey without regard.

With violent thugs and unruly mobs all around, wits and courage are not enough. Effie must become something more than herself, an Oak Seer, a fey mantle long lost. But can she survive long enough to claim it?

BARROW WITCH
The Fey Matter, Book III

City Owl Press, ISBN: 978-1648980282

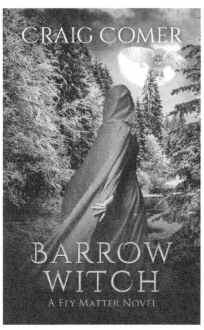

The treaty that will bring peace to the fey of Scotland is within Effie of Glen Coe's grasp. Yet the lords of London will not consent to such an accord until the madness spreading across the empire is halted and its source destroyed.

As Effie and her allies hunt for the ancient being known as the Barrow Witch, they uncover her sinister plot. The Barrow Witch has found an alchemic means to transform fey into devilish creatures bent on her will. Using these marauding bands, she seeks to enslave not only the empire, but all of fey kind.

Effie's fight takes her from haunted cities to ruined castles, but it is not until Caledon, Steward of the Seily Court, is captured that she must finally confront her own self-doubts and the legacy of her family's treacherous past. For only by accepting she has become the very heart of the Scottish fey can she learn to unravel the schemes of their enemy and rally the empires of man and fey toward an ultimate confrontation with the Barrow Witch.

THE ROADS TO BALDAIRN MOTTE

Knight Owl Publishing, ISBN: 978-0359207572

Three novellas linked by a common field of battle...

The king is dead and all shall suffer for it.

In the North, Henry Barlow plots to replace him using the might of the wild Marchers.

In the South, Terryll Payce sails into dark harbors to commit dark deeds.

And amidst it all, Trask the crofter and Hem the miller hope only to survive the schemes of mighty lords.

THE ROADS TO BALDAIRN MOTTE is a mosaic fantasy novel composed of three long tales interspersed with short scenes and historical documents. Events are sometimes told out of sequence, or are told multiple times from different vantage points. Characters central to some stories, completely disappear from others.

THRALLS OF THE FAIRIE & OTHER TALES

Copper Pot Books, ISBN: 979-8826377437

In these tales of high adventure and low fantasy, thieves quest for lost honor, the abandoned hunt for justice, and common farmers struggle merely to survive.

TALES OF LOST LANDS
To reclaim the heart of her god, Mior bargains with mages and delves deep into the temple of a cult. Caita Halftallow finds strength amongst the herd, the better to crush her enemies, while Jaelyn's song lends her the strength to slay fiends.

TALES OF KUTHAHAAR – In Kuthahaar, the Sultan lords over imprisoned oracles, wraith-like assassins, and underground rivers filled with the dead. For Saja and Akil, uncovering these mysteries will seal their fates, whether they wish it or not. For Rajheb, it is enough to wander the city, and remember what was.

TALES OF BALDAIRN MOTTE – Far away in Baldairn, the king is dead. As armies march and lords grasp for an empty throne, the villagers of Burn Gate find themselves caught between protecting their families and defending their lands. For the crofter, Trask, the decision is simple, but the cost will shape the fortunes of those he loves.

Made in the USA
Monee, IL
30 July 2023